ULTIMATE STORM

RICHARD CASTLE

ULTIMATE STORM

A Derrick Storm Omnibus

TITAN BOOKS

ULTIMATE STORM
Print edition ISBN: 9781783291861
E-book edition ISBN: 9781783291878

Published by Titan Books
A division of Titan Publishing Group Ltd.
144 Southwark Street, London SE1 0UP

First edition June 2015

3 5 7 9 10 8 6 4 2

This edition published by arrangement with Kingswell, an imprint of Disney
Book Group.

A CIP catalogue record for this title is available from the British Library.

Printed and bound by CPI Group (UK) Ltd, Croydon, CR0 4YY.

Did you enjoy this book? We love to hear from our readers. Please email
us at readerfeedback@titanemail.com or write to us at Reader Feedback at
the above address.

To receive advance information, news, competitions, and exclusive offers
online, please sign up for the Titan newsletter on our website:

WWW.TITANBOOKS.COM

ULTIMATE STORM

CONTENTS

A
BREWING
STORM

CHAPTER ONE

Current Day
SILVER CREEK, Montana

He could feel it coming long before he heard it, descending like a sudden chill that swept through his bones, causing every muscle to tighten. It was a primal response, sharpened by years of experience. This, he thought, must be how dogs feel in those quiet moments before the earthquake hits, when they alone know the devastation of what's coming. When they alone know that everything is about to change.

For a split second, he considered tactical evasion, but out here among the pines and Rocky Mountain junipers, he knew it was a fool's errand. How far could he get? Maybe to the shore of the river before they arrived, maybe to the tree line, if he was lucky. And then what? He was easily fifty miles from the nearest town, equipped only with what could fit in his backpack.

But what did it matter? They'd already found him. And if they'd found him, that meant they knew.

He looked over the rolling water of the mountain stream.

How long did he have? A minute? Maybe two? Scratching at the worn military cap covering his dark brown hair, his eyes fell on a rainbow trout swimming lazily near the surface, eyeballing the red-and-black fake bug dancing on the stream's surface. He'd spent the past hour luring the trout from the shadows. Maybe he had time enough for that. After all, if there was anything he hated, it was unfinished business.

"Come on. Come to papa," the man whispered. The trout, hypnotized by the hand-tied fly, drew closer.

But just as the fish was ready to strike, the water began to churn and rise upward around him, accompanied by a growing apocalyptic roar.

It was too late. They had arrived.

High above him the churning blades of the monstrous machine eclipsed the sun before sweeping over the tree line and coming to an imposing hover just above him. Droplets of water spattered onto the pepper-like stubble on his chin.

The sound of a Bell UH-1Y Venom helicopter is something that no soldier who has heard it ever forgets. It is what a man hears going into battle and what he hears when he is done fighting—if he is still alive.

The pilot landed in a clearing next to the stream and a twenty-something kid wearing an off-the-rack suit jumped from it, the blades of the aircraft still cutting though the clear air.

"Derrick Storm?" he called. "Is that you?"

The fisherman glanced at the kid with disdain.

"Never heard of him," he growled.

Unsure what to do next, the young courier looked over his shoulder at the helicopter. A side door slid open and an older, pudgy man stepped to the wet ground. He slowly made his way to the creek's edge, cupped his hands around his lips, and yelled: "Jedidiah sent me."

"Don't know him."

"He said you'd say that." The speaker hollered, "Jedidiah says he's calling in *Tangiers*."

Tangiers. Tangiers had been bad. Even after all of these years, whenever the fisherman thought of Tangiers, he could still feel the cold linoleum pressed against his cheek, sticky and wet with his own blood. He could still see the mangled bodies and hear the unanswered cries for help. If it weren't for Jedidiah...

Reeling in his line, the man started toward the creek bank. He did not talk to the two strangers waiting there. He gathered up his gear and boarded the helicopter.

Tangiers. It was a hell of an IOU to call in. Jedidiah knew how difficult it had been for him to disappear. To go off-the-grid. To die, at least to be dead to a world that he had once known. A world that had tried to kill him, not once, but many, many times. Jedidiah understood why it had been important for him to no longer exist. And now Jedidiah was calling him back, dragging him back, to what he had worked so hard to free himself from.

Now inside the chopper, the man looked outside at the creek, the meadow, the blue sky. He was leaving it all.

"Let's go," the fisherman told them.

"Then you are Derrick Storm!" the younger man gushed. "You aren't dead like everyone said."

The older envoy gave the pilot a thumbs-up and the

helicopter lifted from the ground.

"What's it been, Storm?" the older man asked. "How many years have you been dead?"

It had been nearly four. Four years of solitude. Of peace. Of self-assessment. Of reevaluation and reflection. Jedidiah knew Storm better than any man alive. And he had known that he would come back if the trump card was played. Jedidiah had played it. Tangiers. Derrick Storm always paid his debts.

Even in death.

CHAPTER TWO

A black stretch limousine was idling near the tarmac at Joint Base Andrews in Maryland when the air force C-21A Learjet carrying Derrick Storm landed. Now clean-shaven, dressed in a tailored Caraceni suit and black Testoni shoes, Storm walked directly from the jet to the car's rear passenger door. An officer from the Central Intelligence Agency's internal police force, called the Security Protective Service (SPS), opened the door for him.

Sliding into the back leather seat, Storm found himself sitting across from Jedidiah Jones, the director of the agency's National Clandestine Service—a fancy name for the CIA division that recruited spies and did the nation's dirtiest jobs overseas.

Jones inspected Storm over half-glasses perched on a nose that had been broken so many times that it had been impossible for surgeons to fully repair. Although Jones was old enough to be Storm's father, the NCS director was military-fit, built like a pit bull, with a shaved head and a raspy voice that sounded angry even when he was paying a compliment, which was rare.

"You look a hell of a lot better than the last time I saw you," Jones said.

"It would be difficult to look worse," Storm replied, as the limo began making its way into Washington, D.C., along a route that was all too familiar to Storm.

Jones grunted. "Tangiers was a bitch. Didn't work out the way we planned. Shit happens. Anyway, I'm glad you're back."

"I'm not."

"I don't believe that, Storm," Jones said. "A guy like you needs the adrenaline rush. A guy like you thrives on the danger. You weren't really happy in Montana. Deep down, you know it. And so do I. You knew this day would come."

"You're wrong. I was at peace."

"Bullshit, you're lying to yourself!"

"Look, I'm here," Storm said. "But when I've done whatever you want this time, I'm going back. I'm done. We're even."

Jones took a fat cigar from his coat jacket, nipped off its end, looked at it lovingly, and fired it up.

"What about Clara Strike?" he asked. "You saying she doesn't matter to you anymore?"

Concealing his emotions had always been something Storm did well. It was a necessity in his line of work. He would not give Jones the satisfaction of a reaction now. Or ever. Still, Jones had struck a blow. Storm and Clara had worked together. They'd been perfect partners on assignment—and in bed. She was part of the reason he'd decided to disappear. She was part of the reason he still wished that he were a ghost.

It was an ironic twist. Clara had been declared dead once, too. There was even a death certificate filed in Richmond that verified she had been killed. He'd believed it when Jones had first told him. He'd been crushed. She'd been ripped from his life, and for one of the first times in his memory, he'd grieved. He'd actually felt tremendous and overwhelming loss because of her death.

Then he'd discovered it was a lie. Jones had engineered it. Her death was for the good of the company. For the good of the country. But it had not been for his good. It had taken him a long time to accept that Clara had not died, that she had been somewhere breathing, eating, possibly making love with someone else, while he was grieving. Yet she had not contacted him. She'd let him believe that she had been killed. Why? Being dead seemed to be an occupational hazard when you worked for Jones. It was a professional requirement; only her death had cut him deep.

Storm wondered, Had his death caused the same reaction in her?

"Don't worry," Jones said. "Clara is out of country."

"Do me a favor," Storm said. "Don't tell her I'm still alive. It'd make things... complicated."

Jones smirked, revealing rows of perfectly crowned teeth.

Did Jones have a heart? Or was he the ultimate Machiavellian company man? Ice-cold. Storm wasn't sure, even after all of the years that he had worked from him.

"Whatever you want, Derrick," Jones said, inhaling deeply.

"I want another promise from you," Storm said. "When

I've done whatever it is that you want, promise me that you'll let me be dead again—this time forever."

Jones leaned forward and stuck out his right hand to shake.

"You've got my word," he said.

"My debt is paid?"

"In full. After this time, you're done." And then Jones added, "Besides, you're getting too old, too soft for this."

Storm returned his smile. "What's so important that you called in Tangiers?"

"A kidnapping here in Washington, D.C."

"You called in Tangiers because of a kidnapping?" Storm repeated in an incredulous voice.

"There's more to it."

With Jones there always was. His mind was already racing. He knew Jones would not be calling him out of his self-imposed retirement because of a kidnapping. It didn't make sense. The CIA was not authorized to operate inside the borders of the United States. Kidnappings fell under the jurisdiction of the Federal Bureau of Investigation, and although in public the CIA and the FBI always presented a united front, Storm knew there was an intense rivalry between them. That was putting it mildly. Jones despised the FBI's current director, Roosevelt Jackson.

"Who's been kidnapped?" Storm asked.

"The stepson of a U.S. senator," Jones replied. "His name is Matthew Dull, and his stepfather is Senator Thurston Windslow from Texas."

Thurston Windslow. The first player in the Kabuki play

that was about to begin. Windslow was one of the most powerful senators on Capitol Hill and chair of the U.S. Select Committee on Intelligence—the oversight committee charged with keeping an eye on the CIA and Jedidiah Jones. No wonder Jones was interested. But there had to be other players and more to this than a kidnapping.

"Who kidnapped his stepson?" Storm asked.

Jones waved his cigar in his hand, dismissing the smoke around him and Storm's inquiry in one move. "We're on our way to Windslow's office. He can fill you in. That way you will go into this fresh without any preconceived impressions."

It was classic Jedidiah Jones. Storm had been here before. Jones liked his officers to assess situations on their own—to come up with their own opinions. He wanted to see what they would learn. He wanted to see if they might discover something that he might have missed. Jones would give them just enough to get them started and then feed them information if they needed it, when he felt they needed it, and only if he felt that they needed it. Jones played it close to his vest, and even when you had completed a job, you were never really sure of how it fit together with some grander plan. Only Jones understood the master plan. He operated in a world of smoke and mirrors where nothing was what it appeared and nothing could be taken at face value. Even those closest to him were never confident that they knew what Jones was orchestrating.

Storm said, "What about the FBI?"

Jones shrugged. "What about them? They're on the case. The special agent in charge is a woman named April Showers."

Another player enters the game.

"April Showers? Is that her real name?"

"Yes, it is. Her folks must have had a sense of humor. Or they were hippies from the sixties. Either way, she'll be at the senator's office when we get there."

"And who am I supposed to be?"

"You're a special advisor. You're name is Steve Mason. That way Derrick Storm can remain dead."

"And if something goes wrong, there's no Steve Mason to be found."

"Exactly," said Jones.

"It seems like a lot of trouble—bringing me back and giving me a false identity—just for a kidnapping."

Jones blew out a series of perfect smoke rings. "It's sad really," he said. "Smoke rings. With everyone banning smoking, it's becoming a dying art."

CHAPTER THREE

Through the bullet-resistant windows of the black limousine, Storm saw the U.S. Capitol dome rising before them as they rode east on Constitution Avenue. It was an impressive sight, especially brightly floodlit at night.

The car passed the Russell Senate Office Building (SOB), which was the first of three ornate office buildings used by the nation's one hundred elected U.S. senators. In a city obsessed with acronyms, Storm had always thought the shorthand SOB seemed a fitting description for where senators did their business.

The Dirksen SOB was next. Opened in 1958, it had been known for nearly two decades simply as SOB Number Two, until Congress decided to name it after the late Illinois Republican Senator Everett M. Dirksen, an orator so famous that he'd been awarded a Grammy for an album of his patriotic speeches called *Gallant Men*.

Senators loved naming buildings after their own.

When the limo stopped at the Dirksen SOB's western

entrance, the SPS security officer in the front seat jumped out and darted inside to alert the Capitol Hill Police officers on duty that two VIPs were arriving. Jones and Storm would not be delayed by security checks. There would be no walk-through metal detectors, no searching of briefcases and emptying of pockets. Instead, both men were quickly escorted to Senator Windslow's office, where a secretary immediately led them into the senator's inner chamber.

As with most other things on Capitol Hill, senate offices were doled out based on seniority and power. The bigger the office, the more important the senator. Windslow had been assigned the largest office in the Dirksen. His private domain had fifteen-foot-tall ceilings, ornate carved wooden bookcases, and thick carpet. Expensive brown leather sofas and overstuffed chairs faced an executive desk made of polished mahogany that had clearly not come from some General Services Administration warehouse. One wall was covered with framed photographs that showed the senator posing with foreign presidents and dignitaries. It was proof that Windslow relished his power and clearly enjoyed taxpayer-funded junkets to exotic locales. Another wall was decorated with the Texas state seal and a pair of mounted longhorns from a Texas steer.

The senator rose from behind his desk but made no effort to walk forward and greet them. He let them come to him with outstretched hands.

"About time you got here, Jedidiah," Windslow snapped, as he shook the CIA spymaster's hand. "You've kept me waiting ten minutes."

Windslow looked at Storm, and the two men immediately sized each other up, like two schoolboys squaring off during recess.

Tall and thin, Windslow was in his early seventies and instantly recognizable. He was a familiar face on Sunday morning television talk shows and evening newscasts. But it was his haircut and voice that made him memorable. He had pure white hair that he wore in an outdated, carefully coifed pompadour swept back from his forehead and held firmly in place with a glossy shellac spray. He spoke with a slow, deliberate Southern drawl that was sprinkled with homespun sayings that he frequently used to remind voters that he was one of them, a yellow-dog Democrat. In Texas, which he had represented for more than thirty years, he was considered undefeatable.

"So this is your man," Windslow said.

"Senator Windslow," Jones said, "this is Steve Mason. He doesn't work for me, but he occasionally does piecework for me. He's a private detective."

"You're the fixer?" Windslow asked bluntly. "You're the man who gets things done no matter what—am I right?"

Storm didn't like the fact that there were three others in the office. He'd identified FBI Special Agent April Showers as soon as he walked in. A telltale bulge under the jacket she was wearing had given her away. He'd recognized the senator's wife from news articles. But he had no idea who the twenty-something-year-old girl was sitting nearby.

"I'm here to lend a hand," Storm said, dodging the senator's questions.

"I've already got enough hands," Windslow replied. "I've

got the entire FBI lending a hand, and so far, it hasn't done any good. What I need is someone with a fist."

No one spoke for a moment, and then the senator's wife said in a quiet voice, "My husband seems to have forgotten his manners. My name is Gloria Windslow." She rose gracefully from her seat, showing the emotional control of a well-trained politician's wife. Even in times of great emotional stress, she knew that she needed to be composed.

Her grip was soft. Her fingernails manicured. She was at least thirty years younger than her husband and was dressed in a pricey New York designer outfit that had been tailored to accent her figure.

Storm had read about her in the media. As soon as she'd finished high school, Gloria Windslow had fled the poor, rural Texas town where she'd been born. Her ticket had been her breathtaking good looks and unbridled ambition, which had led to her winning a spot on the Dallas Cowboys cheerleading roster. She'd gotten pregnant, married a star NFL quarterback, and then divorced him two years later, after claiming that he'd abused her. She and her newborn had made the covers of both *People* and *Us* magazines, where she'd been portrayed as a determined single mom who'd refused to be bullied by her famous husband. Gloria and the senator had met two years later at a Dallas political fund-raiser where supporters had paid three thousand dollars a plate to hear him speak. She'd arrived on the arm of one of the city's most eligible bachelors, a prominent lawyer, but had traded up, leaving with Windslow. A month later, he hired her to work in Washington as his personal secretary. A year later, Windslow filed for divorce from his wife of thirty years, causing a dustup back home. The new couple's age difference raised eyebrows, but Windslow hired a Manhattan public relations firm to salvage his well-crafted reputation as a good Christian family man, and by the time the Madison Avenue spin masters were finished, Gloria was no longer a home wrecker. She was now a confident and trusted advisor to her husband, with a passion about education, libraries, and women's issues. At Christmas, she invited special needs children to a party at their estate, and gave them pony rides in a heated barn.

She was still stunning in her mid-forties, thanks to a strict starvation diet, cosmetic surgery, and regular Botox injections.

After introducing herself, Gloria directed Storm to the other women in the office.

"This is Miss Samantha Toppers," she said, directing his attention to the youngest. "She and my son, Matthew Dull, are engaged to be married."

As Toppers rose from her seat on a sofa to meet him, Storm realized that he was looking at an architectural marvel. She weighed less than a hundred pounds and was under five feet tall, but she was so top-heavy that Storm wondered how she kept herself from tumbling facedown when she reached out to shake his hand.

"Nice to meet you," Toppers said in her childlike voice.

When he finally got around to looking at her face, he saw that her eyes were swollen and red from crying.

"And this is Special Agent April Showers," Gloria continued. In her green eyes, Storm saw a look of irritation. She

couldn't have been any more opposite in appearance to
Toppers. The FBI agent was six feet tall and had a world-
class marathoner's body, which meant she averaged two
pounds per inch. In her mid-thirties, she had porcelain white
skin and wore her red hair tied in a bun.

"Now that you've met everyone," Senator Windslow
said, "let's get to it. My stepson, Matthew, has been
kidnapped. They grabbed him while he and Samantha were
walking across the Georgetown campus."

"Fortunately," Gloria interrupted, "they didn't bother
Samantha, but they did kidnap my son."

For the first time since Storm had entered the office, he
saw a crack in Gloria Windslow's veneer. Tears began to
form in her eyes. She removed a tissue from her purse and
dabbed them.

"The kidnappers," Windslow continued, "left Miss
Toppers hysterical on the sidewalk."

Storm looked for some sign of sympathy in Windslow's
face, but there was none. *Had he expected the top-heavy
Toppers to fight the assailants?*

Toppers lowered her eyes, avoiding contact with
Windslow's glare.

"I think it would be best," Gloria said, between sniffles,
"if Special Agent Showers gave you the details. It is difficult
for me to discuss the facts without becoming emotional."

Taking her hint, Agent Showers said, "The kidnapping
happened three days ago. A white van pulled up at an
intersection on the edge of the Georgetown campus where
Mr. Dull and Miss Toppers were waiting for a red light to

change. It was shortly after fourteen hundred hours. Three men, all wearing ski masks, leaped out of the vehicle. One stayed behind the wheel. The first assailant fired an automatic weapon in the air to scare onlookers. The other two overpowered Matthew and forced him into the van. We found the van abandoned six blocks away."

"No fingerprints or trace evidence, I assume?" Storm said.

"That's right. Wiped clean."

"How about the shell casings left behind?"

"It's all in my report," she replied curtly.

"Which she'll be happy to give you after we are done," Windslow declared. "I spoke to FBI Director Jackson this morning, and he has instructed Agent Showers to cooperate fully with you. No questions asked. Isn't that correct?"

"Yes," Showers said. "I've been ordered to help you."

"Agent Showers doesn't think bringing you into the investigation is a good idea," Gloria Windslow said. "My husband and I feel differently."

"That's because the FBI hasn't done a damn thing so far," Windslow declared.

Storm saw Showers's jaw muscles tighten. He suspected she was biting down hard to keep her response from slipping out.

"I got a ransom note," Windslow said, "the day after those bastards snatched him. They demanded a million dollars, which I immediately agreed to pay." Windslow shot FBI Agent Showers a disgusted look. "Agent Showers here assured me that if I played along with these sons-of-bitches, the Bureau would be able to catch them when they picked up my money."

"But that's not what happened," Gloria Windslow said,

cutting in on his account. The two of them made quite a tag team. For not wanting to discuss the case, both seemed eager to do it.

"The Bureau here screwed up," Windslow said.

"With all due respect, Senator," Showers replied. "We followed standard procedures. The ransom was left exactly where the kidnappers had told us to put it. The entire place was under surveillance."

"That money just sat there," Windslow said, "and no one showed to get my million dollars. They knew it was a trap. Someone tipped off the kidnappers. I just know it."

"We don't know that," Showers said.

"Well, young lady, something spooked them—like a mule deer sniffing the air when you're hunting," Windslow said. "The next morning, I got another ransom note; only now these bastards have decided to play hardball."

Gloria began to quietly sob. Toppers left the couch and knelt down next to the chair where her future mother-in-law sat. Rising from behind his desk, Windslow walked over, too, and put his right hand on Gloria's shoulder. "This is a terrible thing for my wife to be going through." He stroked her hair.

Continuing, Windslow said, "Those bastards pulled out four of Matthew's front teeth and sent them to me in that ransom note, along with a photograph. That's when I decided to talk to Jedidiah. That's when I decided we needed your help."

Storm looked at Agent Showers. She had placed her right leg over her left one and then wrapped them so tightly together that she now had her right toe tucked behind her left ankle. Her arms were crossed against her chest. Even someone completely unfamiliar with body language would have recognized how frustrated she was.

"I'd like to see the two ransom notes," Storm said.

"Agent Showers will get them for you," Windslow said. "Now, I'd like all the women folk here to skedaddle for a few moments so I can talk to Jedidiah and his man in private."

"C'mon, ladies," Gloria said, rising slowly from her seat. Toppers instantly fell in line, but Showers didn't move.

"Senator," she said sternly, "as head of this investigation, I need to be involved in every discussion that you might have that involves the kidnapping."

"I have things to say in private, Miss Showers," Windslow snapped. "I was assured earlier today by Director Jackson that I would have your total and full cooperation. Do I need to have him replace you?"

"For the record," Showers said, "I think you are making a mistake bringing this outsider into the case."

"For the record," Windslow replied, mimicking her, "I asked you to leave my office."

Showers walked out the door.

"Jedidiah tells me," Windslow said to Storm when she was gone, "that you're a man who knows how to find people who don't want to be found and that you can handle yourself in extremely difficult situations."

Jones said, "He's my go-to guy. If it were my stepson, I'd call him."

"That's exactly what I wanted to hear," Windslow said. "I need someone who can track down these bastards and do whatever is necessary to free my stepson. Do you understand what I am telling you?"

Storm said, "You want results and you don't care how I get them."

Windslow smiled. "Finally, I'm getting the sort of answers I wanted. Yes, this is exactly what I want from you, Mr. Mason, or whatever the hell your name might be. I asked Jedidiah to get me someone who isn't worried about legal niceties. I asked him to get me the best."

Storm didn't respond.

"First, I want you to track down these bastards, and then, I want you to kill every one of them. I'm not worried about you reading them their legal rights and arresting them and getting them some fast-talking lawyer whose going to bottle this up in some long, drawn-out trial. I want them dead. I want you to get it done before they send more of my stepson's body parts to my wife."

CHAPTER FOUR

t was 8:30 P.M. by the time Storm and Jones left Capitol Hill and arrived at the Willard InterContinental Hotel on Pennsylvania Avenue, less than a block from the White House. Before they parted, Jones handed Storm an envelope stuffed with hundred-dollar bills, a fake Nevada driver's license, private investigator credentials under the name Steve Mason, a cell phone that was a direct line to Jones at the CIA, and the keys to a rental car parked in the hotel's lot. Storm reached his fifth-floor suite at the same moment the phone inside it began to ring. It was FBI Agent Showers calling from the lobby. She'd come to brief him.

"Come on up," Storm said.

"I'll wait for you in the hotel's restaurant."

Storm joined her five minutes later at a secluded table.

"I've never stayed in this hotel," she said as he was sitting down. "But it is famous. Mark Twain wrote two books here."

"We can go up to my suite and I'll give you a tour," he said.

"I was being polite, making chitchat," she said. "I've no interest in going to your bedroom."

"Too bad," he intimated. "I was hoping for a full debriefing."

Storm glanced around the mostly empty restaurant. "This hotel is much nicer than the places Jedidiah typically sends me," he said.

The waiter arrived. Showers ordered coffee. Storm ordered a sixteen-dollar hamburger and an eight-dollar beer. When their server left, she said, "And where would some of those places be—where Jedidiah has sent you?"

"If I told you, I'd have to kill you."

"That's an old line."

"In my case, it happens to be true."

"Look," she said sternly. "I've been ordered to brief you and work with you. I think I deserve to know who you are."

The waiter interrupted with their drinks. After he'd left, Storm said, "I'm a private investigator—just like Jedidiah said. I used to work for him on occasion when I was in the military."

"Oh really," she replied skeptically. "I did some checking earlier today after Jedidiah told us that he was flying you into town. He said you were from Nevada. If that's true, why is there no record of you being a licensed private investigator in that state?"

Storm shrugged. "I've been meaning to get a license. I just haven't gotten around to it."

"*You do* have a Nevada driver's license though, right?"

Storm didn't answer. She was supposed to be briefing him, not interrogating him. But Showers wasn't about to stop now.

She said, "I checked the photos of all the Steve Masons who have Nevada driver's licenses. You don't look like any of them."

Storm was disappointed. Jedidiah usually did a better job backstopping legends.

"I got a haircut," he replied.

"I ran an FBI background check and there is nothing in any public record about a Steve Mason that fits your description. Who are you—really?"

Storm leaned in close and whispered, "I'm the man who's been brought in to clean up your mess. That's all you need to know."

The waiter brought him his burger. Storm hadn't realized how hungry he was. He took a big bite and another long gulp of cold beer.

In a resigned voice, Showers said, "What exactly do you need to know about the kidnapping?"

"Everything."

Between bites, Storm questioned her. Showers elaborated on the basics that he'd already heard in Windslow's office. Matthew Dull and Samantha Toppers had finished their last class for the day at Georgetown University and were walking across campus to get something to eat when a white van pulled to the curb and three attackers leaped from it. One fired an automatic weapon in the air to intimidate would-be heroes. He then pointed it directly into Topper's terrified face. The other two assailants overpowered Dull and forced him into the van. The entire abduction had taken less than a minute.

"Why hasn't this been all over the national news?" Storm asked.

"Strings were pulled. The media was told that it was a college prank. Georgetown officials went along. Said it was a fraternity gag that got out of hand."

"What kind of automatic weapon was used?"

Showers opened a black leather briefcase that she had brought with her and removed a clear plastic bag that contained about a dozen brass shell casings.

"There were no fingerprints on them," she said, putting the bag on the table.

Storm didn't bother opening it as he finished the last bite of his burger. He'd seen enough 7.62 x 39mm ammunition casings to recognize them by sight.

"The assailant used an AK-47," he said.

"Yes," Showers replied, impressed. "Unfortunately, there are about seventy-five million AK-47s being used right now in the world. The Soviet Union did a hell of a job exporting them to every terrorist and revolutionary group in the world, as well as every nut in the U.S. who found a way, legally or illegally, to get his hands on a firearm capable of firing six hundred rounds a minute."

"It sucks being Bambi nowadays."

He smiled. She didn't.

Storm said, "These guys went in fast, hard, deliberate, and left nothing behind that could be used to identify them. They were pros. Possibly ex-military." He said, "Let's see the ransom notes."

She removed two letters from her briefcase. Both were protected in plastic. The first was written in block letters, similar to what a draftsman would use on blueprints.

"WE WILL KILL YOUR STEPSON UNLESS YOU PAY US $1,000,000."

The note went on to order Windslow to pay the ransom in hundred-dollar bills. The cash was supposed to be placed in a briefcase left in the fast-food dining area of Union Station, the city's major subway and Amtrak station, near Capitol Hill. The kidnappers had drawn a diagram on the note that pinpointed where the briefcase was to be left, underneath a table near a back wall. The ransom was supposed to be delivered by Dull's fiancée.

"Samantha Toppers was terrified," Showers said. "I kept telling her that she was fine. We had the entire train station flooded with agents—nearly a hundred—coming and going. We used interns and retired agents so the kidnappers wouldn't have a clue who was a civilian and who wasn't."

"And no one showed up to grab the case?"

"No one showed any interest in it even after she walked away from that table."

"I'm surprised. Not because of the kidnappers. But that you could leave a briefcase in Union Station without someone stealing it."

Continuing her briefing, Showers said, "We found a partial print on the corner of that first note. There weren't any prints on the second one. It arrived the next day."

Like the first, the second ransom note was handwritten, but not in block letters. There was no mention of a ransom— only a cryptic threat.

"Your son dies if you continue toying with us."

Storm said, "Obviously, these were written by different people. Not only is the handwriting different, so is the paper they used. The first note had a partial print on it. The second didn't. There's also an error in the second message. In the first, Dull is correctly described as Windslow's stepson. In the second, he's called his son."

"Yes, I noticed those contradictions, too," Showers replied. "But we know that at least four kidnappers were involved. One of them could have written the first note, and another the second, simply to throw us off. The same could be true about the discrepancies. They might have been intentional."

Storm wasn't so sure, but he decided to move on. "Tell me about Senator Windslow. Does he have many enemies?"

"Does he ever. He's probably one of the most hated senators in Washington. He's blunt and he's been around so long that he's untouchable. He knows it. He's a bully, and when he doesn't get what he wants, he gets angry—and he always gets even. Other politicians fear him. Even the White House. He has a reputation for being ruthless and vindictive."

"Sounds like every politician I've known," Storm said.

"No, Windslow is in a league of his own. You would expect Republicans to hate him because he's a Democrat. But half the members of his own party can't stand him. And that's just on Capitol Hill. Outside of Congress, the groups that probably hate him the most are the environmentalists. Windslow is a shill for Big Oil. Always has been. He doesn't believe in global warming, thinks oil companies should be able to drill holes anywhere they damn well please, and once voted against a bill that would have levied fines on visitors who littered in state parks."

"It's hard for me," Storm replied, "to imagine that an armed gang of environmentalists kidnapped the senator's stepson."

"You asked me to identify his enemies. That's what I'm doing. Being thorough."

Storm called over the waiter and ordered another beer. "OK, besides the tree huggers, who's next on the enemies list?"

"As chair of the Senate Intelligence Committee, Windslow wields tremendous power. He's always been a strong advocate of Israel. That makes him hated by Middle Eastern extremists."

"Any particular terrorist cell?"

"All of them despise him. He's also managed to alienate the Russians, the Germans, and the Greeks. He's a rabid anti-Communist and doesn't trust the new Russian leaders; he believes all Germans are closet Nazis, and he dislikes socialist countries."

"How can anyone hate the Greeks?" Storm asked. "All they ever do is break plates and spend Euros that they don't have."

Showers didn't smile. "There's also your people—the intelligence community. Senator Windslow and Jedidiah were all buddy-buddy tonight in the senator's office, but there are rumors they're fighting about a covert operation. And their dispute has gotten nasty."

"What covert operation?"

"Don't know. It's above my pay grade. Maybe you can find out."

"Do you honestly believe Jedidiah is behind the kidnapping?" Storm said skeptically.

"At this point, I'm not counting out anyone. I think you CIA types are capable of anything. Even your arrival here today could be part of a ruse."

She finished her coffee and carefully placed the cup back on its saucer.

Although Showers had already given him a long list of suspects, Storm suspected she was holding back. He'd learned a long time ago that during interviews, it was the last thing that people told him that often held the most important clue.

"If our roles were reversed," he said sympathetically, "I'd be pissed. I'd think, 'Who the hell does this guy think he is barging into my investigation?' I wouldn't be as helpful as you have been just now. But a crime's been committed, and there's a chance that Matthew Dull may still be alive. We owe it to him to put all of our cards on the table, so if there is anything else that you can tell me, anything at all, please share it."

He sounded sincere. He was very good at sounding sincere. It had always served him well—at work and in bed.

Showers sat quietly for a moment. "About a year ago, the bureau began hearing reports that Windslow was on the take. Bribes. Big ones. The first complaint came from a Texan who had bid on a lucrative military contract. One of Windslow's staff members demanded a kickback. When the Texan refused, the contract went to another company. The Texan called us, but all we had was his word and that wasn't enough—not to build a criminal indictment against a U.S. senator."

"You began digging."

She nodded. "I wasn't going to let it go. I discovered Windslow was adding riders to legislation that permitted oil companies to move millions of dollars from their overseas operations into the U.S. without paying federal income taxes."

"But that's not illegal," Storm said. "Senators screw with the IRS all the time to help out their friends."

"Right. But I discovered that Windslow was collecting a fee based on how much money he helped the oil companies get back into the country tax-free. Or, I should say, I got several people to talk about kickbacks. But nothing on paper. Windslow is smart. And then I found a smoking gun. I discovered a wire transfer that I felt certain was a bribe paid to Windslow by someone overseas."

"Who? A government, a corporation, an individual?"

"I'm not sure. Bribery is difficult to prove. The person who paid it isn't going to talk. The person who got it isn't going to talk. Most times, you can only make a criminal case if you have a money trail."

Storm didn't interrupt. He wanted her to keep talking. But he was very familiar with how bribes worked and how to hide them. He'd helped Jedidiah distribute millions of dollars in Iraq and Pakistan. The agency had handed out hundred-dollar bills as if they were Halloween candy—all unbeknownst to Congress and the American taxpayer.

Showers said, "I was able to trace a six-million-dollar payment from a London bank account to the Cayman Islands, where it was converted into cash and brought to Washington, D.C. I'm fairly certain it ended up in Windslow's hands."

"Fairly certain or positive?"

A pained look appeared on her face. His question had hit a nerve. She said, "I feel confident that I had developed a sufficient circumstantial case—enough to indict. But when my file reached the director's office, it was put on ice. No one would tell me why. That was three weeks ago."

Showers glanced at her watch. It was eleven and the restaurant was closing. She collected the two letters from him. "I've done what I was told," she said. "I've briefed you. I'll pick you up tomorrow at eight A.M. sharp. We have set up a command post at FBI headquarters. If you have additional questions, then you can ask them to my bosses tomorrow at the briefing."

"I do have more questions," he replied. "Since the restaurant is closing, let's go upstairs to my suite so we can talk more."

"I don't think talk is what you have in mind."

He grinned. "Depends on the kind of talk. At least let me walk you to your car."

"I'm armed, and I think I can make it through the hotel lobby to the valet without your help." Then, for the first time since they'd met, she actually smiled and said, "Besides, I think I have more to fear from you than I do from any strangers."

"Ouch," he replied, touching his heart as if he'd been shot. "Just trying to be gentlemanly," he said, intentionally repeating her words.

"Then you can pay the check—Mr. Steve Mason."

He watched her walk away from the table, admiring the dazzling results of her yoga routine hidden under her tailored slacks. As soon as he'd signed the bill with his room number and fake name, Storm followed her. But by the time he reached the lobby, she was already behind the wheel of her BMW. He stepped outside the hotel's double doors just as she was driving away. As he watched, he saw a black

Mercedes-Benz sedan pull from a side street near the hotel and begin to follow her.

Storm recognized the red, white, and blue license tag. It was a diplomatic plate.

Hurrying back to his suite, he used his portable computer to log on to the Internet. Diplomatic plates contained a two-letter code that identified which country had been issued the plate by the U.S. State Department. Periodically, the code letters were changed and reassigned. GB was never used on tags from Great Britain and IS was never used for Israel, because that would make it too easy for potential enemies to identify the car's occupants.

Storm had seen the letters YR on the plate of the Mercedes following Showers. Within seconds, he'd broken the code.

What had Jedidiah Jones gotten him into? Why would a diplomatic car from the Russian embassy be tailing Special Agent Showers?

CHAPTER FIVE

The hotel phone in Storm's suite woke him from an alcohol-induced slumber. Several jigger-sized whiskey bottles pillaged from the hotel's minibar littered the nightstand. He'd stayed up late trolling for information on the encrypted computer network that the CIA and other federal intelligence services could access via the Internet. His searches had led him to several clues. But what he'd uncovered remained disjoined pieces of a puzzle that still needed to be assembled.

At around 3 A.M., Storm had gone to bed, but he'd found it difficult to sleep. He'd known why. It wasn't the kidnapping. There were two reasons, and both had to do with his return to Washington, D.C. *Clara Strike* and *Tangiers*. Sometimes only Jack Daniel's could help a man black out his past.

A woman's voice on the telephone line said, "Senator Windslow is calling."

Storm checked the clock next to the king-sized bed. It was a few minutes after 6 A.M. His head was throbbing. The next voice he heard was Windslow's. "Those bastards left me another note—this one at my house."

"Did they send anything else?"

"No teeth or body parts, if that is what you're asking. But they raised their ransom demand."

"How much?"

"Six million! I'm at my house in Great Falls. Get out here now!"

Storm jotted down the address and asked, "Have you called Agent Showers?"

The question was met with silence. Finally, Windslow said, "I don't want her or the FBI involved. I'll explain when you get here. Don't call her, that's an order."

An order? That was something Storm would need to clear up with Windslow. Only Jones gave him orders, not a politician.

Storm went downstairs to claim his rental car. The valet brought him a white Ford Taurus. It was not what spies in movies used, but it was perfect for blending in around Washington and its suburbs. He drove to Constitution Avenue, turned right, crossed the Potomac River, and headed north on the George Washington Parkway until he reached the Capital Beltway, a major highway that encircled the city. Exiting west onto the beltway, he went farther into Virginia. It took him another ten minutes to reach Great Falls, a heavily wooded, rolling suburb dotted with multimillion-dollar Colonial estates. He assumed he was being tracked electronically—if not by the CIA then by the FBI. There was probably a bug planted somewhere in the Taurus, or they were using the cell phone that Jones had given him. At this stage, he didn't care.

Senator Windslow's driveway was barred by an ornate,

monogrammed iron gate. Storm pushed a button on a speaker mounted at the driveway entrance, and when the gates swung open, he drove along a circular driveway bordered by a carefully manicured lawn. An older black maid answered the front door and escorted Storm into the grand foyer, which had an imported Italian marble floor and a massive Versailles chandelier made of crystal and oxidized brass. Rising directly in front of him was an elaborate double staircase. A portrait was hung next to the first step on each side. One painting was of Senator Windslow and the other was of Gloria Windslow. Because each painting was hanging next to the first step, it gave the impression that the senator used one flight of stairs and his wife the other. The artist, Storm noted, had been shrewd enough to recognize that his patrons placed a higher value on flattery than realism. Both of the Windslows looked like British royalty.

Senator Windslow appeared in a dark blue nylon workout suit with a curled up towel resting on his shoulders and his forehead beaded with sweat.

"I ride my stationary bike for an hour every morning," he explained. "Gives me a chance to exercise while I read the papers and watch the news."

Storm followed him through a side door into a wood-paneled study where the maid had placed a pot of coffee and two mugs on a table edged by three leather chairs. They matched the brown leather chairs in Windslow's office. Storm spotted another pair of Longhorn steer horns mounted on the wall, just like the ones that he'd seen on Capitol Hill. Obviously, the senator's decorating taste was the same whether he was at home or work.

"Hattie, our housekeeper, fetches me the newspapers each morning from the box at our gates while I'm exercising," Windslow said, as he poured himself coffee and took a seat. He nodded at Storm, indicating that he could pour himself a cup, too, if he wished. "This morning," Windslow said, "Hattie found this at the gate."

Windslow nodded toward an opened manila envelope on the coffee table, along with a pair of yellow rubber gloves.

"Has anyone checked the note for prints?" Storm asked.

"No. Put on those gloves there before you handle it. I had Hattie get them from the kitchen."

Storm pulled on the gloves. They were tight. He removed the letter and asked, "Does your wife know about this new demand?"

Windslow shook his head. "She's still sleeping upstairs in her bedroom."

Her bedroom. He hadn't said "our bedroom." Apparently using different staircases was not the only thing that the couple did separately.

This new note—the third from the kidnappers—looked much like the first ransom demand. It was handwritten in block letters and contained specific instructions.

"GO TO YOUR SAFETY DEPOSIT BOX AND REMOVE THE SIX MILLION YOU HAVE STASHED THERE."

While Storm was reading, the senator said, "My stepson must have told them about the six million. I should've known that little bastard couldn't keep his mouth shut. Probably told them about it when they were jerking out his front teeth."

Six million dollars in a safety deposit box. Storm marveled at the way the senator had just let that drop, as if having that kind of money just sitting around in cash was the most natural thing in the world. Showers had been right about Windslow. He was indeed on the take. No wonder the Great Man had wanted to see him alone. Seeing as things were just starting to get interesting, Storm decided to play along.

"Why'd your stepson know about it?"

"The box is rented under his name."

The note instructed the senator to remove the six million from the bank before closing time today. It was to be divided into four equal piles of $1.5 million, and each pile was to be put into a gym bag. At exactly 6 P.M., the kidnappers would call Samantha Toppers on her cell phone with instructions on where to deliver the bags. She would need a car because the bags would be dropped at different locations around Washington, D.C. If the FBI attempted to monitor the deliveries or to intervene, the kidnappers would kill Matthew Dull.

Jabbing his bony finger at the ransom demand, Windslow said, "Make sure you read that last line carefully!"

"HAVE STEVE MASON DRIVE SAMANTHA TOPPERS TO THE BANK AND ON THE DELIVERIES TONIGHT."

"How in the hell do the kidnappers know about *you*?" Windslow asked in an accusatory voice, "and why do they want *you* driving my future daughter-in-law around with *my* six million in cash?"

Storm had to admit it was an interesting question. *Clearly there was a leak, an informant, tipping off the kidnappers.* But Storm didn't like Windslow's tone. The senator might have gotten away with bullying his way over others, but not Storm.

"I've got a few questions of my own," Storm replied, ignoring Windslow's question. "Why don't *you* want the FBI to know about this note?"

The senator replied, "Because that six million is what we call 'walking around money' in politics. Texas is a big state. Lots of people have their hands out come election time. I don't think Agent Showers or the Justice Department would understand."

"Neither would the IRS," Storm said. "It's bribe money."

"C'mon, son. Jedidiah told me you had street smarts. How do you think campaigns are run? I use that cash to grease a few palms. It's no big deal. It's expected."

"I'm not talking about greasing palms in Texas," Storm replied. "I'm talking about your palms getting greased."

A flash of anger washed over Windslow's face. No one talked to him like this. But he kept his temper in check. "Where that money came from is none of your goddamn business," he said. "You're not here to investigate me. Look, what choice do I have? The kidnappers are demanding six million or they're going to kill my stepson. I can't go to the FBI because the six million is off-the-books income. I need you to do this for me. I need you to do it without telling the FBI."

Having carefully returned the ransom note to its envelope, Storm removed the rubber gloves and said, "The kidnappers know where you live."

Windslow said, "Everyone knows where I live. It's no goddamn secret."

"The kidnappers know you've got six million in cash in a safety deposit box and you can't tell the FBI about it."

"Yeah, and they also know about you, Mr. Steve Mason, or whatever your real name is."

"They seem to know an awful lot."

"We got a leaky faucet," Windslow said.

"Any idea who?"

"No. I've been going over names since the note arrived."

"How about Samantha Toppers?"

"Samantha?" Windslow repeated, breaking into a toothy grin. "That girl's bra size is twice her IQ. She's not smart enough to be involved in this. Where would she find four men to kidnap Matthew? Kidnappers don't advertise on Craigslist. Besides, she's a trust fund baby. She's got no need for my money."

"My experience has been that the richer you are, the more you want. The kidnappers have asked her to deliver the ransom twice now. Why her?"

"She loves Matthew and she isn't going to take my money and disappear. I told you, she's loaded. Her parents died in an accident and left her millions. Besides, she's not exactly a threat to them since she's so puny. "

"Could she and your stepson have dreamed up this entire scheme?" Storm asked. He watched Windslow's face for a reaction. Surprise. Anger. Anything. But there was nothing, and that suggested the senator had already considered the idea.

"Matthew is too vain to let someone pull out his four front teeth," Windslow said. "Also, the safety deposit box is in his name, and he knows I can't complain in public if that cash vanishes. He could have gone in and taken it without faking his own kidnapping."

"What about your congressional staff? A disgruntled employee, maybe?"

"Haven't fired anyone in years, and only a couple of them know Matthew is missing."

"That leaves only two other people who could've tipped off the kidnappers about my arrival last night," Storm said. "You and your wife."

Windslow smirked. "Why would I kidnap my stepson and demand six million in cash—money that's already mine."

"That narrows it down to your wife."

Windslow set down the coffee mug that he'd been cradling. "I'm going to tell you a story. A year ago, I had a heart attack and it almost killed me. Gloria never left my side. She nursed me back to health. By that time, we'd been married for nearly twenty years. Marrying a younger woman caused tongues to wag. Everyone thought Gloria was a gold digger waiting for me to die. But that woman really loves me. She proved it when I got sick. After I recovered from my heart attack, I tore up our prenuptial agreement. If I kick off today, Gloria gets everything and that's more than the six million walking around money that these bastards want. Besides, Gloria wouldn't put her son through this. She spoils that kid rotten."

"Where's the leak then?" Storm asked.

"Why are you assuming it came from my turf? Those instructions—telling us to divide the money into four piles so they can be delivered at four different sites—that sounds like something the CIA would dream up."

"Jedidiah Jones?"

"Son, I've been dealing with the agency for a long, long time, and you never can be certain what Jones and his buddies are doing. For all I know, Jones could be playing some sort of game here."

"I owe my life to that man."

"That don't mean he wouldn't use you—to get to me."

"For what reason? Why would he risk kidnapping the stepson of a U.S. senator on U.S. soil?"

Windslow shrugged. "All I'm saying is he's the one who brought you here, and he has contacts with plenty of ex-military who would know how to pull off a kidnapping. Plus, the kidnappers want you riding around with my money."

"Motive? Jones could steal millions at his job. He doesn't need to rip off you."

"Maybe he's got other reasons."

"Since you've opened that door," Storm said, "what's the covert mission that you and Jones are fighting about?"

A flash of surprise appeared in Windslow's eyes.

"I'm not opening any doors. Our disagreement has nothing to do with this, nothing. Don't try to go there."

"How about Ivan Petrov?" Storm asked. "Could he have something to do with your stepson's kidnapping?"

The Russian was one of the names that Storm had come across during his late night probe on the intelligence network. Petrov was an oligarch who the CIA was monitoring. He'd recently had several dealings with Windslow, according to CIA INTEL bulletins.

The mention of Petrov's name sparked an instant reaction that Storm hadn't expected.

Windslow sprung from his seat toward the chair where Storm was sitting. Towering over him, the senator said, "You're sticking your nose where it doesn't belong now. Who the hell do you think you are? How dare you come into my house and accuse me of taking bribes! How dare you accuse my wife of being in cahoots with the kidnappers! How dare you ask about private intelligence matters between Jones and me! Why did you mention Ivan Petrov just now? Did Jedidiah put you up to that? Is that why he brought you in—to investigate Petrov and me?"

Windslow hesitated for a second, clearly thinking about his next step. Still fuming, he said, "Listen, son, all I need to know from you right now is whether you're in this thing tonight or you're out. I can arrange for Toppers to get the six million from the bank. But I'm going to need time to find someone else to drive her around if you back out. Are you in this thing or not?"

"What about Agent Showers and the Bureau?" Storm asked.

"I've already answered that. No FBI. Period."

"Even if Agent Showers and the Bureau are your best shot at saving Matthew Dull's life?"

Windslow's face was now turning red with both frustration and anger. "You're supposed to be my best shot. But, so far, all you've done is flap your jaws and question my integrity. I've destroyed men much more powerful than you are. I crushed them like bugs under my boot heel. If you want out of this, then get the hell out of my house and go back to whatever rock you crawled out from under. But you'll keep your damn mouth shut about the six million—if you know what's good for you. Either way, I need to know if you are in or out."

Storm rose from his seat and stood directly in front of Windslow's age-lined face. "Don't threaten me, Senator," he said calmly. "The last guy who did didn't survive his 'heart attack.'"

For a moment, neither flinched, and then Windslow broke into an odd smile. "Fair enough," he said. "In Texas, we admire a man who stands his mud. But while the two of us are having this little pissing contest, time is wasting."

Common sense told Storm to walk away. The kidnappers had an inside source. The fact that they wanted him to drive tonight was suspicious. Was he being set up? Ever since Tangiers, Storm had trusted Jones completely. He still did. But was it possible that Senator Windslow was right about the CIA's involvement? People were expendable. Storm had learned that early on. And that applied to him, too. For the good of the country, he could be sacrificed.

From the beginning, Storm had been curious about why Jedidiah had brought him back to help solve a kidnapping. There had to be more involved here. Jedidiah had admitted that to his face. But what was being hidden in the shadows? What was the game that he was being drawn deeper into?

During his overnight Internet investigation, Storm had learned about Ivan Petrov. The Russian was another suspect that he'd added to the long list of suspects identified by Agent

Showers. She had told him that the senator and Jedidiah were involved in a nasty dispute about a covert operation. Windslow had reacted violently when questioned about that operation and about Petrov. Showers had mentioned a six-million-dollar bribe from a foreigner. The kidnappers were demanding a six-million-dollar payoff. Were they the same six million, and if so, was that significant or a coincidence?

Only one thing was perfectly clear—the longer Storm stayed, the more he discovered, the more difficult it would be to walk away. Senator Windslow had just offered him an out. To the world, Derrick Storm was still dead. He could catch a flight back to Montana that afternoon and disappear. He could be fly-fishing at sunrise tomorrow. The big trout was still there waiting for him.

It really could be that simple. That easy. All he had to do was walk away now, which is what anyone with any shred of common sense would do.

"I'll drive tonight," Storm said.

"What about Agent Showers?" Windslow asked. "Are you going to tell her about what's happening—about the money and the four bags?"

"No," Storm said. "I'll deliver the money tonight with Samantha Toppers on my own. Without backup—either from the FBI or Jones."

CHAPTER SIX

Storm had gone about a mile from Windslow's Great Falls estate, when the cell phone that Jedidiah Jones had given him began to ring.

"Out on an early morning drive," Jones said when Storm answered. "How's our friend this morning?"

Jones was tracking him. Was the FBI, too?

"He's a bit rattled," Storm said.

"Why don't you drop into my office? The exit is clearly marked."

Jones was referring to a green exit sign on the George Washington Parkway that read: "George Bush Center for Intelligence CIA, Next Left."

So much for secrecy.

Storm took the exit and soon reached a stoplight where Georgetown Pike intersected with the entrance to the CIA's vast compound in Langley. Someone had placed freshly cut flowers next to two wooden crosses in the median. The sight of them brought back a memory.

It had been cold in January 1993 when an Islamic

fundamentalist from Pakistan stopped at this intersection and casually stepped from his Isuzu pickup. He'd lifted an AK-47 rifle to his shoulder and started shooting motorists and passengers in the vehicles that had stopped behind him at the stoplight, waiting to turn into the CIA compound. They were employees on their way to work. The shooter had spared the women because he'd considered murdering them a cowardly act. In all, the Pakistani killed two CIA employees and wounded three others before he returned to his truck and drove away. It had taken a special CIA team five years to track down the gunman. They'd caught him while he was asleep in a three-dollar-a-night Pakistan hotel. The terrorist had been brought back to the U.S., put on trial, and executed in Virginia's electric chair. The flowers were a reminder of the nation's many enemies out there.

When the red light changed, Storm turned into the CIA entrance and out of habit stayed in the left lane as he approached a large guardhouse. Suddenly, he caught his mistake and swerved into the right lane. The entrance on the left side was for employees. As directed by signs, Storm stopped at a speaker and announced that his name was Steve Mason and he was coming to see the director of the NCS.

"What's your Social Security number?" a male voice asked.

"You'll have to ask the director for it," he replied.

For several minutes, Storm sat in his car at the now silent speaker, imagining what was happening in the guardhouse, which was about a hundred yards directly in front of him. It was unusual for someone to withhold their Social Security number.

Finally, the male voice said, "Mr. Mason, drive forward slowly."

Two armed security officers stepped from the guardhouse, both cradling semiautomatic weapons. When he reached them, one of the officers compared his face to a picture. It was an old shot from Storm's CIA files, only the name on it now was "STEVE MASON." Satisfied, the officer let him pass.

Storm drove the Taurus through a maze of waist-high concrete pillars designed to prevent motorists from speeding through the main gate. He parked in the visitor's lot outside the 1960s-era Old Headquarters Building at the top of a gentle hill. Inside, Storm walked across the CIA emblem embedded in the gray marble lobby floor. To his left was a white stone wall inscribed with a quote from the Holy Bible: John, Chapter 8, Verse 32:

"And ye shall know the truth, and the truth shall make you free."

To his right were five rows of stars on a wall, each representing a CIA officer who had been killed in the line of duty.

An attractive middle-aged woman dressed in a dark gray business suit was waiting to escort Storm through Security. Storm found Jedidiah perched behind his GSA-issued executive desk, which had been cleared of all papers, a routine practice whenever someone not officially employed by the Agency entered a room.

"Why'd the senator call you this morning? Was he having nightmares?" Jones asked gleefully.

Déjà vu. How many times had Storm sat across from

Jones in this office? How many times had they discussed black ops? But that had been then. This was now.

Ignoring Jones's question, Storm replied, "When were you going to tell me about Ivan Petrov?"

Jones leaned forward and raised his interlocked fingers, placing them directly under his chin with his elbows now resting on his desk. He seemed to be in deep thought. "I wondered when you would identify Petrov. What have you learned?"

It was as if Storm were still in training, being dropped off with only the clothes on his back in a frozen wilderness as part of a survival exercise.

"Ivan Petrov," Storm said, "was once best friends with Russian President Oleg Barkovsky. It was Barkovsky who helped Petrov become a multi-billionaire by letting him privatize the nation's largest bank after the collapse of the Soviet Union. He became one of Russia's first oligarchs. Private jets, a yacht in the Mediterranean—Petrov bought all the toys. He even owns an English castle outside London formerly owned by the Duke of Madison. And then two years ago, Petrov started biting the hand that was feeding him. How am I doing so far?"

Jones nodded approvingly. "Go on," he said.

"Petrov began publicly criticizing Barkovsky. He developed political ambitions of his own. That's when President Barkovsky brought down the hammer. He sent the Federal Security Service into Petrov's bank and seized all its records. He accused Petrov of embezzlement and crimes against the state. He was about to have him arrested when Petrov somehow managed to slip out of Moscow."

Storm paused and said, "His escape looked like something you might have had a hand in."

Jones smiled slightly and said, "More likely MI-6. The Brits. They've done that sort of thing before, remember? But you're the one telling this story."

"Petrov surfaced in London, where he surrounded himself with bodyguards and began a personal crusade to get Barkovsky ousted from the Kremlin. The Russian president didn't take the attacks well. There was a sensational murder. The poisoning of a top Petrov aide. Radionuclide polonium-210, I believe. Nasty stuff. Next came a car bomb. Petrov decided to come here. Probably felt safer. That's when he really began showing up on your radar. Correct?"

Jones leaned back in his chair, which squeaked loudly. He rested his hands in his lap. And waited, without comment, for Storm to continue.

"Petrov makes a big splash in Washington. He buys a mansion on Embassy Row. He begins throwing elaborate parties for the city's political elite. And he continues his verbal attacks on Barkovsky. He continues plotting ways to undermine him. He starts making friends on Capitol Hill."

"Money and power," Jones said. "They're magnets in this town."

"Petrov has the money. Billions," Storm said. "Windslow has the power. A perfect marriage."

Leaning forward, Jones began rapping his right index finger on top of his desk as if he were playing a drum. He was becoming impatient. "That all?" he asked.

"Is there more?" Storm replied coyly.

"I was hoping you could tell me."

Cat and mouse. You go first.

Storm shook his head, indicating that he was done.

"You've uncovered the basics," Jones said, taking over the story. "Everyone began getting nervous when Petrov and Windslow became so chummy. Officially, the White House has good relations with Russian President Barkovsky, so the President didn't like having the chair of the Senate Intelligence Committee becoming bosom buddies with an oligarch whose mission in life is to destroy a sitting Russian leader."

"I'm sure Petrov's billions made the White House nervous—given Windslow's light fingers."

Jones gave Storm an approving smile. "So you do know more. Shall I assume you also know about Agent Showers's investigation and her recent claim that Windslow was paid a six-million-dollar bribe."

"Showers said the six million came from London via the Cayman Islands. Petrov was granted political asylum by the Brits after he was forced to flee Moscow," Storm said. "It's an easy connection to make."

"But it's a circumstantial connection at best. There's no proof that Petrov paid the bribe or that Windslow got it."

For a second, Storm considered telling Jones about the six million in cash that Windslow had hidden in a bank safety deposit box. But he decided against it. He wanted to see what else Jones was willing to tell him.

"What was Petrov hoping to buy with his six-million-dollar bribe?" Storm asked.

"We don't know. At least, not for certain."

"Could it be the covert operation that you two are fighting about?"

"So you know about that, too," Jones said. "You are a resourceful student."

"That's why you love me, isn't it? Now, what is it—the covert operation that you are fighting about?"

"It's a 'need to know' operation, and you don't need to know."

"Is it linked to the kidnapping?"

Jones gave Storm a blank look. "I said you didn't need to know."

"Do you think Petrov is responsible for the kidnapping?"

"You tell me," Jones said.

It was a difficult game to play with someone as experienced as Jedidiah Jones. He knew secrets about secrets about secrets. And he kept them carefully concealed until he needed to use them. Obviously, he was keeping the covert operation and his opinion of Ivan Petrov to himself. At least for now.

"Is Petrov even in the country?" Storm asked.

"He's in London or on his yacht. It hardly matters. A billionaire can hire anyone to do his dirty work."

"Why is a car from the Russian embassy tailing Agent Showers?"

"Now, that's a good question—that you should ask her."

"I will." Changing subjects, Storm said, "Senator Windslow suggested this morning that you brought me here as a ruse. He said you don't really care about solving the kidnapping. He suggested that you wanted me to investigate his relationship with Petrov. He thinks you might even have engineered this whole thing—the kidnapping—as part of some elaborate agency ploy."

A look of disgust came over Jones's face. "Please, do you think I would put this agency at risk by abducting a senator's stepson in broad daylight in Georgetown and then jerking his teeth out? My hands are clean. But he's right about me wanting you to find out more about his relationship with Petrov. The White House also wants to know more."

Storm asked, "Is that why Agent Showers's bribery case against Senator Windslow has been put on ice? The White House doesn't want the public to know that Petrov bribed Windslow?"

"Let's just say everyone believes it is prudent to wait right now until we know for certain that Petrov bribed Windslow and, if he did, what Petrov expected to get for his money. The White House wants to know the answers to that before it's made public. There could be international consequences."

"And the covert mission—the one that you don't want to discuss—could that be something that Windslow got you and the agency to do for Petrov? Are your hands really clean?"

Jones raised his palms in front of him. It was a gesture that was intended to show that his palms were washed and also to stop this line of questioning. "Let's focus on the kidnapping," he said.

"'And ye shall know the truth, and the truth shall make you free,'" Storm taunted.

"Sometimes too much truth is not a good thing when it comes to international politics," Jones replied. "Find out who's behind the kidnapping. And do it without causing the White House or this agency embarrassment."

"One last question," Storm asked. "Where'd you hide the bug? In the rental car or are you using the cell phone?"

"You're the private detective," Jones said. "You figure it out."

CHAPTER SEVEN

S torm could hear the muffled sounds of a television playing inside his hotel suite as he approached its locked door. Someone was inside. He knew it was her as soon as he smelled her perfume. Swiping his room key through the electronic lock, he walked in, expecting to see Clara Strike.

But she was not there. It was Agent Showers.

A coincidence that both women wore the same fragrance? Or was it him? How many times had he and Clara met in hotel rooms? How many sweaty mornings, afternoons, and nights had they made love? Was he having some Pavlov's dog reaction? Was Agent Showers replacing Clara in his thoughts?

"You were supposed to meet me at eight o'clock," Showers said, clearly irritated. "I was scheduled to take you to our FBI command post."

She was sitting on the suite's sofa watching CNN on a flatscreen while sipping a Diet Coke from the recently restocked mini-bar.

"A bit early to be drinking Diet Coke, isn't it?" he asked,

walking to the minibar. He took out an imported beer.

"A bit early to be drinking a beer, isn't it?" she shot back.

He sat in a chair near the sofa. "I'm glad I finally got you in-suite," he said, glancing toward the bed.

"Don't get your hopes up," she replied.

"I was hoping you'd get them up for me," he answered.

Ignoring the innuendo, she said, "Where have you been? I've been waiting."

"Sightseeing."

"Are you going to tell me about your meeting this morning with Senator Windslow? How about your meeting with Jedidiah Jones? We're on the same team, right?"

So the FBI was tracking his movements, too.

Storm took a swig and then said, "Agent Showers, when were you going to tell me about Ivan Petrov?"

She looked surprised. "Did Windslow tell you about Petrov or did Jones?"

"Neither. This might surprise you, but I am a private detective."

"Does Jones think Petrov is behind the kidnapping?"

"You'll have to ask him," Storm replied. "Do you think Petrov had the stepson kidnapped?"

"Yes, I do. I think that's why the kidnappers didn't try to pick up the one-million-dollar ransom in Union Station. Petrov's a billionaire and he doesn't need the money. He kidnapped Matthew Dull because he's pressuring the senator to do something for him—something that I think your buddy Jedidiah Jones knows about. I think it's all tied to some covert operation they're fighting about. But every time

I ask about it, I'm told it's 'above my pay grade.' The same old shitty excuse that I'm always told."

"I'm surprised," Storm said.

"Why? You think I'm wrong?"

"No, I think you're probably right. Petrov is the most likely suspect. And I also think something strange is going on between Windslow and Jones. But the reason why I'm surprised is because you just said the word 'shitty.'"

She gave him a puzzled look.

"That's such rude language," he continued, "coming from someone who got her undergraduate degree at Marymount University. Isn't that suburban Washington, D.C., school a Catholic enclave, founded by the Religious of the Sacred Heart of Mary? I doubt the good nuns allowed you to swear on campus."

"Is this your clever way of telling me that you ran a background check on me last night?"

"Editor of the *Georgetown Law Review*, top in your graduating class at the FBI Academy in Quantico. The Bureau sent you to Seattle first, but you were too good to stay long in the field. The brass wanted you at headquarters. The best and brightest. A go-to agent in high-profile cases. Smart. Clever. Someone who understood this city. A workaholic. No time for hobbies. No time for fun. No time for marriage or even a boyfriend. Your mother doesn't like that. She wants grandkids."

"There's nothing in my personnel record about my mother wanting grandkids," she said.

"Doesn't need to be. Flaming red hair. Emerald eyes. You've

got Irish written all over your face. I've never met an Irish mother, especially a good Catholic, who didn't want her only daughter married and pregnant. She must be so disappointed."

"It's none of your business."

"You asked me about my past."

"And you didn't tell me a damn thing."

"Ah, more profanity. Did the nuns slap your knuckles? How did they feel about premarital intercourse?"

She started to respond but caught herself. "Let's cut the bull, er, crap," she said.

He had gotten to her. Unnerved her. Irritated her. He was enjoying this.

She asked, "Did the kidnappers contact Windslow this morning? Is that why he got you up so early and you went to his house?"

She had good instincts. She suspected something was up.

Storm took another long swig and noticed that he'd almost emptied the bottle. "The senator specifically asked me to keep our meeting this morning confidential," he replied. "If you haven't noticed, he's lost faith in the FBI."

Showers hit the television remote hard with her right thumb, flipping off the CNN newscast. "What did Jones tell you at the CIA?"

"Why aren't you married, Agent Showers?"

"Are you?" she shot back. "Do you have an ex living in Hawaii, a girlfriend in Pocatello? Oh, maybe you like boys?"

She was getting warmed up now. He could see fire in her green eyes and he liked it.

Continuing, Showers said, "Are you going to tell me

about your meetings with Windslow and Jones? Or are we going to keep trade insults?"

"Insults? I thought we were engaging in foreplay," he replied. "Tell me something juicy about yourself—something dirty."

He could tell that she wasn't enjoying this. He was.

"You think you're clever, don't you?" she asked. "You roll into Washington like some big, bad hero brought in to save the day and impress everyone while giving me and the Bureau the finger."

"Yes. But with you I mean it in the nicest way."

Rising from her seat, she said: "You need a reality check. No one is above the law. Not Senator Windslow, not Jedidiah Jones, and certainly not you. If you're not going to cooperate, then I'm not going to watch your back. You should think about that. And think about this, too. If I discover that you intentionally withheld evidence or did something illegal for the senator—even something just a teensy-weensy against the law—I'm going to come down on you with the full weight of the Justice Department. You're not a federal employee. You're a civilian, just like any other asshole on the streets."

With a look of fake innocence, Storm replied, "How did they define 'teensy-weensy illegal' at Georgetown Law? I'm not familiar with it as a legal term."

Her face flushed red. She started walking toward the suite's door.

"Agent Showers," he called after her.

She paused, glancing over her shoulder.

"This is the second time that I've been threatened today

and it's not even noon," he said.

"Maybe instead of being an ass," she replied, "you should start cooperating with the people who can help you. You're a fool if you try to handle this on your own." She reached for the doorknob and turned it. "I'll tell them at the command post that you are being less than forthcoming."

"Before you go," he said, "I have a question. Why was a car from the Russian embassy tailing you last night after you left the hotel?"

She turned to face him but kept her hand on the doorknob. "It's interesting that you know when someone is being tailed, but you don't know when you're being played. Did it ever dawn on you that the reason Jones brought you into this case is to be a fall guy?"

"How would I end up being a fall guy, Agent Showers?"

"Quid pro quo," she replied.

"Oh, I'll show you mine if you show me yours. No, thanks. Unless you actually do want to see mine."

As before, she ignored his sexual flirtation. "There'll be a scapegoat if Matthew Dull ends up dead," she said. "This is Washington. Someone will have to take the blame."

"You did learn something at Georgetown Law," he said.

"One of the first lessons was that it's always the person who's in the weakest position who gets hung out to dry. That's you."

Storm put his now empty beer bottle down and looked up at her from his chair. *There was a magnetism about her. A passion. His father had warned him to stay away from red-haired women. "They're nuts!" he'd said. Storm thought about what she was saying. Was he really in the weakest position? It was not an unusual position for him to fall into. All of his training had been aimed at teaching him how to strengthen his position, how to overcome any type of obstacle. If he were in a weak position, he knew that he could find a way out. Could she? It was clear to him that Agent Showers was playing a game of checkers, when everyone else around her was playing chess. Did she realize it?*

"Since you graduated magna cum laude," Storm replied, "You know that what you just said is—to use your own term—bull crap."

He was mimicking her. He was continuing to push her buttons.

Storm said, "Yes, the weakest player is always the fall guy. But in this investigation, I am not him. It is not Senator Windslow and it certainly is not Jedidiah Jones. It's you, Agent Showers."

April Showers slammed the suite's door as she exited.

He gave her ten minutes to vacate the hotel. After that, he went to the lobby and spoke to the concierge.

"I'd like to rent a van. Can I get it before lunch?" Storm asked.

"Of course. How long will you need it?"

"I'll return it tomorrow morning. I'd prefer something with no windows, or heavily tinted ones."

"I'll arrange it immediately."

When he returned to his suite, he could still smell the remnants of her perfume.

CHAPTER EIGHT

Storm left the hotel shortly after 12 P.M. in the rented, white Ford E-series commercial van that the concierge had arranged for him. The van had seats for a driver and a passenger, but its cargo bay was empty. There were no windows except for the windshield and the front doors. After driving through the Virginia suburbs for a half hour to make certain that he wasn't being followed, Storm bought four women's gym bags at a sporting goods store and then returned to the District. He drove to the Thomas Jefferson Memorial, located at the southern end of the National Mall, adjacent to the Tidal Basin in West Potomac Park. He parked the van there and flagged down a taxi, which brought him back to his hotel with the gym bags.

Storm grabbed a shower and dressed in loafers, khaki pants, a blue shirt, and a navy sports coat. He tucked his Glock .40-caliber semiautomatic into the special holster that he wore in the center of his back and made certain he had extra ammunition. Now ready, he went downstairs and gave the valet his parking stub. A few minutes later, Storm was driving east toward the Capitol in the Taurus sedan that Jones had rented for him. He was scheduled to meet Samantha Toppers and Senator Windslow in the Dirksen SOB at 4 P.M.

Toppers was pacing nervously inside the senator's inner office when he arrived. Senator Windslow was seated at his desk.

"I've called the president at Riggs Bank and arranged for Samantha to have access to the safety deposit box," Windslow said. "Did you get the gym bags?"

"They're in the car," Storm replied.

Windslow suddenly shouted at Toppers. "Stop fidgeting, girl! And make sure you have your damn cell phone with you."

"I've got to use the bathroom," she stammered. She ducked into the senator's private toilet that was connected to his office.

"You haven't told the FBI about this, have you?" Windslow growled.

"No. I told you that I'd keep it confidential."

"Does Jedidiah know?"

"No."

"Good."

A still visibly frantic Toppers joined them. "I'm not sure I can go through with this!" she said. "What do you think is going to happen tonight?"

"They'll make us drive around the city," Storm answered. "We'll be sent down one-way streets and then they'll have us reverse our route so they can see if anyone is following us. They'll probably select routes that don't have much traffic so it will be obvious if we are being tailed. And when they are convinced that we are in the clear, they'll have us make the deliveries."

"What if they take us hostage?" she asked. Storm noticed that her hands were trembling.

"Don't worry, dear," Windslow said. "You have him to protect you—and my six million."

Storm added, "I'll make certain nothing happens to you. Let's go."

Riggs National Bank was located about a block from the White House and could be seen on the back of a ten-dollar bill, behind the U.S. Treasury Building. Naomi Chatts, a senior bank official, met Storm and Toppers at the entrance and escorted them to the safety deposit vault in the building's basement. Storm stayed outside the giant walk-in chamber, which was protected by a huge swinging stainless steel door. It was an older Diebold model that was three and a half feet thick and operated on a time lock. A beefy security guard was stationed at a desk next to the vault's entrance, and Storm made small talk with him.

Ms. Chatts escorted Toppers inside the massive vault and then joined Storm and the guard outside the chamber's entrance. About ten minutes later, Toppers appeared at the vault door lugging the four gym bags, two per each hand. Storm took the stuffed bags from her while Ms. Chatts ducked into the vault to make certain Toppers hadn't accidently left anything behind.

"Can you have two of your guards escort us to our car?" Storm asked Chatts. There would be no way for him to carry the four bags and defend himself.

"Yes," Ms. Chatts said. She had the guard make a telephone call, and by the time that Storm and Toppers had gone upstairs, there were two armed, uniformed officers waiting at the entrance for them.

"Please give my best regards to Senator Windslow," Ms. Chatts said cheerfully as they exited the bank. The Taurus was double-parked directly outside the door. Storm put all four bags into the rear seat while Toppers took a seat in the front.

So far, so good. It was show time now. He needed to stay alert. To watch for some tip off, some clue to the kidnappers' identity. Something he could use.

As he merged into traffic, Storm checked his rearview mirror and spotted an unmarked Ford sedan behind them. He drove the Taurus to K Street, which was often referred to as the city's main street because of the many law firms and lobbyist offices that bordered it. The Ford stuck with them. Storm was going West on K Street along with a steady stream of rush hour drivers.

Suddenly, he swerved off the main thoroughfare into the entrance to an underground parking garage. He turned so quickly that he nearly hit a woman walking on the sidewalk. She jumped back and shot him the finger as the Taurus raced down the lot's ramp.

As soon as the car reached the garage attendant's station, Storm leaped from it, tossed the keys to one of the workers there, and grabbed the four gym bags from the backseat.

"C'mon!" he hollered to Toppers.

"Where are we going!" she shrieked.

"Follow me! Now!"

Storm rushed down the parking ramp to a basement exit. With Toppers chasing after him, he ran up two flights of concrete steps to a street exit that opened into an alley behind the office building. He dashed out and hurried down the alley to Nineteenth Street NW—a one-way street filled with southbound traffic. The bored taxi driver who stopped for them didn't bother getting out of his cab. Instead, he pushed a remote button to pop the car's trunk. Storm tossed the four bags into it and got into the backseat with a now breathless Toppers.

"Where to?" the driver asked.

"State Department and we're in a hurry."

"Everyone is," the cabbie said. "That's what's wrong with this country." The driver, whose taxi license was on display, was from Ghana, and he launched into an immediate monologue about the ills of America's rushed society. Storm ignored the mindless chatter. He was looking at the alleyway to see if anyone had followed them. He didn't see anyone.

The cabbie abruptly stopped talking, and when Storm looked at the car's rearview mirror, he saw why. The driver's eyes were locked onto Topper's breasts, which were heaving as she struggled to catch her breath from running.

"You might want to redirect your eyes to the road," Storm suggested.

Storm again glanced behind the cab to see if the Ford was behind them. It wasn't. He had a hunch that the men inside it were now in the parking garage having a frantic conversation with FBI Agent Showers. She would have known that a ransom drop was being made as soon as Storm traveled from the Dirksen SOB to Riggs National Bank. Why else would he go there? Storm assumed that she had immediately sent two special agents to tail them. At that point, Agent Showers had made a critical error. She'd felt a false sense of security because of the monitor in the Taurus. She had not felt a need to flood the area with agents or call in air surveillance. Storm had not only abandoned the car in the underground parking garage, he'd also left the cell phone that Jedidiah Jones had given him on the vehicle's front seat. It was probably ringing right now.

When the taxi was about a block from the State Department, Storm announced that he'd changed his mind. "Take us to the Jefferson Memorial," he said.

As the cab continued south into the traffic traveling around the National Mall, Storm checked for tails. There were none. They had gone "black."

"You guys married?" the cabbie asked when the cab stopped at a red light.

"No, we work together," Storm said.

The cabbie caught another peek at Samantha's cleavage. She was wearing black wedge leather slip-ons without stockings, a tight denim blue jean skirt, and a bright pink, short satin jacket that was layered over a cream-colored silk blouse and sexy black lace camisole.

"You're a lucky guy," the cabbie said as the light changed. "To work with such a pretty lady would be a pleasure indeed."

Samantha smiled and said, "Thank you!"

Ten minutes later, the taxi reached the Jefferson Memorial parking lot. Storm took the four gym bags from the trunk and eyeballed the lot while the driver got out of the car to open the rear passenger door to Samantha, anxious to take a mental snapshot of those architectural marvels, no doubt.

Confident that they hadn't been followed, Storm led Toppers to the Ford cargo van that he'd parked here earlier.

"We're taking this," he explained, unlocking the doors. "Get in."

Storm had just stored the four gym bags in the cargo area when the rhythmic voice of Rihanna could be heard coming from inside Toppers's Lilly Pulitzer handbag.

"Your phone?" he asked her.

"Yeah." It was 6 P.M. The kidnappers were calling right on time.

Toppers was so nervous that she dropped the phone while she was removing it from her handbag. She bent forward and snatched it off the floor mat.

"Give it here," Storm ordered. He answered it.

A deep voice that sounded like Darth Vader said, "You got our money?" The caller was using some sort of voice changer software.

"That's right. Where do you want us to go?"

"Arlington National Cemetery. Robert E. Lee mansion. Leave the first gym bag in a public trash receptacle about fifty feet from the house's front entrance. There's a National Park Service sign next to the trash can."

The line went dead.

A trash container in a public park. It was an odd place for a drop. Or was it?

Pulling from the memorial's parking lot, Storm headed west across the Potomac River into Northern Virginia. He glanced at Toppers. Her face was ghost white. She looked as if she were about to faint or vomit. When he lowered his eyes, he noticed that her tight jean skirt had risen up when she'd bent over to retrieve her cell phone from the floor. She was wearing a tiny red thong with white polka dots. She'd either not noticed or felt no need to readjust her skirt.

She was a distraction and he needed to be focused. He decided to do what he always did when a woman was distracting him, especially sexually. He would talk with her. He would calm her down. Then he could focus on what was important and not her taut little body, her freshly shaved legs, her muscular thighs.

"You're doing fine," he said. "Think about something else. Tell me about Matthew. Where did you meet?"

"We were in the same first-year English class. He asked me to have coffee. He kept his eyes on my eyes the entire time. Not many boys do that."

Her candor surprised him. Why? Did he think she was so naïve that she didn't understand how her figure affected men? How she could use it to manipulate them?

"What are you studying in school?"

"No one believes me when I tell them, because they assume that someone who looks like I do has to be dumb, but I'm studying mechanical engineering." She laughed.

Good. He was breaking the tension. Helping her relax. Mechanical engineering. Curious.

Continuing, she said, "I know Senator Winslow thinks I'm stupid. He told Matthew that I was an airhead. But I've always been good with math and designing. I'm a whiz at reading and drawing blueprints."

"Good for you," Storm replied. "The senator's a jackass."

"Where did the kidnappers tell you to stash the money?" she asked him.

Her question set off an alarm bell. Although he'd heard her, he acted as if he hadn't. He wanted to make sure that he'd heard exactly what she'd said.

"What did you say?" he asked.

"Where did they tell you to stash the cash?"

He had heard her correctly.

"In an outside trash can," he replied. "How long have you been engaged to Matthew? Tell me a little about your background."

"He asked me three months ago. It was a total surprise. He wants to have a big wedding in Texas on a ranch."

"You aren't getting married in your hometown?"

"No. I lost my folks when I was a teenager. In an accident."

"An accident?"

"An awful car accident. We were vacationing in Spain, where my parents had a house. My mom and dad and a friend of mine who was on vacation with us were killed by a drunk driver who swerved into the wrong lane. It was horrible."

"You weren't with them?"

"No. Everyone said I was lucky." Tears began to fill her eyes. "I had a bad cold that night and stayed home when they went to dinner. I'd rather not talk about it."

The Taurus reached a traffic circle. Storm turned from it into the entrance to Arlington National Cemetery.

"Is that where we're going?" Toppers asked, looking at a house directly in front of them on a hill.

"Yes," he replied. "That's Lee's mansion."

A guard stopped them at the cemetery's gated entrance.

"Sorry, you missed the last tour of the house," he said. "It was at four-thirty."

"I've got friends buried here. Iraq," Storm said. "We'll pay our respects and tour the house some other time."

"Take this," the guard said, handing Storm a pamphlet. He waved them through.

The Robert E. Lee house was built in the early 1800s, in the Greek Revival style. Designed by one of the architects who worked on the U.S. Capitol, the stone mansion had six large columns holding up the front of its massive portico. When the Civil War started, the Union began burying fallen soldiers near the house because President Lincoln wanted the Lee family, including the Confederate general's wife, who was living there, to see the graves when she looked out her windows each morning.

Storm weaved through the acres of white tablets, eventually making his way up the hill to the front of the mansion.

"There's the drop site," he said, pointing to a dark green outdoor trash container. It was overflowing with garbage.

Storm drove to it and scanned the area. No one was watching them. He picked up a gym bag and unzipped it. Toppers had carefully stacked one-hundred-dollar bills in neat rows. Closing the bag, Storm stepped from the still running cargo van and shoved the money deep inside the debris, covering the top with discarded newspapers.

Toppers's cell phone rang as soon as he returned to the driver's seat. It was Darth Vader again.

"Time for the next drop."

Storm sensed that they were being watched. It was a sixth sense that had served him well in combat. There wasn't anyone near the Lee house, but there was a large group of people several hundred yards down the hill. Storm had been to enough funerals to recognize that the departed had just been given full military honors. The flag-draped coffin had been carried on a horse-drawn caisson to the grave site. A color guard had escorted it there. A military band had sounded a farewell, followed by a three-rifle volley. It was dusk and that was late for a graveside service, which meant someone important had pulled strings to arrange it. The evening sun was setting, but from the grave's vantage point, a mourner could glance up the hill and see the white cargo van.

Had one of the kidnappers blended into the crowd of mourners? Was Darth Vader among them?

The scrambled voice said, "Head to Georgetown. The canal on Thirty-first Street. Walk down the path to Wisconsin Avenue. The first trash can on the right. Leave the second bag in it."

Storm exited the cemetery and crossed the Potomac back into the District, where the van was immediately stuck in traffic. A woman talking on her cell phone nearly collided with them when she cut in front of the van.

"Stupid broad," Toppers snapped. "It's against the law to use a cell phone in the District unless you've got a hands-free device. Someone should arrest her. She could have killed us."

An accident was all that they needed. A cop further stalling traffic. A fender bender disrupting their delivery schedule.

"Senator Windslow said you were a trust fund baby," Storm said, casually probing. "That's one reason why he knew you wouldn't run away with his six million."

"It's not polite to talk about money," Toppers said. "My parents had houses in Connecticut, Spain, and in Palm Beach, too. I loved it there. You ever been?"

"It's too rich for my blood," Storm replied. "I was there but not during the Season."

"The summer," she said. "That's the best time. Me and a friend of mine had a wild time there. Actually, we had a bet to see who could lose their virginity first!" She took a stick of gum from her purse and offered him a piece.

"No thanks," he said. She put two in her mouth and began chewing.

The Season. In Palm Beach, that term had special meaning. It was a five-month whirlwind of parties, balls, and charity events that no one who was anyone dared miss. It was a timeless ritual for America's most wealthy, the Old Guard's most treasured social event. It was a tradition carefully passed down from generation to generation. And it was not during the hot summer months. It was when the snowbirds ventured south to escape the cold.

When they reached 31st Street NW, Storm slipped into an alleyway and left Toppers in the van while he walked briskly to the Chesapeake and Ohio Canal. The man-made canal had been constructed because the Potomac was considered too unpredictable for safe travel. Merchants needed a safe way to transport tobacco and other commodities some 185 miles west. By the time the canal was dug, it was already obsolete because of the railroad. Now couples used the pebble-strewed path next to the canal for evening strolls, while bicyclists and joggers hurried by them.

Storm waited until the path was empty, and then he stuffed the gym bag into the trash receptacle, covering it with discarded cups, cans, bottles, and papers.

As had happened after the first delivery in Arlington Cemetery, Rihanna's voice greeted Storm as soon as he returned to the van.

Four kidnappers had abducted Matthew. Was it possible that a different one of them was monitoring each delivery? How else would they know where he was?

"What took you so long?" Darth Vader asked.

"There were people on the path," Storm replied. "What happens if a stranger gets one of the gym bags by accident?"

"Your boy dies."

Darth Vader told them to drop the third bag at Hains Point, located at the southernmost tip of East Potomac Park—a good twenty-minute trip from Georgetown during rush hour.

Bordered by the Potomac River on one side and the Washington Channel on the other, Hains Point was at the tip of a man-made island composed of dirt dredged from both rivers. When they reached it, Storm hid the bag in a public trash container just as he had hidden the others.

The final drop-off point was at Battery Kemble Park, a tiny area of grass and woods in Northwest Washington, smack in the middle of expensive homes. The park was a former Civil War battery built on high ground so that Union troops could look down during the fighting and fire canons if enemy soldiers attempted to cross the Potomac and enter the city. Now it was popular with local dog walkers. Storm dumped several bags of discarded poop onto the gym bag.

Samantha's phone rang as if on cue.

"Okay, we've done our part," Storm said. "Where's Matthew?"

"Wait in Union Station for my next call."

"We've played by the rules," Storm told the caller. "If you don't, you'll never live to enjoy your money."

The line went dead.

He looked at Toppers. She'd pulled down her skirt. She was still chewing her gum.

She had no idea that he had been interrogating her.

CHAPTER NINE

Storm and Toppers found seats at a bar on the main floor of the Union Station terminal. She placed her cell phone in front of them so they would not miss any calls. She was jittery.

All around the bar, there was motion. Commuters rushed to catch trains. Tourists gawked at the restored rotunda, wandered from shop to shop in search of souvenirs, and snapped photographs. A homeless man begged for quarters. Neither Storm nor Toppers paid attention to the whirlwind. Their eyes were on the pink cell phone resting on the bar. They were waiting for Rihanna's voice.

"What's taking them so long?" Toppers complained.

It had been nearly a half hour. Something caught Storm's attention. It was a news reporter on the flat-screen television behind the bar. Storm motioned for the bartender to turn up the volume.

"Park police do not believe the explosion was the work of terrorists," the petite blond news reporter breathlessly announced. As the camera pulled back, viewers could see that she was standing outside the Robert E. Lee mansion. Red and blue strobe lights from emergency vehicles flashed against the house's marble columns.

The reporter said, "Once again, this does not seem to be a terrorist attack. However, a spokesman for the National Park Service said the explosion was not the result of some natural cause, such as a garbage fire. An explosive device was put into the trash can, but it was more like a powerful Fourth of July firecracker than a bomb, the spokesman said. At this point, we don't know why someone would want to blow up a trash can here. There's speculation it might be part of a protest against the memory of Robert E. Lee and the Confederacy. However, no damage to Lee's home was done. The explosion was loud and strong enough to destroy the trash can and all of the trash inside it. But there was no serious damage."

An anchorman's face appeared on the screen, and it looked as if he were about to make a joke when his face turned somber. "I've just been told there has been a second explosion in a trash receptacle," he said. "This one in Georgetown on the C and O Canal path. There are no apparent injuries, but the blast has alarmed businesses and homeowners in the area. A bomb disposal unit is en route to the scene, and police have roped off the area and urged people to stay away from the canal path. Bomb-sniffing dogs are being sent in to search for other devices that may be hidden in trash cans by the canal."

The anchorman paused and then said, "A third explosion has been reported. This one in a trash can at Hains Point. I repeat, this is the third confirmed report of an explosion in a trash can. We have been told that the chief of police, the National Park Service, Homeland Security, and the mayor have agreed to hold an emergency meeting, but, once again, it is not believed that this is a terrorist attack. There have been no injuries because of the explosions, which the police have stressed are more like giant firecrackers than they are bombs. The purpose of the explosions, according to one fire department official, was to make a loud noise, destroy the containers, and burn whatever was inside them—rather than to injure persons or cause property damage. One source speculated that this could be a misguided prank by someone who understands basic chemistry and simply wanted to do something to frighten this city."

Because Battery Kemble Park was more isolated, it took a few more minutes before the fourth blast made the news. When the anchorman announced it, Toppers said aloud, "They're destroying the money."

The bartender and several customers gave her curious glances.

"Let's go," Storm said, gently taking her elbow and maneuvering her through the crowd that was now congregating around the bar's television.

By the time that they reached the terminal's exit, Toppers looked terrified.

"This was a mistake," she said. "Something horrible is going to happen to Matthew. I just know it!"

CHAPTER TEN

Storm and Toppers went directly from Union Station to Senator Windslow's SOB. Agent April Showers was already there. So were Senator Windslow and his distraught wife, Gloria, who was crying in her husband's arms.

"We found Matthew Dull," Showers said quietly.

"Is he okay? Where is he?" Toppers asked.

Then she realized why his mother was in tears. Toppers gasped and whispered, "Oh my God!" She collapsed on the floor. Storm helped her to the couch, and Gloria hurried over to hug her. The two women held each other and sobbed.

"His body was found floating in the Anacostia River," Showers said.

"Executed?" Storm asked.

Before Showers could reply, Gloria turned on them.

"You two were supposed to keep my son alive! I trusted you!" she shrieked.

Senator Windslow stepped between his angry wife and

the targets of her fury. "It would be better if you two left us alone for right now," he said.

Both started to leave, but the senator asked Storm to stay behind for a moment. When he did, Windslow leaned in close to his ear so that neither his wife nor Toppers could hear what he was whispering.

"What the hell happened?" he asked. "I saw the news flash. Why did you let those bastards blow up my money?"

"Later, Senator," Storm replied.

"Easy for you to say. You just didn't have six million bucks blown to pieces."

Agent Showers was waiting to ambush Storm in the hallway outside Windslow's office.

"You went behind my back," she said, her eyes ablaze. "We might have been able to save that kid if we'd worked together. The shit is going to hit the fan when the media finds out that Matthew Dull is dead."

Continuing her tirade, she said, "You need to tell me what the hell happened after you ditched my men in that parking garage on K Street this afternoon."

"Are you arresting me?"

He already knew the answer. Jedidiah Jones would not allow Storm to be arrested. Or interrogated. Survival of the fittest. Jones would not permit it because it would tie him and the Agency to this mess.

"Not yet," she snapped. "But if you don't come with me right now to headquarters and tell me what happened—I am going to recommend to my superiors that you be arrested."

She was bluffing. He knew it.

"I'm not going with you," Storm said quietly. "I have more important things to do."

He wanted to tell her, but he was not yet ready. There were still a few pieces that he needed to gather.

"I hope you have a damn good lawyer," Showers said, "because I'm going to nail your ass to the wall."

Now she was beginning to irritate him.

"Since you mentioned it, what do you think of my ass, Agent Showers?" he asked. "Most women like it."

For a moment, he thought she might actually slap him. Instead, she walked away enraged, her three-inch heels smacking the marble floor like a stick beating a snare drum.

Showers finally got it. She understood that he was right. She knew that she was on the bottom of the totem pole. She was in line to become the scapegoat, the fall guy, the weakest link. It wasn't fair, but it was what would happen. What she still didn't seem to realize was that Storm was the only person who could save her.

CHAPTER ELEVEN

The J. Edgar Hoover Building on Pennsylvania Avenue was considered such an architectural eyesore after it opened that there had been talk for years about demolishing it and moving the FBI's headquarters into the suburbs. Hoover, himself, had reportedly bullied the architects into adding several unusual safeguards to the building's boxy design. At the time, race riots were rocking Washington and other major cities, and 1960s antiwar protestors were threatening the tear down the "establishment." Fearing the FBI building might come under siege, Hoover demanded that the street level of his new headquarters be constructed without any windows or offices. Built of concrete mixed with crushed limestone for extra strength, the first level resembled a castle wall. It protected an open mezzanine where there were a limited number of elevators leading to the upper floors. There was no second floor. Instead, the second level was an ugly open gap with only structural supports and reinforced elevator shafts and stairways linking the ground and third floors. The second floor was missing to deter rioters from using ladders to scale the building. At one point, rumors surfaced that Hoover had put razor wire in the branches of the trees that lined Pennsylvania Avenue outside his building to stop attackers from climbing them to reach the headquarters' upper floors.

It was two days after the trash can explosions had alarmed the city and Matthew Dull's body had been found floating in the river. Storm was sitting alone in a conference room on the FBI headquarters sixth-floor, waiting for Agent Showers. In an upside-down move that would have been unthinkable in any major city except for Washington, D.C., Storm had come to the headquarters today—not to be questioned—but to interrogate Agent Showers.

Things had played out much as Storm had anticipated. Within minutes after Dull's corpse had been found, Jedidiah Jones had started pulling strings. FBI Director Jackson had guaranteed Jones that Storm would remain invisible and untouchable—at least for now. Senator Windslow had circled the wagons around Samantha Toppers.

Agent April Showers had been stonewalled.

At a news conference held on the morning after Dull's body was found, an FBI spokesperson told reporters that the senator's stepson had been kidnapped, held for ransom, and murdered, apparently by a foreign gang. The spokesman said Senator Windslow had cooperated fully with the FBI during the tragedy. The lead investigator on the case, Special Agent April Showers, had been removed from the investigation and was going to be reassigned to a field job.

There was no mention at the press conference of the four

trash can explosions that had happened that night, no mention of the six-million-dollar payment that had been destroyed by the blasts and fire. Instead, the agency mouthpiece had said that Dull had been executed by gang members, possibly from Mexico or Ukraine—even though the Windslows had agreed to negotiate.

Agent Showers walked into the conference room where Storm was waiting, with a thin file in her hands and a scowl on her face. She dropped the paperwork in front of him, where it landed with a thud.

"Are you going to sit down?" he asked.

Showers pulled a chair from the conference table and took a seat across from him.

"They're sending me to Tulsa," she said.

"You're not gone yet," he replied.

Storm carefully thumbed through the documents that she'd brought him. The first was her final report about the kidnapping/murder. In the classified, secret section of her report, she theorized that Dull had been kidnapped because of a sour business deal between Senator Windslow and Ivan Petrov. She claimed that the Russian oligarch had paid Windslow a "fee," believed to be six million dollars, but the senator had later broken their deal. Petrov had reacted in typical Russian fashion, by abducting the senator's stepson as a threat to force Windslow to comply. Petrov also had demanded his six-million-dollar payment back in the form of a ransom.

Although Agent Showers had been kept from interrogating Storm and Toppers, the clever FBI agent had figured out the link between the ransom demand and the exploding trash cans. In her report, Showers explained that destroying the cash had dovetailed perfectly with Petrov's criminal mind-set. Not only had he taken revenge by killing Windslow's stepson, Petrov had destroyed the original six-million-dollar bribe that he'd paid the senator.

While Showers's report was nice and neat, it did not contain any evidence to justify her theory or an arrest. Her account mentioned that immigration records from the night of Dull's murder indicated that four Ukrainians had boarded an international flight for London. Yet no one attempted to stop them from fleeing. Further investigation showed that all four were former KGB agents.

When Storm finished reading Showers's analysis, he asked, "Do you feel confident that Petrov was behind the kidnapping and it was carried out by hired thugs?"

"That's what I wrote, isn't it?" she replied in a sarcastic voice. "Not that it matters. It doesn't appear that anyone is really interested in the truth."

Storm removed a second report from the case file. It was an autopsy. Dull had been shot twice, once in the back of his skull and once in his heart. Both rounds had been fired behind him at close range, based on the entry and exit wounds. The shot through his head had passed completely through his skull and had not been recovered. However, the damage caused by the slug revealed it had been made by a hollow-point round. This meant the bullet's tip had mushroomed upon impact so it would cause maximum damage as it ripped through brain tissue and destroyed Dull's once handsome face. The bullet fired into his skull had been shot at a downward angle, which suggested the gunman had been standing behind Dull, who was most likely sitting in a chair. The location of the two wounds further suggested that Dull had been shot first in the back of his skull and then fallen forward onto the floor, where the gunman had fired the second shot straight down while standing over him. The second slug had entered through Dull's back, caused his heart to literally explode, and had exited through his chest. Because Dull had collapsed onto a hard-surfaced floor, the slug had been stopped when it attempted to exit his body. In an odd move—most likely caused by its mushroom shape—it had ricocheted back into Dull's chest, where it had lodged. The FBI had recovered this slug and discovered attached to it microscopic slivers of tile and concrete that had come from the floor. An examination of Dull's lungs confirmed that he had been dead before his body had been dumped into the river.

The report found that the bullets that killed Dull had been 9mm rounds. FBI ballistic and firearm experts had determined that the bullets had been manufactured by the JSC Barnaul Machine-Tool Plant in Russia, a leading maker of Russian military ammunition.

Storm returned the autopsy to the folder and closed the case file, which he pushed across the table to the still bitter Agent Showers.

"Do you have any files about the four trash can explosions that happened that night?" he asked.

"Why would you want to see them?" Showers asked, not trying to hide the contempt in her voice.

"Don't play dumb," he said. "It doesn't suit you."

"Are you now telling me that those four explosions were related to the kidnapping?" she asked. "Are you admitting that you and Toppers put money in those trash cans?"

"Let's just say I'm curious about everything odd that happened that night. I want to be thorough."

"Then you should contact the D.C. police," she said sarcastically. "Maybe someone stole an elephant from the National Zoo or ran naked down Pennsylvania Avenue."

"Stolen elephants and naked people do interest me," he quipped. "Naked people more than stolen elephants, unless midgets and butter are involved. But for now I'll settle for the file about the four explosions."

A clearly irked Agent Showers left the conference room. When she returned, she jabbed another case folder at Storm as if it were a knife.

"You and I both know," Showers said, "that the kidnappers blew up the ransom money after sending you and Toppers on an elaborate goose chase. Ivan Petrov spit in Windslow's face. Petrov took back his bribe money and killed his stepson. But I can't prove any of this—thanks to the higher ups protecting you, Toppers, and Senator Windslow."

Storm took the file and asked, "Did the FBI work the blasts that night or was it some other agency?"

"The explosions happened on parkland so the National Park Police and the District of Columbia police were responsible for the investigation. The actual bomb investigation was done by the federal Bureau of Alcohol, Tobacco, Firearms and Explosives because of its expertise."

Storm removed the BATF analytical report. All four explosions had been caused by identical homemade devices. The explosions had come from small amounts of ammonium nitrate packed tightly into plastic bottles. A cell phone had been used as the trigger. The devices resembled the improvised explosive devices (IEDs) used against U.S. troops in Iraq, but they packed much less power. This similarity prompted BATF investigators to speculate that the bomb maker had some military training. The IEDs were missing the projectiles that insurgents normally used to cause maximum damage. Instead the bombs had been designed to cause a loud noise and ignite fires.

Included in the report was a list of debris that had been collected at each blast site. Despite the explosion and resulting fire, numerous remnants of one-hundred-dollar bills had been found. Newspaper fragments had been collected, too, along with other debris from items commonly found in trash cans, such as plastic bottles and aluminum soda and beer cans.

Although the four cell phones used to trigger the bombs had been destroyed, investigators had been able to glean that they were identical Motorola models.

With the report still in his hands, Storm asked, "Did you read this list of remnants?"

"Of course," she replied. "Do you think you're the only one who wants to be thorough?"

"Did you notice anything odd?"

"I assume you're talking about the large amount of newsprint."

"The report says there was four times more newsprint

found at each blast site than there was remnants from hundred-dollar bills," Storm said.

"At first, I didn't think that was significant," Showers admitted, "but then I remembered that newsprint is made of wood pulp."

"And currency is made from cotton and linen," Storm said, completing her sentence.

"Which means," she said, "that the newsprint should have burned faster than the currency. Less newsprint should have survived. But there was more of it."

Storm closed the file and handed it to her.

She said, "What are you saying—that something happened to the money?"

"I'm saying this case is far from over."

He stood to leave.

"Hey, where are you going?" she asked. "What do you mean, 'This case if far from over'? What aren't you telling me?"

"I'll be in touch. Thanks for your cooperation."

"You can't just walk out of here like this," she said.

But that was exactly what he was doing.

"You're a son of a bitch—whatever your name is," she said.

The coldness in her voice was strong enough to have chilled shots from an entire fifth of Jack Daniel's.

CHAPTER TWELVE

Matthew Dull's funeral was held in the prestigious Washington National Cathedral and attracted the sort of attention you would expect when the deceased had been murdered and was related to a powerful U.S. senator. The President of the United States was traveling overseas, but he sent the vice president to represent him. At least forty members of Congress took seats in the front pews. Georgetown socialites, who knew Gloria and her son, intermingled with the politicos. Every member of the Washington press corps who mattered was covering the event. While most mourners came to genuinely pay their respects, Storm knew a few had shown up simply to curry favor or rub shoulders with the city's crème de le crème. He arrived late and stood at the rear of the church. He spotted Jedidiah Jones in a second-row seat.

A colleague of Senator Windslow had just started the eulogy when there was a ruckus in the front of the cathedral. Samantha Toppers had fainted and was sprawled on the floor. Everything stopped while security officers administered first aid and carried her outside to an ambulance. She was driven to an exclusive, private hospital on Capitol Hill.

After the service, television news reporters doing stand-up reports outside the cathedral could be overheard telling viewers that Toppers had collapsed because of her "broken heart."

Storm didn't stick around for the funeral processional to the famed Georgetown Tall Oaks cemetery. Dating back to 1849, Tall Oaks had run out of room long ago, but its owners had recently dug up the cemetery's paths and walkways to create more space. Matthew's body would be interred in a double-decker concrete crypt covered with slate and used as a new footpath. A tasteful marker would be placed beside the walkway, noting who was buried beneath it.

The local newscast that night revealed that Toppers was being held overnight for observation at the St. Mary of the Miracle Hospital. It was standard procedure. She was suffering from situational depression, her doctor said, and needed rest.

Visiting hours at St. Mary's, which only accommodated fifty patients in its private suites, ended at precisely 8 P.M., which is exactly when Storm walked through the hospital's entrance. The lobby was designed to look as if it were a living room. All visitors were required to sign in with a kindly looking elderly woman stationed behind a mahogany desk. The white-haired matron would press a concealed button that opened a solid oak door that led into the ward.

"I need to speak to the security officer on duty," Storm told her.

"Oh, that'll be, Tyler Martin. He's a real nice fellow, but

he's always late. He's supposed to be here now because my shift ends at eight o'clock."

At that same moment, an overweight, balding middle-aged fellow wearing dark blue trousers, a light blue button shirt, and a black tie burst into the lobby and hurried toward them.

"Sorry, Shirley," he said, puffing from his rushed pace, "traffic is a mess out there."

"You know it always is, Officer Martin," the woman replied, "especially since they got the streets around the hospital torn up with construction. You'd think all that construction work would stop drivers from racing by here, but I almost got hit last night crossing at the intersection. Someone's going to get hurt."

"The good news is that if they get hit, they'll be outside a hospital," Martin quipped.

The older woman didn't smile. She said, "Officer Martin, this man wants to speak to you." Collecting her purse, she walked to the exit, calling over her shoulder, "See you tomorrow and please don't be late again."

"Give me a moment please," Martin said as he popped behind the reception desk and put a paper bag and thermos bottle into a large drawer. Sucking in a deep breath, he looked up at Storm and said, "OK, now, how can I help you?"

Storm handed Martin a thin black wallet that contained the fake private investigator credentials that Jones had given him earlier. "Senator Windslow sent me over," Storm explained. "He wants to make certain Ms. Samantha Toppers is protected from the media. He's worried some tabloid photographer is going to sneak in here and take pictures of her while she's distraught."

"I heard about her on the radio driving to work," Martin said, "but the senator doesn't need to worry. We keep things pretty tight around here, especially at night. I'm the only officer on duty and all the doors except the front entrance are locked. No one gets by me."

Retrieving his false credentials, Storm extended his hand and gave Martin's a firm shake. "Officer Martin, I'm glad you're on duty. It'll be a pleasure working with you. Now, I'll just take a seat in your lobby, and if someone asks to see Ms. Toppers, you can signal me."

Martin hesitated. "I'll need to call my supervisor about this."

"No problem. Tell him I'm here in case one of those photographers manages to slip by you. They're sneaky bastards, and this way, it will be my dick, not yours, on the chopping block if the senator gets angry."

The thought of Storm taking the blame seemed to remove any doubts Martin might have had. "I guess there's no reason to bother my boss. He gets cranky when I call at night."

Storm smiled reassuringly. "I'll just take a seat over there." He pointed to a brown leather chair near the lobby wall where he would have a clear view. "If someone comes in who you don't know—anyone—even a doctor or someone who claims they're a new employee on your janitorial staff—you give me a nod."

"We should have a code word," Martin volunteered. "I'll tell them, 'You'll have to wait a moment before I buzz you in.'"

"That would be great. I hope your boss knows how

fortunate he is to have you working here."

"He doesn't, but you're right, he should," Martin said, beaming.

Storm had dealt with people like Martin all of his life. All they wanted was a little respect, a little appreciation and some encouragement. If you gave them that, most would turn over state secrets to please you.

Storm took a seat and picked up a copy of the *Washington Tribune* from a nearby coffee table. During the next two hours, a handful of doctors arrived to see patients, but Martin recognized each of them.

Around 11 P.M., a rail-thin man, who looked to be in his late twenties, entered carrying a large bouquet of fresh-cut flowers. Dressed in blue denim jeans, sneakers, a T-shirt, and a light tan jacket, he went directly to the reception desk without noticing Storm and spoke so softly that only Officer Martin could hear him.

The next sound Storm heard was Martin's loud voice. "YOU HAVE A DELIVERY FOR SAMANTHA TOPPERS—IS THAT WHAT YOU JUST SAID?"

So much for the code. Why would a flower shop be making a delivery so late at night?

Storm sprang from his seat. Uncertain why the security guard had hollered so loudly, the deliveryman glanced around and saw Storm. Their eyes met and Storm sensed that the man recognized him, although Storm had never seen him. The man pitched the glass bowl of flowers at Storm's face. Storm ducked and instinctively raised his right arm to block the vase while the deliveryman scrambled out the front door. The bowl struck Storm's forearm and exploded when it hit the floor.

The deliveryman was fast, but Storm caught him twenty yards from the hospital entrance, just as he entered a nearby intersection. Storm tackled him from behind in a move that would have made a great NFL film highlight. The two men's bodies hit the black asphalt hard near the center of the street. When Storm loosened his tackle around the man's ankles, the suspect kicked him in the jaw.

Slightly stunned, Storm rolled backward to avoid another punishing blow and pushed himself up from the asphalt. His target was up on his feet, too. Storm lunged forward, but the deliveryman moved quicker than Storm had anticipated and was out of reach. In a well-practiced move, the man pulled a pistol from his belt.

Completely in the open and unprotected, Storm knew his assailant couldn't miss at such a close range. With lightning quickness, Storm dove to his left just as the gun fired. The bullet sliced across his right shoulder, ice skating across the skin as if it were a surgeon's scalpel.

Storm rolled as he hit the street and came up in a crouched position with his Glock in his right hand. He was now protected behind a three-foot-tall concrete barrier that construction crews had installed temporarily near the curb to protect themselves from traffic while on the job.

Suddenly, from behind him, Storm heard Officer Martin yelling an expletive. The security officer was lumbering toward them, his watermelon belly bouncing with each step. His voice caused the deliveryman to momentarily glance away from Storm and redirect his pistol at the oncoming security guard. He fired. Martin froze and screamed in terror.

Storm was about to return fire when there was a brilliant flash directly in front of him that blinded him temporarily. Simultaneously, he heard the sound of steel smashing into concrete, the breaking of glass, the last-second squeal of brakes and felt a sharp pain in his shoulder.

The driver of a speeding BMW had swerved to miss the deliveryman, who'd been standing in the intersection, directly in the car's path. The driver had lost control and the BMW had smacked into the concrete barrier protecting Storm. The impact had destroyed the car's distinctive grill, peppered the air with shrapnel-sized pieces of broken headlight, and sent a narrow piece of chrome sailing into Storm's left arm like a jagged arrow. Steam and smoke gushed from the engine and the car's horn blared loudly.

Storm had not flinched or moved from where he was standing with his raised Glock. But the collision had blocked his view, and he now had a pencil-sized chrome spear stuck in his left bicep. He shifted his position for a better look into the intersection. The deliveryman had vanished. With disgust, Storm holstered his Glock and used his right hand to remove the chrome dart from his arm.

Lights popped on in the old row houses surrounding the hospital. A dog yelped. Through the car's cracked windshield, Storm could see air bags. They'd saved the lives of the male driver and female passenger, but both were bloody and clearly dazed.

Storm looked behind him. Martin was still standing frozen on the sidewalk. The bullet had missed him.

"Get a doctor!" Storm called.

Storm tossed the tiny chrome spear in his hand to the ground and walked toward the terrified security guard.

"The people in the car need help," Storm said. "Go back inside and get a doctor and nurses out here."

Martin stared blankly ahead. "I've never had anyone shoot me!"

"You still haven't. He missed."

Martin noticed that both of Storm's arms were bleeding. "He didn't miss you."

"Actually, he did. It's just a flesh wound. We're both lucky. Now you need to get help from the hospital. The people in the car are conscious but they're injured. I'll go check on them while you go inside. Call the police and fire department, too. And make sure no one sneaks in while everyone is paying attention to this accident."

"OK, OK," Martin replied. "You can count on me." He started back toward the entrance.

Storm noticed a glint of light in the intersection. He assumed it was debris from the car crash until he saw that it was illuminated. As he got closer, he realized it was a cell phone. It had been knocked from the fleeing deliveryman's belt when Storm tackled him.

Picking it up, he pushed its recent calls button. Storm recognized the first name that flashed on the tiny screen.

It was the final clue that he'd needed. Now he had all of the evidence. He had solved the puzzle, or at least a key part of it.

CHAPTER THIRTEEN

Special Agent April Showers exited FBI headquarters and made her way to the curb on 10th Street NW at exactly the same moment as Storm arrived in the rented Taurus.

"I'm crazy for doing this," she said as soon as she got into the car.

"You made the call for me?" he asked.

"Yes, the senator and his wife will meet us at six-thirty in his office, and they promised that Samantha Toppers would be with them. She was discharged early this morning from the hospital."

Agent Showers was not as angry as she'd been during their last meeting. That was good. He'd told her earlier today on the phone that he'd uncovered evidence about the kidnapping and murder, but he'd not revealed it. He'd only asked her to get everyone together. He told her that what he had to say might redeem her with her bosses. She might not have to go to Tulsa.

"Are you going to tell me now," Showers said, "or is this another secret?"

"There won't be any reason for secrets after this meeting."

"Does that mean you'll tell me your real name?"

Storm shook his head, indicating no.

He had misspoke. There were parts of his life that would always be secret, especially if he wanted to remain dead and return to Montana.

Storm made a left onto Pennsylvania Avenue and drove east toward the U.S. Capitol, whose brilliant white exterior looked slightly pinkish from the orange sun setting behind them.

Agent Showers entered the Dirksen SOB office first, with Storm trailing behind her carrying four heavy gym bags.

"What's this about?" Senator Windslow said, rising from behind his desk. "Why are you carrying those bags?"

Storm dropped them on the carpet.

"He knows who kidnapped Matthew," Showers said.

Gloria rose from the sofa, where she had been sitting next to Toppers, and hurried over to Storm. "Is it true?" she asked. "Have you found the men who murdered my son? Tell me, please!"

"I will," he replied, "but it is complicated." He took Gloria's hand and led her to a chair. "Why don't you sit here while I explain it." Gloria was now to his right. Toppers was on his left, and he was facing Windslow, who was seated behind his desk. Agent Showers was standing behind him near the door.

He had everyone where he wanted them. Divided.

Storm began. "Agent Showers already has solved half of this kidnapping."

"What the hell are you talking about?" Windslow asked incredulously.

"Yes," said Gloria. "What is half a kidnapping?"

"Let's start at the beginning," Storm said. "The day after Matthew was kidnapped, you received a ransom note demanding one million dollars. The note was handwritten in block letters. The writing on that note was completely different from the writing on the second note, which you received the next day. The second note didn't include a demand for money, but it did contain Matthew's teeth."

"We know that," Windslow said impatiently. "Get to the point. Who killed Matthew?"

"Let him talk," Gloria said.

"The second note contained a mistake," Storm recalled. "It identified Matthew as the senator's son. The differences in these two notes were the first tip-off that you were actually communicating with two different groups."

"Two kidnappers?" Windslow bellowed. "How could two different groups kidnap one person?"

"Please, Thurston, stop interrupting," Gloria chided.

"Let's call one group the real kidnappers," Storm said. "They are the armed men who actually abducted Matthew. The second group was trying to take advantage of his kidnapping. They didn't have anything to do with his actual abduction. Their goal was to get your money. That's why they sent you a third handwritten note demanding six million in cash."

Senator Windslow glanced nervously at Agent Showers and then gave Storm an angry look. "That third note was supposed to be kept confidential," he said. "You weren't authorized to discuss it. I'm going to have my lawyers—"

Gloria cut him off. "You can threaten him later. I want to know who killed my son. Go ahead."

"Thank you," Storm said. "It was this second group—the criminals who wanted your money—that had me confused at first. I knew it was someone inside your inner circle, because they mentioned my name in the third note."

"Someone close to us betrayed us?" Gloria said.

"I had a hunch but wasn't certain until Samantha and I were delivering the money."

"Samantha?" Gloria repeated. Everyone looked at Samantha, who locked eyes with Storm and then looked at Gloria and said, "It's not me."

"During our ride," Storm said, "Samantha used the word *stashed*. That was the same word printed in the third kidnap note, ordering the senator to use the six million *stashed* in the safety deposit box to pay the ransom. It's slang that Russians don't use."

"What Russians?" Gloria asked. "Are you saying that Samantha was helping Russians?"

"I don't even know any Russians," Samantha said. "He's not making any sense."

"I'll explain the Russians in a minute," Storm said. "Let's get back to the night when Samantha and I were making the deliveries. She told me that she was studying mechanical engineering."

Agent Showers jumped in. "Which means she knows how to write in block letters on blueprints like the ones on the ransom notes."

"Lots of people know how to do that," Samantha protested.

Gloria fixed her eyes on Samantha and said, "Is this true? I thought you loved my son."

"Yes, I do, I did," she stammered. "I didn't do anything wrong."

"This is ridiculous," Windslow complained. "Why would she steal money from us?"

Storm continued. "The most obvious clue was that each time I dropped off one of the gym bags, the kidnappers called Samantha's phone. It was as if someone was telling them exactly what I was doing. Someone who was sitting in the van waiting while I was dropping off the bags. Someone sending text messages."

"Why are you attacking me?" Samantha exclaimed. "Why are you lying about me!" She stood from the sofa. "I want to leave. I don't feel well."

"No one is leaving," Agent Showers said. "Not yet."

With a frustrated look on her face, Toppers sat back down. "This isn't fair," she said and pouted.

"The first time," Storm said, "when Samantha took a million dollars to Union Station, she knew Agent Showers had flooded the train depot with agents. So she warned her partner. That's when the two of them came up with a new scam. They thought of an ingenious way to get the money."

"What money?" Windslow said. "The kidnappers blew it all to pieces."

"No," Storm said, "they didn't. Again, let's look at the facts. The third note instructed Samantha to take six million from the safety deposit box and put it into four gym bags. But that's not what you did when you were alone in that vault, is it, Samantha?"

"That's exactly what I did," she protested. "You saw me come out of that vault carrying the gym bags. You looked in the bags and saw the stacks of bills there."

"I did. But I didn't look deep enough," Storm replied. "Here's what happened. When Samantha was alone in that vault, she opened a different safety deposit box—one that she had rented. She had newspapers cut in the same shape as hundred-dollar bills hidden in her box. She put those fake bills in the bottom of each gym bag and covered them with a top level of actual hundred-dollar bills. Then she put the rest of the six million into her safety deposit box."

"My six million wasn't blown up in those trash cans?" Windslow said.

"Those explosions blew up counterfeit bills made of newsprint," Storm said.

"You have no proof," Toppers objected, but her face looked panicked, as if she were an animal caught in a corner.

Storm picked up the four gym bags and carried them over to her. "A hundred-dollar bill weighs roughly one gram," he explained. "A million dollars in hundred-dollar bills weighs a hundred grams or the equivalent of twenty-two pounds. Six million dollars weighs a hundred and thirty-two pounds."

"I can count," Toppers said.

"Yes, you told me that you were good in math." He dropped the bags at her feet. "I've placed the equivalent of one hundred and thirty-two pounds into these four gym bags. When you came out of the bank vault, you were carrying all four bags— two in each hand. You should have no problem lifting all of these bags right now—if the six million was in those bags."

"What's this going to prove?" Windslow asked.

Agent Showers answered. "Obviously, newsprint weighs less than currency. If she can't lift the bags, then it would have been impossible for her to carry six million in hundred-dollar bills out of that vault. That will prove that the bags were stuffed with newsprint—not money."

"Pick up the bags," Storm said. "Prove me wrong."

Toppers didn't move.

"Damn it, girl. Pick up those bags," the senator ordered.

She didn't flinch.

"If you want us to believe you weren't involved, pick up those bags," Gloria said sternly.

Toppers rose slowly from the sofa. She looked at each of them and then reached down and put her fingers around the straps on the four gym bags. With a huge grunt, she gave them a tug.

For a second, it looked as if she were going to lift them. But they were simply too heavy and she was too petite, too weak. She nearly fell forward on her face.

Gloria shot from her chair, lunging at Toppers. The older woman slapped the young girl's face and grabbed her hair. Both women tumbled onto the floor. Storm grabbed Gloria, who was swinging and kicking Toppers. Showers pulled Toppers to one side.

"You little bitch," Gloria screamed. "How could you do this to us? How could you do this to our son? We treated you like family. Why did you do this?"

Agent Showers said, "Samantha, was there newspaper in those bags when you brought them out of the vault?"

Looking completely defeated, she said, "Yes. I made the switch just like he said."

Showers handcuffed her and gave Storm an appreciative smile. "Smart thinking putting a hundred and thirty-two pounds in those bags," she said.

"Actually, there's two hundred pounds in them. It was a trick. I have no idea how much newsprint weighs."

Toppers face turned bright red. She burst into tears, overcome with pent-up emotions.

"Who helped you?" Windslow demanded. "Who was your partner? You may have written those notes, but you didn't make those bombs."

Between sobs, she stammered, "I never liked you, and your stepson didn't like you either. You're a bully."

Storm removed a cell phone from his pocket and pushed the last number dialed feature. The voice of Rihanna could be heard coming from Topper's handbag.

"This cell phone belongs to the man who tried to get into the hospital last night to see Samantha," Storm explained. "I knocked it from his belt just before he fired a shot at me. The last number that he'd called was Samantha's."

He hesitated and then said in a sympathetic voice, "This phone belongs to your brother, doesn't it, Samantha? He was coming to see you because he wanted to get the money."

"You have a brother?" Gloria said. "I thought you were an only child."

Between sobs, Toppers said, "His name is Jack, Jack Jacobs."

"I'll be goddamned," Windslow said. "How'd our background investigators miss that?"

"The woman we all know as Samantha is actually Christina Jacobs," Storm said. "She and her brother were born in Vermont and lived there until the courts took them away from their drug-addicted, abusive mother. I'm not sure how or why, but Christina ended up living with Charles and Margarita Toppers, a wealthy couple in Stamford, Connecticut. They had a daughter the same age whose name was Samantha."

"You told us the Toppers were your parents," Windslow said.

"Charles, Margarita, and the real Samantha were killed in a car accident in Spain while on vacation," Storm explained. "Their bodies were burned beyond recognition. Christina was sick at home that night, and when the police told her that everyone was dead, she decided to assume Samantha's identity. She told the authorities that the girl killed was a family friend named Christina Jacobs, an orphan."

"How could she pull that off?" Windslow said.

"She never went back to Connecticut. Margarita had relatives in Spain, so all three bodies were buried there. The 'new' Samantha contacted the bank that was the trustee of the Toppers estate and told the executor that she was distraught and wanted to live in Europe for a while. He had dealt only with Charles Toppers and had no idea what Samantha looked or sounded like. He sent her monthly checks to a bank in Paris. She stayed abroad for six years, posing as Samantha, only dealing with the Stamford bank by e-mail and letters. By the time that she returned to the U.S., she had transformed herself—adopting the same hair color, the same signature as Samantha. She fooled everyone—it seems—but her brother."

"I never thought I'd see him again," Samantha said. "After the accident in Spain, I sent word to him that his sister was dead. I'd heard he enlisted in the marines and had been to the Persian Gulf to fight in Iraq. He was Army Intelligence. Then out of nowhere, he showed up at my apartment on the very night that Matthew was kidnapped. I was an emotional wreck and I told him about what I'd done and how I was engaged and about how Matthew had been kidnapped. I thought he would be sympathetic, but he told me this was his big chance. He said, 'You had your chance to start over. I want mine.'"

"It was your brother's idea to write that first ransom note, wasn't it?" Storm said.

"He thought if we acted fast, we could beat the real kidnappers to the punch. He told me if I didn't help him, he would expose me and I would go to jail. But then, I told him the FBI was everywhere in Union Station. There was no way for him to get the money. I thought he'd give up on the entire idea after that, but I made a stupid mistake."

"You told him about the real kidnappers' note, the one with the teeth in it," Storm said.

"I wanted him to know the kidnappers had contacted the Windslows. I told him the CIA had brought in a real expert to help the FBI. I wanted to scare him. But instead he realized the kidnappers weren't after money. They were trying to get the senator to do something else. That's when he came up with the idea of getting money out of the safety deposit box and making everyone think it got blown up."

"How did you know about the six million hidden in the

safety deposit box?" Agent Showers asked her. "Did Matthew tell you about it?"

"He did more than tell me. Matthew took me to the vault and showed me all that cash. He told me it was bribe money that his stepdad got from some Russian."

"Wait a minute, girl!" Windslow exclaimed. "Bribe money? There's no proof that I took a bribe. You need to watch your tongue!"

Gloria said, "What have you done, Thurston? Are you responsible for Matthew getting kidnapped? Who are these Russians and why did they pay you a bribe?"

Nervously eyeing Agent Showers, Windslow said, "This is not something that we need to be discussing right now, Gloria."

Showers said, "Senator, I can help you if you tell me the truth about that money. We can work out a deal. It's not too late to do the right thing."

Windslow's face became flush. "Don't you dare tell me what I can and can't do. I have no idea what this woman is jabbering about. I've never taken a bribe in my political career."

Addressing Toppers, Showers said, "Did your brother rent the second safety deposit box where you put the newspapers or did you?"

"He did. The six million is still there, or most of it is. You can get it as evidence against him." She nodded at Windslow. "Matthew told me it was bribe money. My brother told me that taking it was like ripping off a drug dealer. I kept thinking, 'OK, if I do this for Jack and he gets the six million, he'll be set for life. He'll leave me alone. Jack gave me the key to the second box on the day that we went to the bank. He told me nothing could go wrong. I thought the kidnappers would free Matthew as soon as the senator did what they wanted."

"This is outrageous!" Windslow declared. "She's trying to implicate me to make herself look good. How do we know that her brother didn't kidnap Matthew? All this talk about Russians is nothing but speculation and hearsay."

"Where's Jack now?" Storm asked Toppers.

"In a motel in Virginia. After Matthew was killed, I was never alone. So he was waiting until after the funeral to get the key back from me so he could go get the money. He came to the hospital to get it last night, but he couldn't get in. He never cared about me. All he wanted was that stupid money."

Agent Showers said, "I'm going to send a team to arrest your brother." Looking at the senator, she added, "I think you better call your lawyers."

"That money was in a box rented by my stepson," Windslow said. "You can't tie it to me. You can't prove where it came from."

"Don't you dare try to blame this on my son," Gloria snapped. "You selfish son of a bitch, how could you let this happen." She turned to speak to Storm. "If Samantha—or Christina—or whatever her name is—and her brother didn't have anything to do with actually kidnapping Matthew, then who are these Russians and why did they kill my son?"

Storm looked at Senator Windslow. "About time for you to come clean, isn't it, Senator? Tell your wife what you did. Tell us all."

Windslow rose from his desk. "I am a United States senator and you are in my office. I think it is time for all of you to get out of here. You think you're so smart. You've got it all figured out, don't you? But you really don't."

Gloria screamed, "Did you get my son killed?"

A darkness settled on Windslow's face. "This is so much bigger than you know. None of you have any idea who you are dealing with or how high this goes. These people are—"

But a thunderous crack and the crash of shattering glass cut the senator's sentence short as the window behind him exploded. His right shoulder jerked forward as the lone sniper bullet burst from his chest. The stunned look on his face lasted only a millisecond before his body gave way and he collapsed in a jumbled heap.

Almost without thinking, Agent Showers threw Toppers to the floor, out of harm's way, while Storm leaped behind the senator's desk, where Windslow was now gasping his final breaths. As blood gushed from the exit wound and Storm peered into the eyes of a man who knew he was only seconds away from death, Windslow whispered: "Midas. Jedidiah knows."

Just as those words had barely escaped his lips, Storm watched as the life left Windslow's eyes. The senator was dead.

Screams and shouts filled the room, but all Storm could hear were those last couple words of Windslow's, echoing over and over in his head.

Jedidiah knows.

To be continued in *A Raging Storm*…

A
RAGING
STORM

CHAPTER ONE

WASHINGTON, D.C.
Present day, 7:15 P.M.

A dead United States senator was in his arms.

Derrick Storm had been the first to reach him and the only one who'd heard his dying words: *Midas—Jedidiah knows.* Seconds earlier, Senator Thurston Windslow had been alive and angry. He'd leaped from his chair and was about to reveal who had abducted and murdered his stepson when a bullet sent him crashing to the floor. From his crouched position, Storm could see the bullet hole in the large window directly behind the elderly statesman's desk.

It was dusk outside, and the window had turned into a mirror, making it impossible for Storm to spot the assassin. Along with the three women with him inside the Dirksen Senate Building office, Storm was a sitting duck.

"Get down!" he yelled at Gloria Windslow, the senator's newly widowed wife. She was standing in the center of the room in shock.

Storm needed to act before the sniper fired again. Springing to his feet, he dashed around the desk in a blur of motion. Like an attacking lion, he lunged at Gloria, throwing his right arm around her waist in mid-flight, pulling her down onto the thick carpet out of harm's way.

FBI Agent April Showers and Samantha Toppers were already prone on the floor. Showers was clutching her .40-caliber Glock semiautomatic in one hand. The other was gripped around a pair of stainless steel handcuffs that she had snapped onto Toppers's wrists before the shooting.

As in all Capitol Hill buildings, the senator's office had been refitted recently with bullet-resistant glass windows that were supposed to prevent the sort of assassination that they'd just witnessed. By composing them of five thick pieces of shatterproof glass, the manufacturer had guaranteed the windows would stop bullets fired from guns as powerful as a .44-caliber magnum revolver—even if they were shot at close range. But the window had offered little real protection from a professional killer using a high-powered sniper's rifle. The layers of safety glass may have slightly altered the slug's path, because it hit the senator's left shoulder rather than what was surely its intended target—his heart. That shift had kept him from dying instantly and given him seconds to whisper his dying words.

Jedidiah knows was clearly a reference to Jedidiah Jones, the cranky director of the CIA's National Clandestine Service and the man responsible for dragging Storm into this thorny mess. What the word *Mida* smeant was less clear, but since Jones was involved, Storm suspected it was the name of a covert CIA mission.

"The drapes," FBI Agent Showers called out.

Storm followed her eyes to a red button on the wall next to the office window. Releasing his hold around Gloria Windslow's waist, he shot forward, punching the button with his palm and dropping to the carpet just as another bullet pierced the glass—this one aimed at his head. The slug sailed by his left ear and smacked into the senator's desk, causing splinters of polished mahogany to spray through the air.

That was close.

How many times can a man cheat death?

"You OK?" a concerned Agent Showers hollered.

"Piece of cake," he replied. "But thanks for caring."

"If anyone is going to kill you," she replied with a smile, "it should be me—for you pushing yourself into my case."

"But we're having so much fun together, aren't we?" he called back.

With the heavy drapes now drawn, Agent Showers rose to her feet, pulling Toppers with her up from the floor. "Don't move!" she ordered Toppers, a twenty-something college student whose entire body was trembling.

Storm started for the office door just as a uniformed U.S. Capitol Police officer burst through it, followed by another. Both had their guns drawn and they instinctively divided their targets. One aimed at Showers, the other at Storm.

"Freeze!" the first cop yelled.

"I'm FBI!" Showers shouted. "Special Agent April Showers. The shot came from outside, not here. The senator is down."

Not sure how to react, one officer kept his pistol leveled at her while the other rushed over to examine Windslow's body.

"He's dead!" the officer confirmed.

"She just told you that," Storm said.

"Show me identification!" the cop with his gun aimed at Agent Showers commanded.

"Take it easy," Showers replied as she slowly holstered her pistol and fished out her FBI credentials.

"How about you?" the other officer asked Storm.

"Don't mind me. I'm a nobody—just ask her."

"He's with me," Showers declared. "He's a private detective named Steve Mason, hired to help the senator."

Steve Mason was the pseudonym that Jedidiah Jones had given Storm when he brought him to Washington to help solve a tricky case.

Looking down at Windslow's limp body and then back at Storm, the cop asked, "Is this the senator you were supposed to help?"

Storm grimaced and said, "Actually, things were going rather well—until he just got shot."

"This woman is under arrest," Showers said, nodding at the traumatized Toppers. "Watch her, seal off this crime scene, and call the number on this card." She jabbed her FBI business card at the officer. "Tell the person who answers that the senator's been murdered."

"What buildings are across from this office window?" Storm asked.

"Only one building is out there," the officer at the doorway replied. "The Capitol Police Building—our headquarters."

"That's got to be where the shot came from," Storm said, moving toward the room's exit.

"Call your dispatcher," Showers said, falling behind him. "Tell him to lock down your entire police headquarters. Stop anyone who's coming down from the roof."

A bewildered look washed over the officer's face.

"Do it now!" she yelled. "And get a doctor for Mrs. Windslow. She's in shock."

"Wait," the officer said as she scooted by him. "You two shouldn't leave, should you? I mean, you're witnesses."

But she and Storm were already halfway down the building's corridor. The killing had all the traces of a professional hit. Every passing second was working against catching the killer. Storm reached C Street first, with Showers on his heels. The eight-story police headquarters was about four hundred yards ahead of them. It sat in the center of a vast parking lot and was the only structure tall enough to accommodate a sniper.

The assassin must be wearing a disguise. How else would he have gotten onto the rooftop of a police headquarters without being noticed?

Storm and Showers reached the building's front entrance just as a Containment and Emergency Response Team, the equivalent of a police department's SWAT squad, burst through the double glass doors on its way to the Dirksen Building. Flashing her credentials, Showers exclaimed, "A sniper fired from your rooftop!"

Speaking into his headset, the CERT's leader said, "Dispatch CERT Two to check the rooftop. Armed suspect may still be there. No one gets in or out of our building. Lock her down. Now!"

Addressing Showers, he said, "We have jurisdiction here. You need to stand down."

Before she could respond, his team began racing across the parking lot.

Storm, meanwhile, was scanning the area, confident that the shooter had already fled from the building. To their immediate left was a city park that separated Capitol Hill from Union Station, the main rail hub in Washington, D.C. It served both Amtrak and subway lines, was always filled with travelers, and was exactly where Storm would have gone to disappear into a crowd.

"There!" he yelled, pointing a finger north toward Columbus Circle, the traffic interchange directly in front of the train station. Showers spotted the lone figure as he walked under a street lamp. They couldn't see his face from this distance, but they could see that he was wearing a blue shirt and black pants—a U.S. Capitol Police uniform. All of the other officers either were locked inside the headquarters building or were scurrying as quickly as they could toward the Senate office building. But this officer was casually walking *away* from the action.

"That's got to be him," Storm said, breaking into a run.

Showers pounded on the headquarters' now locked front doors and pressed her FBI credentials against the glass. "The shooter is getting away. Call the D.C. police at Union Station! He's disguised as one of your officers!"

The officers standing guard behind the glass gave her blank stares. Frustrated, she used her cell phone to call the D.C. police department.

In top physical shape, Storm could run a mile in less than four and a half minutes, even in street shoes. But despite his quickness, his target entered Union Station before he could reach him. Storm eyeballed the crowd as soon as he burst inside the station's massive lobby. No Capitol Hill uniforms were in sight.

I'm dealing with a professional, he told himself.

A D.C. cop was loitering near the entrance to the Amtrak ticket line. Storm dashed over to him.

"There's been a shooting on Capitol Hill," he said. "The gunman is dressed like a Capitol Hill Police officer and he just came in here. Did you see him?"

With a skeptical look, the cop said, "And who, exactly, are you? You got a badge?"

"I'm a private investigator."

"Let's see your ID."

Dealing with this dolt was a waste of time. A men's room. That's where the shooter would go to ditch his disguise. Emerge as someone else. Someone who wouldn't stick out. A tourist. A businessman. A janitor. A construction worker. Anyone but a Capitol Hill cop.

There was a large "RESTROOM" sign to his left. Storm ran past it into the room. A long string of startled men peeing at urinals glanced up. When Storm drew his handgun, they panicked and scrambled past him out the exit, some not bothering to zip their pants. There were seven stalls across from the urinals. Storm could see beneath the doors that three were occupied.

He pounded on the first stall's door, and when the

occupant let loose with a profanity, Storm stepped back and kicked it open.

"What the—" the startled man sitting on the commode exclaimed, his sentence cut short when he saw Storm's Glock.

"Sorry," Storm said. "You can go back to your business."

He moved to the next stall, but when he knocked on the door, its occupant opened it and immediately raised his hands. It was a teenage boy. The last occupant was an old man. None of them had been changing out of a Capitol Hill uniform. None of them had looked suspicious.

"Drop it!" a voice behind Storm yelled. It was the D.C. cop from the lobby.

Raising his Glock above his head, Storm slowly turned to face him.

"Are you crazy, man?" the cop asked him. "What the hell you doing, busting in here, waving around a gun? You're lucky I didn't shoot you just now."

"I'm looking for a sniper," Storm said. "Like I told you, he's dressed as a Capitol Hill cop. We need to close off the exits before he escapes."

"Then you *are* crazy," he replied. "Even if I wanted, there's no way to shut down this building in time. We got entrances out onto the street, downstairs to the subway lines, and out back to the trains."

A second D.C. cop came running inside with his gun drawn.

"What's happening?" he asked his partner.

"He says he's a private eye looking for an assassin."

The newly arrived officer asked Storm, "You high on something?"

"Get his weapon," the first cop declared.

Holstering his sidearm, the second officer stepped forward, took Storm's Glock, and ordered him to "assume the position."

Storm placed both hands flat against the wall and spread his legs. Resigned, he said, "Don't tickle."

Agent Showers came flying into the men's room. "FBI!" she said, waving her badge. "You've got the wrong guy. He's with me."

"Then you can have him," the first officer said, lowering his gun. The second officer stopped frisking Storm, who turned and said, "My gun please."

The officer handed it back.

Storm walked over to a nearby trash container and flipped open its lid. But there was nothing inside it except crumpled paper towels and trash. He checked a second one. There was no Capitol Hill policeman's uniform inside it either.

"We'll check the lobby," the first officer announced.

"Great," replied Storm, knowing the killer was probably long gone.

"What exactly are we looking for?" the second officer asked.

"At this point?" Storm replied. "A ghost."

Storm and Showers stepped from the men's room together. A third trash container was a few feet away, located between the entrances to the men's and women's restrooms. Storm checked it. A blue Capitol Hill Police officer's shirt was stuffed inside, complete with a badge and pair of black slacks.

Pulling the shirt from the bin, Storm said, "It's a small.

We're looking for a man probably under six feet, about a hundred and fifty pounds."

Together they scanned the waves of people scurrying by them in the cavernous station's lobby. Dozens of men fit that description. The shooter could have been anyone, anywhere.

"How'd you know I was in the men's room?" Storm asked.

"Do you think you're the only one who can think like a fleeing criminal?" she replied.

Storm smiled. "It could have been embarrassing for you if I hadn't been in there."

"Not really," Showers said.

"Oh, you've been in a lot of men's rooms, have you?"

She simply smiled and said, "Let's go. We got a killer to catch."

CHAPTER TWO

MOSCOW, Russia,
Mayakovskaya Metro Station

"We are the new Russia!" President Oleg Barkovsky declared, ending his three-hour-long speech. The crowd leaped to its feet. They stomped on the floor. They hollered. They whistled. No one grumbled about the late hour. No one complained that it had been five hours since the evening's meal had been cleared from the tables. The vodka had flowed freely all night. Barkovsky's aide, Mikhail Sokolov, had made sure of it. The many toasts and earlier speeches had been painstakingly choreographed to build momentum for this moment.

Barkovsky's ovation was the evening's grand finale.

The Russian president made no effort to calm the frenzied crowd. He stretched out his arms—Christ-like—behind the podium and drunk in their revelry. In his mind, he deserved it.

Barkovsky was transforming Russia. The reforms of the past—*glasnost* and *perestroika*—were dead. Gone were the leaders who had betrayed Mother Russia by destroying the great Communist Party. Gone were the oligarchs who had raped the nation, stealing billions and billions. Like a mythical Phoenix, Barkovsky had arisen from the chaos of the imploded former superpower. He'd kicked out the money-grubbing foreign capitalists who had arrived promising reforms but had only lined their own pockets. Brilliant and ruthless, he had maneuvered himself into the presidency and reasserted the Kremlin's authority over all aspects of Russian life. Reporters who dared question him were attacked by thugs who left them bleeding and dying on sidewalks. Political enemies were arrested, imprisoned; some had disappeared. Elections were bought. After years of instability, ordinary Russians had silently fallen into line. There had been no complaints when Barkovsky started stripping away the civil liberties that the revolt against the old regime had brought them. Barkovsky's iron fist established order. For the first time in decades, it was safe to walk the streets of Moscow at night; shops were well stocked, homes were heated, people had bread, and Russia was once again demanding international respect.

"Barkovsky!" a dark-haired beauty near the podium screamed. Her cry sparked a chorus. "Barkovsky! Barkovsky! Barkovsky!" It swept through the chamber like a wave. Glancing down from the stage at the woman, Barkovsky brought his fingers to his lips and blew her a kiss.

She fainted. He was a political rock star.

The late night rally was being held not in the ballroom of one of the new, dazzling Western-style hotels that now dotted the Moscow skyline, but in Mayakovskaya Metro Station on the Zamoskvoretskaya rail line. To the unaware, it may have seemed an odd choice. But to this crowd, it was a brilliant selection.

Joseph Stalin promised in 1932, when construction of the Moscow underground began, that the city's railway stops would be artistic showplaces—daily reminders to the masses of the superiority of the Communist system. The Mayakovskaya station was a jewel in the Metro crown. It was such an engineering feat when it opened in 1938 that it was awarded a Grand Prize at the New York World's Fair. It was designed to calm even the most claustrophobic traveler. Buried more than one hundred feet underneath the city, the station's ceiling contained thirty-five individual, round niches with filament lights hidden behind them. The lights burned so brilliantly that it looked as if the summer sunshine were streaming through the panes. The station's steel support beams were covered with pink rhodonite. Its walls were decorated with four different shades of granite and marble. Artists had created thirty-four mosaics in the ceiling, each glorifying the Soviet Empire. During World War II, the station had served as an air raid shelter and had escaped unscathed. But it was another historic event that had caused Barkovsky to select the station for this evening's banquet. When Moscow was under siege in 1941 by the Nazis, Stalin had addressed a crowd of party leaders and ordinary Muscovites inside this very station, giving what would become known as his "Brothers and Sisters" speech. In it, Stalin predicted that although the Nazis seemed invincible, they would be defeated. Barkovsky's speech tonight had mimicked Stalin's famous remarks. He had attacked "outside invaders" who were threatening the new Russia—just as the Nazis had once done. He'd made thinly disguised attacks on the United States and NATO. Stalin had promised that the Motherland would rise triumphant, but only if it held "true to the moral principles" that had first guided the Communist revolution. Barkovsky repeated that same cold line.

It was Barkovsky's goal, and that of his New Russia Party, known simply as the NRP, to turn Russia backwards and, in doing so, restore it as a world superpower, capable of protecting its people from the threat of the U.S. and its newer rivals: China and India. Suspect everyone. Destroy all enemies. Use any means at your disposal.

Wooden chairs and tables had been placed on the station's boarding platform and train service had been suspended for tonight's rally. Blood-red and bright yellow banners—the very colors of the flag of the old Soviet empire—dangled from the ceiling. The entire station had the feel of an old time Communist rally. It was all well planned. Most of the crowd of four hundred had been members of the *apparatchiki*—the Communist Party apparatus. They had reaped the spoils of the *nomenklatura*—the party system of rewarding people who were in political favor. As a child, Barkovsky had grown up envying these privileged party members, wanting desperately to be one of them. But his parents had not been invited to join. They had been poor factory workers south of Leningrad. Because they were not party members, they had been doomed to lives of obscurity and poverty. Their only son should have suffered their same dreary fate, but Barkovsky had found a way to pull himself up from the squalor. Through sheer determination, a total lack of conscience, and an unquenchable lust for power, he had risen to become the most powerful leader in Russia since Joseph Stalin. Now he used his humble origins to his advantage. He had become a hero to the masses by pretending to be one of them. They loved him even as he was picking their pockets and constructing a palace for himself along the banks of the Black Sea, at a cost of a billion dollars. Some nights, when he was alone, Barkovsky wondered if he could be the living reincarnation of Stalin. There were moments when he imagined that he could feel Stalin's blood pulsating through his veins.

Standing before the crowd, soaking in the hoopla, Barkovsky felt a hand gently touch his shoulder, followed by the familiar voice of his chief aide whispering.

"Senator Windslow is dead."

Without showing the slightest glimmer of a reaction, Barkovsky cocked his head slightly to his right and asked. "Where is Petrov?"

"London."

"Why is he still alive?"

CHAPTER THREE

Duke of Madison's estate,
SOMERSET COUNTY, England

The startled ring-necked pheasant burst from its hiding place in the knee-high grasses. The blood red circling its eyes gave the bird a terrified look as it flapped its wings to gain speed. A brown-and-white spotted cocker spaniel had flushed it. Like many game birds in England, the pheasant had been bred and reared by a professional gamekeeper and then released to roam the rolling hills of the Duke of Madison's vast estate until its master came hunting.

The pheasant had flown about twenty feet above the ground when the boom of a 12-gauge shotgun broke the early morning silence. Dozens of blackbirds in nearby trees took wing, scattering in different directions.

The buckshot broke the pheasant's right wing, causing it to careen to the ground, where it flapped desperately as the dog raced toward it. The spaniel expertly snatched the wounded bird in his mouth and shook it violently, snapping its neck and ending its misery.

"Good boy, Rasputin," cried the dog's owner, Ivan Sergeyevich Petrov. The spaniel dropped the pheasant at Petrov's feet and was rewarded with both a treat and pat on its head. One of Petrov's two bodyguards took the bird and deposited it in a satchel. It was the first kill of the morning.

"Nice shooting, Ivan Sergeyevich," Georgi Ivanovich Lebedev said. He was Petrov's best friend and morning hunting companion.

Petrov opened the breech of his 12-gauge shotgun and inserted a new shell. He considered it unsportsmanlike to hunt with anything other than a single-shot rifle. If he couldn't kill a bird with one round, the creature deserved to escape.

"The next bird we see will be yours," Petrov promised.

Lebedev was smart enough to always allow Petrov the first kill. It was one reason why the two men had stayed close friends for so many years. Lebedev was content being second fiddle. It had been this way from the time when they were boys growing up in the northwest Moscow neighborhood of Solntsevo, one of city's toughest areas. When the teenage Petrov took a sudden interest in a girl named Yelena, Lebedev stepped aside even though he had a crush on her. When Petrov became best friends with Russian president Barkovsky, Lebedev gladly turned into the third wheel. When Petrov and Barkovsky became sworn enemies, Lebedev supported Petrov, eventually following him to London.

While Lebedev played the role of a supplicant well, Petrov played it not at all. It was fair to say that he never put his own wants or needs aside for anyone. It was a luxury he could afford, given his net worth of a reported six billion dollars. The fact that his fortune had come not because of hard work or brilliance but because of good timing and connections did nothing to deflate his grandiose ego.

It was his bloated self-esteem that had ultimately led to him clashing with President Barkovsky. To escape being arrested and thrown into prison, Petrov had been forced to flee Moscow at night, concealed behind a false panel inside a Russian SUV. British foreign intelligence had arranged his escape and in return had demanded that he snitch on his Kremlin friends. Petrov had done so with relish. He had known where lots of bodies were buried.

In truth, only his money made him attractive to the young women who frequently accompanied him to London's most posh clubs. A big man, standing six feet, two inches tall and weighing nearly three hundred pounds, Petrov's had a puffy, white, and round face. At age forty-two, he was balding, although his personal stylist did her best to disguise it by combing long strains of hair from the side of his head across his naked scalp. He favored loose-fitting, hand-tailored clothes and only wore black and white because he was colorblind. This morning, a pair of handmade platinum rimmed sunglasses copied from a photograph of a bespectacled Johnny Depp sat on his nose.

His hunting partner was shorter, standing five feet, six inches, and considerably thinner. Lebedev had a full head of bushy black hair, as well as two caterpillar like eyebrows. He was both a lawyer and an accountant, two trades which served him well as Petrov's most trusted lackey and advisor.

Shortly before daybreak, they had left the forty-thousand-square-foot manor house that Petrov had purchased from the cash-poor heirs of the Duke of Madison. Walking side by side, they had crossed the lush fields and rolling hills of the Cotswolds.

With Rasputin racing a few feet in front of them, they had entered a tall grass area near a brook and trees. It was here that Petrov had killed the first bird. Afterward, he celebrated by opening a thermos bottle filled with black coffee mixed with vodka, Kahlúa, and amaretto. Lebedev had brought coffee, too, but it contained no alcohol. As the two men drank, Petrov's bodyguards walked in a circle around them, safely out of hearing distance as they scanned the landscape for possible flashes of sunlight—reflections from a camouflaged shooter's telescopic gun sight.

"The Americans will be sending people to question you about Senator Windslow," Lebedev said solemnly.

"Should I see them?" Petrov asked. "Or go to the *Daria*?" He was referring to his 439-foot-long yacht that had cost one billion dollars to build and was named after his mother. He kept it anchored in the Mediterranean Sea off the French Riviera. "It will be more difficult for them to interrogate me there."

"I think you should meet with them. Otherwise, it will look as if you have something to hide."

Petrov chuckled. "I do."

"I should be present as your lawyer."

"Perhaps, it was a mistake telling the CIA about the gold, instead of my British friends," Petrov said.

"I disagree," Lebedev replied. "The Americans have longer arms and are not as timid as MI-6. It was right to tell them. The Americans also have more to gain by helping us."

Rasputin, who was waiting patiently at Petrov's feet, began to pant loudly and whine.

"You have a scent, don't you, boy?" Petrov said to his dog. He finished his drink. "Are you ready?" he asked Lebedev.

Tossing away the remains of his coffee, Lebedev put his stainless steel cup into his knapsack and said, "I'm ready."

Leaning down, Petrov gave his dog the command: "BIRD."

The spaniel bolted along a hedgerow, his snout floating inches above the ground. The sound of rustlings feathers and a cry of alarm caused both men to shoulder their shotguns. Another pheasant exploded into the sky, this one much smaller and faster than the first.

Petrov fired. His shot stopped the bird in midair. Bits of feathers blew away from its breast. It fell dead.

Cracking open his shotgun, Petrov said, "I promised you the second kill, my friend, but my instincts overruled my obligation."

Lebedev shrugged. "There will be other birds for me."

Rasputin arrived with the dead bird clutched in his mouth. Petrov petted the dog.

"You have someone watching the Americans," he said.

"Yes, of course. One of our best."

Lebedev reloaded and snapped the shotgun shut.

"Do you think Jedidiah Jones has told the FBI what he knows?"

Lebedev replied, "We can't be certain. This is why you

must meet with the Americans."

Petrov grinned. "They think they are coming to interrogate me but I will be interrogating them."

CHAPTER FOUR

CIA headquarters,
LANGLEY, Virginia

How many layers does an onion have? What had brought Storm to this moment?

Jedidiah Jones had called Storm back to Washington, D.C., two weeks earlier to help solve a "simple" kidnapping. But that crime had proven to be more than a kidnapping and not simple at all.

Matthew Dull, the stepson of Senator Windslow, had been abducted while he and his fiancée, Samantha Toppers, were walking near the Georgetown University campus. Four hooded men overpowered him, forced him into a van, and sped away, leaving a hysterical Toppers on the sidewalk.

When the FBI failed to find Dull, Windslow had asked Jones to bring in a "fixer"—someone who knew how to track missing persons and didn't mind coloring outside the lines. Jones had reached out to Storm and had cashed in a favor. A big favor.

Storm had been fly-fishing in Montana when the helicopter arrived. He was a man seemingly without any cares. This was because he was dead—at least to the world. He had successfully faked his own death four years earlier and gone off the grid. He'd done it to escape from Jones and a clandestine world that had tried to kill him, not once, but several times.

There had been a time in his life—before he'd met Jones—when Storm had been just another down-on-his-luck private detective with too many bills and not enough clients. He'd spent his days and nights peeping through windows at no-tell motels photographing cheating spouses and spying on able-bodied men who'd filed false workman's compensation claims citing "bad backs." Storm had scraped by. Barely.

But then Clara Strike had entered his world and turned it upside down. The CIA field officer had enlisted Storm's help in a covert operation being run on American soil. Technically, the CIA was forbidden to operate inside the U.S., so she'd needed Storm as a front man. She'd taken advantage of his expert tracking skills, his patriotic spirit, and his *then*-trusting nature. She'd introduced him to Jones, and it had been Jones who'd drawn him further and further into the CIA's web. One of his assignments had gone terribly wrong. Tangiers! It had ended with Storm lying severely wounded on a cold floor in his own blood.

Jones had rescued him. Storm had survived, but Tangiers had changed him. After that, he'd decided that he wanted out. And the only way for him to quit was for Derrick Storm—the roguish private eye and conscripted CIA operative—to die. In poetic fashion, he'd gone out in much the same way that he'd come into Jones's world. Storm had perished in the arms of Clara Strike. She'd watched in stunned disbelief as the light in his eyes dimmed. He'd reached out for her, and she had taken his hand, squeezing it for the very last time. His death had seemed legitimate because it had been as close to a real death as possible—thanks to the wizards inside the CIA's Chief Directorate of Science and Technology. The CIA scientists had used their magic to stop his heart and show no discernible brain waves. Storm didn't know how they'd done this. He hadn't cared. Death had freed him.

Or so he'd thought.

Jones had brought him back by cashing in Tangiers. Storm owed his life to Jones, and so he'd returned, supposedly for one final mission.

He had now come full circle. He was sitting across from Jones in his Langley office the day after Senator Windslow's assassination.

"I warned you this might get complicated," Jones said.

"Yes, but you somehow forgot to mention the Russian element when we first talked," Storm said.

Jones smiled slyly. "Must have slipped my mind."

Storm knew better. Nothing slipped Jones's mind.

"Since you seem to have overlooked that part," Storm said, "why don't you tell me about the Russians now?"

"I've got a better idea," Jones said. "You tell me what you've learned about the kidnapping and the Russians."

This is how Jones played the game. Ask him a question and he answered with two questions of his own. Ask him two questions and he responded with a dozen more.

"There were actually two groups of kidnappers," Storm said. "The kidnappers who really abducted Matthew Dull were ex–KBG officers."

"And the second ones?"

"They turned out to be Samantha Toppers and her brother."

"She's the short blonde with the big—" Jones started to say.

Storm interrupted. "Yes, Toppers is rather well endowed. She and her brother tried to profit from the kidnapping by sending Senator Windslow and his wife ransom notes even though they didn't have Dull. It was a pretty clever scam."

"That you figured out," Jones said.

It was as close to a compliment as Jones ever gave.

Continuing, Jones said, "Sadly, you weren't able to save Dull. The real kidnappers killed him and now someone has assassinated a U.S. senator."

"Hey, I didn't pull those triggers," Storm protested.

"True, but you also don't know why they were pulled."

"The men who did the actual murders were professionals. My guess is they are hired guns. The real question is who paid them? There are two likely candidates: Ivan Petrov and Oleg Barkovsky."

Storm suspected that Jones already knew about both men. Jones always knew more than he shared with Storm. He never revealed more than what was necessary. He listened and expected his operatives to do their own digging, to develop their own clues, to reach their own conclusions. He expected Storm to dig up his own answers. It was Jones's way of insuring that no rock went unturned.

Continuing, Storm said, "FBI Special Agent April

Showers believes Petrov paid Windslow a six-million-dollar bribe. But at some point, Windslow changed his mind and didn't follow through. That's when Petrov had him killed."

"Do you agree?"

"I'm sure Windslow took a bribe, but I'm not sure it was Petrov who gave the order to have him and Dull killed. It could have just as likely been Barkovsky."

"Why?"

"To stop Senator Windslow from helping Petrov. The problem is that I don't know what either man wanted from Senator Windslow. There's always a motive for murder. Until I figure out that motive, I can't identify the killer."

Jones leaned back in his office chair, which squeaked. It had needed oil for as long as Storm had known Jones. The CIA spymaster swept his right hand across his face as if he were trying to wipe away a problem. Built like a bulldog and in excellent physical shape, especially for a man in his early sixties, Jones was both Storm's mentor and tormentor. He was the only man capable of bringing Storm back into the CIA's world of smoke and mirrors.

"The sniper left his rifle on the roof of the Capitol Police headquarters building," Jones said. He leaned forward, causing another squeak, and removed a photo from a desk drawer. He passed it to Storm.

Storm inspected it and said, "It's a photograph of a Dragunov sniper rifle. Military issue, not one of the cheaper, knockoff versions manufactured in China and Iran for sale outside Russia."

Jones smiled. "Go on."

"Does the media know a Russian rifle was the murder weapon?" Storm asked.

"No, but it's only a matter of time. You know how Washington is about leaks and secrets."

Storm did. When it came to the nation's capital, Benjamin Franklin had said it best more than two hundred years earlier: "Three may keep a secret, if two of them are dead."

"Matthew Dull was shot with Russian-made bullets," Storm continued. "Now a sniper shoots Windslow with a Russian military sniper rifle. The killers clearly aren't worried about covering their tracks."

"Which is why the White House is concerned," Jones said. "The American public doesn't give a damn about the private war Petrov and Barkovsky are waging against each other. Who cares if a billionaire oligarch and his former best friend kill each other? But if word leaks out that an American was kidnapped and murdered and a U.S. senator was assassinated by one of them, then we'll be facing an international shit storm."

"How can you hide that fact?" Storm asked.

"The President is holding a press conference later today. He'll assure the American public that the attacks were not acts of terrorism. He'll say the FBI suspects the kidnapping and murders were carried out by a ruthless gang of Eastern European criminals. But there will be no mention of Petrov and certainly no mention of Russian President Barkovsky."

"Which man is worse?" Storm asked rhetorically. "Petrov is an egomaniac and Barkovsky is as flaky as Muammar Gaddafi without the high heels and rouge."

"The White House is more worried about Barkovsky. We can't sit still and allow a Russian president to assassinate a U.S. senator. That's why we have to be discreet."

"Discreet?" Storm repeated. "Congress already is scheduling hearings to investigate and the media is going wild."

Jones let out a sigh. "Yes, it's going to be tricky, but not impossible."

"With you, nothing ever is," Storm said. "But I'm curious. How long before someone gets interested in Steve Mason? How long before some pesky reporter asks why you inserted a private eye into the kidnapping? How long before someone discovers that Steve Mason doesn't exist?"

"The smart thing," Jones said, "would be for you to disappear—to go back to Wyoming."

"Montana," Storm said, correcting him.

Jones shrugged. "Wherever. But the truth is that I need you more now than ever before. I need someone whom I can trust to keep one step ahead of this investigation."

"Do you need me because you want to find out the truth? Or do you need me to help you bury the truth?"

"Probably both."

Jones looked exhausted. The pressures from his job were clearly taking a toll. His face was becoming a road map of worry lines. There was little doubt that Jones would have had pure white hair if he weren't bald. By contrast, Storm was still ruggedly handsome, although his body also was showing the signs of his past. Five scars in his abdomen marked where he'd been shot. There was a knife wound on his back where he'd been slashed from behind. More recently, a bullet had ice-skated across his shoulder, leaving an ugly superficial scar. Of course, the worst wounds had been delivered in Tangiers—physically and mentally.

One reason why Storm had faked his own death was because he'd quietly begun to question his own abilities after Tangiers. The couple helping him had been shot to death in front of him. He had been left for dead. Doctors couldn't believe he'd recovered. But with his recovery had come doubts. Had he missed something? Was he somehow to blame? It was only after he had "died"—while he was alone in Montana fishing—that he had considered another possibility. Someone had betrayed him. Someone inside the agency. He had gone over every minute detail of Tangiers, over and over, and he'd reached the same conclusion each time, no matter how he twisted it. He'd walked into a trap. Storm's first reaction had been to contact Jones and seek vengeance. But he had no proof. In Montana, he had been out of the game. What was the cost of getting back in? Now the landscape had changed. Now they'd let the fox back into the henhouse. Now he could test his hunch and expose the traitor who was responsible for the scars—both physical and mental— that he carried. If there really was a traitor, then Storm needed to unmask him. And he could only find the truth by working from the inside out.

Jones interrupted his thoughts. "You really don't have any idea what motive Petrov or Barkovsky might have for wanting Senator Windslow dead?"

"The senator's final words were *Jedidiah knows* and *Midas.*"

Storm let his answer hang in the air, begging for an explanation.

But Jones didn't immediately bite. Instead, he sat in his squeaky chair and stared blankly at his young protégé. And then, after several awkward seconds, he said: "OK, I agree. It's time for me to tell you a bit more. Only a handful of government officials here in Washington are familiar with what I am about to say. Senator Windslow was one of them and it cost him his life. It can cost your life, too. Before I go any further, I need to ask: Do you want to take that risk?"

"You seem to forget," Storm said. "I'm already dead."

CHAPTER FIVE

Jedidiah Jones walked to a wall safe with a magnetic strip that had the word "LOCKED" on it slapped across its reinforced steel door. Jones flipped over the strip so that the word "OPEN" was visible in bright red letters and punched a combination into an electronic screen that simultaneously verified his fingerprint. From the safe, he withdrew a thick red envelope marked "PROJECT *MIDAS*." He shut the safe's door, flipped the magnetic strip to "CLOSED" and double-checked to make certain the door was locked.

Returning to his chair, he wrote the name "STEVE MASON" in quotations on a log attached to the top secret file's front. He wrote the date, the time, his own name, and then noted that he had authorized Mason to view four photographs from the file. The photos were numbered MIDAS 001, 002, 003, and 004. He asked Storm to sign the log with his pseudonym. After he did, Jones handed Storm three photographs but held one back.

"Tell me what you see in the pictures," Jones said.

He'd played this game before. After Storm had been recruited by Clara Strike, Jones had sent him through a training course at the CIA's legendary facility called the Farm, outside Williamsburg, Virginia. There he'd been shown a photograph, asked to return it, and then asked about it. What did you see? Why was that important? What did you miss? What does it mean? His private eye experience had made him an expert at it.

"The three photographs show a kilobar of gold," he said. "That's a thousand grams of gold or the equivalent of 2.21 pounds. The markings on the bar show that it is 99.9 percent pure, which means it's high quality. But the reason why this bar is so unique is because of where it was minted and for whom."

Jones nodded approvingly. "And who owned it?"

"The impression in the lower center of the bar shows a hammer and sickle, which is the seal used by the former Soviet Union. Cyrillic letters under the seal form an acronym, КПСС, which, when translated to English, stands for the Communist Party of the Soviet Union. The bar in the photo was minted specifically for the Party and belonged in its treasury."

"It's odd really," Jones said, "how little knowledge most Americans have about the Soviet Union even though they grew up being told that it was an evil empire and its leaders planned on burying them. Just last week, I had to explain to a Senate committee that only a limited number of Russians were permitted to join the Communist Party during the Soviet era and that the Party had its own treasury that was completely separate from the Soviet Union's governmental holdings."

Storm didn't interrupt. Jones had a reason for this history lesson.

Jones said, "I couldn't believe U.S. senators didn't know that the Communist Party charged its members dues—just like labor unions do here. The Party deducted a portion of each member's monthly salary for its coffers."

Jones stopped talking and began tapping his finger on his desk as if he were marking time.

Storm knew the drill. It was now his turn to evaluate.

"There's another marking in the photograph," Storm said. "It identified that individual kilobar as being number 951,951. Logic tells us that this means there were 951,950 identical gold bars minted before it was and that those previous 951,950 gold kilobars also belonged to the Communist Party, not to the Soviet government."

"Do you know the price of gold?" Jones asked.

This was more than a simple question. It was a test. CIA operatives chosen for covert missions were expected to know the worth of precious metals. During wars, local currencies were worthless. But gold and diamonds always could be used to buy information, friends, and supplies.

"You're wondering if I still keep track," Storm replied. "Gold is trading today for $1,770 per troy ounce. That means an individual kilogram bar—like the one in the photograph— would be worth just under $57,000. If you were lucky enough to have the other 951,950 kilo bars that were minted before that bar, you'd have yourself a tidy bit of pocket change."

"Nearly five billion dollars' worth to be exact," Jones said.

"No," said Storm, correcting him. "If you want to be

exact, you would have $54,124,326,318. When you've been busted and had bill collectors pounding on your office door like I have, you don't do estimates when it comes to cash. You count it to the penny."

That was something Jones had always admired in his wunderkind operative. Even though Storm had been rough around the edges when Clara Strike recruited him, Jones had recognized that Storm had a lightning-quick mind and an amazing ability to remember the smallest details—especially when it came to money and instructions.

"Any idea where this fifty-four billion dollars in gold came from?"

Jones didn't throw many softballs. But this was one of them.

"The failed 'bathhouse' coup in 1991."

"Exactly."

Storm knew the story well. It had been a defining moment in history. On August 17, 1991, a Saturday, the head of the KGB, Vladimir A. Kryuchkov, summoned five senior Soviet officials to a Moscow bathhouse to discuss how they could overthrow Soviet president and party boss Mikhail Gorbachev. Kryuchkov often held meetings in steam rooms because it was one way he could insure that his colleagues were not secretly recording his conversations. While sitting naked, they decided to put Gorbachev, who was on vacation in the Crimea, under house arrest and then use KGB troops and the Soviet military to seize control of Moscow. At first, the diehards seemed to be winning. But that had changed when Russian soldiers refused to fire at a huge crowd of Muscovites assembled outside the

*White House—the home of Russia's parliament. Kryuchkov
and the others were arrested. Only after they were in jail did
the Kremlin discover that the KGB had secretly moved out of
Moscow several billion dollars of rubles and precious metals
that belonged to the Communist Party. They hadn't wanted it
to fall into the hands of Gorbachev and other reformers if the
coup failed. Gorbachev, Boris Yeltsin, and all of the presidents
who had followed them had searched for the missing billions.
But none of them had succeeded in finding them. Stories began
sweeping through Russia. The gold bars had been transported
by Vympel soldiers—KGB special forces—to a hidden bunker.
The Vympel were much like the U.S. Navy SEALs and were
used by the KGB for clandestine missions. They first gained
notoriety in 1979 when a team of Vympel operatives
assassinated Afghanistan president Hafizullah Amin while he
was sleeping in his bed inside the Tajbeg Palace in Kabul and
being protected by some five hundred guards. Legend had it
that the Vympel officer in charge of hiding the gold had killed
all of his men and then committed suicide so that none of them
would be tempted to reveal where the billions in bullion had
been hidden.*

"When was the photograph taken?" Storm asked. "Was it
while the gold was still in Moscow or after it disappeared?"

"Ah, you've just asked the key question," Jones replied.

He passed the fourth photograph, the one he had held
back, across his desk to Storm. It showed three men
standing together. They were Jedidiah Jones, Senator
Thurston Windslow, and oligarch Oleg Petrov. They were
holding the gold bar that Storm had just seen.

"Somehow," Jones explained, "Petrov found out where the Party's missing fortune is hidden. He brought a gold bar with him to the U.S. as proof and showed it to Senator Windslow because he was head of the U.S. Select Committee on Intelligence. Windslow brought Petrov to me."

"How'd he find it?"

Jones threw up his hands in exasperation. "I wish I knew. Petrov wouldn't tell us, but he claimed that he could take us to where the rest of the gold bullion was hidden."

"All of the gold bars?"

"Actually, Petrov claimed the treasure consisted of one million kilogram bars hidden by the KGB, plus other precious metals. The total worth is about sixty billion dollars."

"Sixty billion!" Storm repeated. "As in B?"

"Yes," Jones said. "Now that's a treasure worth finding, wouldn't you say?"

CHAPTER SIX

Jones collected the four photographs from Storm and placed them back into the thick file, which he inserted back into his wall safe.

"Why did he ask you for help?" Storm said. "Petrov's a billionaire. Why not hire a private army of mercenaries? For sixty billion, he could buy a country."

"If only it were that easy," Jones answered. "Who would you trust to help you recover sixty billion in gold bars and precious metals? Guns for hire? Mercenaries?"

"Good point," Storm said. "I remember a PI case I had. A couple murdered their parents for five grand in life insurance. Imagine what people would do when sixty billion is at stake."

"Petrov hinted that the gold is in a remote, difficult-to-reach location. He needs the kind of manpower and machinery that we can get him. And there's another problem: Petrov is not as wealthy as everyone has been led to believe. Barkovsky froze the oligarch's assets in Russia after they had a falling out and he fled from Moscow. Our analysts believe he only has access to seven to ten million."

"Only seven or ten million," Storm grunted. "Boo hoo. Makes me want to cry."

"It doesn't last long if you have a palatial estate in England, an Embassy Row mansion here in Washington, D.C., and a billion-dollar yacht sitting idle in the Mediterranean."

"So what's in it for you?" Storm asked.

"If we help him get the sixty billion, Petrov will use it to launch an insurgency against President Barkovsky."

"A war?"

"No, but he'd finance protest rallies, bribe officials, plant news stories, and make Barkovsky's life and presidency a living hell."

"Is getting rid of Barkovsky worth going to bed with Petrov?" Storm asked. "Why not just have him killed if you want to get rid of him?"

"We don't really do that anymore."

"Sure you don't," Storm said in a voice dripping with sarcasm. "Does that mean you turned down Petrov?"

"Absolutely, we turned him down," Jones replied. "We can't kill foreign leaders anymore and we can't topple foreign governments either. Congress has passed laws that specifically forbid us from doing that sort of thing. This isn't the 1950s and 1960s when you could put poison in one of Fidel Castro's cigars."

"Yeah, but if I recall, that cigar stunt didn't work."

"It could have," Jones said. "Creative thinking on our part. That's something I've always admired. But back to the gold. There are other reasons why we can't get involved in searching for the gold. One reason is that it still belongs to the Communist Party of the Russian Federation. Even though the Soviet Union no longer exists, the Communist Party in Russia still does. It's the second largest political party in that nation. All those little Commie bastards didn't just disappear overnight. By international law, that money still belongs to them.

"Here's another reason," Jones said. "President Barkovsky has made it clear to the White House that any cooperation our government extends to Petrov will be seen as a hostile act against him and his nation. The guy might be nuts, but he still has his finger on a huge arsenal of nuclear weapons and most of them are pointed at us. We don't want to encourage his paranoid hatred of the U.S."

"And finally," Jones continued, "we've got an internal problem. The day after that photograph of the kilobar was taken inside my office, the Russian ambassador paid an unannounced visit on the secretary of state and specifically stated that any attempt by the U.S. to recover the missing gold would be considered an act of international piracy."

"You got a leak. Someone tipped off the Russians."

"Exactly," Jones said. "Barkovsky knew about our private meeting in my office—this office—within twenty-four hours."

"A mole?"

"Yes, but I don't think the mole is on our side. I think it's in Petrov's camp. Only I can't be sure."

Despite Jones's litany of reasons, Storm could read between the lines. Clearly, Jones wanted to help Petrov, because Barkovsky was a dangerous loony tune. What better way to get rid of him than to have one of his former friends bring him down? Et tu, *Brute? Using the Communist Party's own wealth to destroy a pro-Communist president only made the entire scheme sweeter.*

"If you aren't going to help Petrov," Storm said, "then why tell me about the gold?"

"Because you're dead, remember? No one can be held responsible for the actions of a dead man, can they?"

"But I'm only one man."

Jones gave him a sly look and asked, "Are you sure? Do you really believe you're the only man who has gone off the grid? Do you think you're the only man who has disappeared?"

"Project *Midas*," Storm said, putting two and two together. "That thick file locked in your safe—it has the names of other 'dead' operatives just like me, doesn't it? You want me and the other 'dead' operatives to help Petrov because our country can't afford to leave any fingerprints behind."

"No fingerprints, no footprints," Jones said. "No prints at all."

Jones pulled a large envelope from a desk drawer and said, "I need you to go to London and talk to Petrov. First, try to find out who killed Windslow and why. Second, tell him that I've assembled a team to help him. All we need to learn is where the gold is hidden."

He emptied the envelope's contents onto his desktop. "Here's a passport, cash, credit cards, a cell phone, and airline tickets. Agent Showers is booked on a six o'clock flight to London. She's being sent to question Petrov. She'll be your ticket in to meet him. You'll tag along. I've already arranged it."

Storm's mind was swirling. "What about the mole?"

"If the mole is in Petrov's camp, there's nothing we can do. Just be careful."

"And what if it is on our side—someone inside this agency?"

"I know who you are, but you always worked in the field. No one else here in headquarters knows you or that you're still alive. I've also compartmentalized Project *Midas*."

"Meaning?" Storm asked.

"Meaning that only you and I know that you are involved in it. That's it. To everyone else, Derrick Storm is still a ghost."

The last time that Jones had been so confident about a covert operation, he'd sent Storm to Tangiers. Look how that had turned out.

Jones continued, "Be careful when you meet Petrov. Just because he showed me the gold doesn't mean we can trust him. I want you to find out what you can about the gold, but I also need for you to help Agent Showers solve the kidnapping and murders. Maybe Agent Showers is correct and Petrov killed Dull and Windslow because the senator had gotten cold feet about Project *Midas*. Maybe Barkovsky is behind the killings because he wanted to stop Windslow from pushing Project *Midas*. Or maybe Windslow was trying to extort a bigger share of that sixty-billion pie than what Petrov wanted to give him. Trust no one."

"Just like old times," Storm said.

"I'm still running covert operations," Jones said, "because I trust only a handful of people."

"Does Agent Showers know about the gold?" Storm asked.

"No. Only one handful of people know about it, and she isn't one of those fingers."

"She won't like having me tag along with her to London."

"She doesn't get a vote. Everything has been arranged—although your role will be strictly advisory."

Storm imagined Showers's reaction. This was not a minor case. A U.S. senator and his stepson had been killed. She wouldn't want him interfering. She was shrewd enough to know that Storm would be Jedidiah Jones's eyes and ears. She'd be suspicious of him.

"Weapons?" Storm asked.

"None for you. You'll be traveling on a diplomatic passport as Steve Mason. You'll be posing as a liaison officer from the State Department."

"Some paper pusher in the State Department told you that I couldn't be armed?"

"It wasn't a paper pusher. It came directly from the secretary of state. Tangiers. Remember? Ever since that fiasco, other agencies have been reluctant to let any of our people pose as one of their own, especially if they are armed."

Tangiers. Even in death, it continued to haunt him.

"How about Agent Showers?"

"No one objected to her having a sidearm," he said. "I'm also going to give you a personal letter to take to Petrov. He'll know it's from me."

Jones gave Storm a piercing look. "You were the last piece that I needed for Project *Midas*."

"Why me?"

"I just told you that I trust very few people. You happen to be one of them. I am trusting you to find sixty billion in gold and not let it corrupt you."

"That's a lot of gold," Storm said.

"Yes it is, and if I am wrong in trusting you, then I will see to it that you really do end up dead."

Another layer had been peeled. Jones was sending him down a dangerous path. And yet Storm still wasn't sure that Jones had told him everything. Knowing Jones, he doubted that he had. There were going to be more layers, more surprises, more twists, more turns, and with sixty billion dollars at stake, there were going to be more murders.

Of that, he was certain.

CHAPTER SEVEN

Storm took a seat in a sports bar directly across from Gate 21 at Dulles International Airport so that his back was against a wall and he could see all possible entrances and exits. He was supposed to meet Agent Showers there at 5 P.M. He'd arrived at 4:30 P.M. In his line of work, you never wanted to walk into an area cold, even if you were simply catching a flight to London with an FBI agent.

He'd just sat down when Agent Showers entered the bar. She'd come early, too. He liked that. As he watched her scan the lounge, he was reminded of how attractive she was. Showers was wearing a dark gray pants suit with a short jacket that covered an off-white silk blouse layered over a black camisole. She was a knockout.

Showers carefully weaved through the jumble of chairs and tables occupied by travelers who were taking advantage of a two-drinks-for-one happy hour.

"Hello, Ms. Showers," Storm said, rising politely from his seat.

She was only carrying a backpack.

"Where's your luggage?" he asked her. "I've never known a woman who traveled light."

"Where's yours?" she replied. He glanced at a backpack next to him.

Both of them had checked their luggage for a reason besides convenience. They would not have been able to react quickly during an emergency if they were lugging suitcases with them.

"Whaddaya want to drink, doll?" a busty cocktail waitress, wearing too much makeup and fishnet hose, asked them.

"A diet cola, either brand," Showers said.

"I'll take a beer. Whatever you have on tap."

"Great choice, handsome," she said, winking at him.

As she walked away, Showers said, "You just ordered a draft of whatever they have on tap and she complimented your choice. You must love it when women flirt with you."

"But you don't," he said. It sounded like a question.

"I don't what? Like it when someone flirts with you? Or are you saying I don't flirt with you?"

"Both."

"Don't be a fool," she said. "That waitress is just working you for a tip."

"I'll be sure to tell her that you're paying the tab."

The waitress returned with their drinks, serving Storm first. "Here you are, cutie," she said.

She plopped Showers's cola on a napkin in front of her without comment.

"Thank you," Storm said, beaming. "By the way, my friend here is going to be paying our tab."

"A girlfriend who buys you drinks," the waitress said.

"Be careful, she might be trying to get lucky."

"He's not my boyfriend," Showers said indignantly.

"Too bad for you," the waitress replied.

When she was out of earshot, Showers said, "I'm tipping her zero."

Storm looked smug. He liked Agent Showers.

She got down to business. "I've contacted Scotland Yard, and they're sending a liaison to meet us at Heathrow and take us to the Yard for a briefing about Ivan Petrov."

"Thanks, but I'll skip the introductions at the airport and just meet you later at our hotel. You can brief me."

"I can brief you?" she replied, bristling. "Hey, you're tagging along with me, remember. It's not my job to brief you."

"You're right," Storm said, throwing her a bone. "But I think it's better if I stay in the shadows."

She thought about it for a second and said, "You're probably right. I didn't have a choice about notifying Scotland Yard. It's agency procedure when a law enforcement group visits a foreign government to interrogate someone. I just hope the Brits have enough common sense to keep their mouths shut about us coming."

"I doubt it," Storm said.

"Why? Because they're cops?"

"Of course not. I just love cops, especially women in uniform with nightsticks," he said, grinning. She scowled.

He said, "I'm suspicious because this is a high-profile case and Ivan Petrov is internationally known. Your arrival in England to question Petrov will be big news if word leaks out."

"I raised that issue with my bosses," she said. "But they

assured me that the Bureau and Scotland Yard have a close professional relationship. Actually, they accused me of thinking like someone who worked for Jedidiah Jones rather than like a cop. Cloak-and-dagger versus real police work."

"Real police work," he repeated. "I like how that rolled off your lips."

"I'm not a private detective," she said, "nor am I one of Jones's contract 'fixers.' I'm still not certain who you really are or what you are doing for Jones, and I doubt if you are going to tell me, are you?"

"A deduction made by real police work," he replied, lifting his beer in a mock salute.

She said, "Look, there's something I need to tell you. I told my superiors that it was a mistake sending you along."

"I would have been surprised if you hadn't."

"It's nothing personal. You're kind of likable."

"Kind of likable, not adorable?"

"The reason why I said I didn't want you tagging along is because you're a cowboy. You don't follow the rules and that means I can't depend on you. When we first met—when Senator Windslow first demanded that you be brought into the kidnapping investigation—I put all of my cards on the table. I was completely honest with you and treated you like a professional. But you didn't put your cards on the table. You didn't treat me like a professional. You hid information from me."

"You're right," Storm said. "I did hide information from you."

"At least you're honest about that," she said. "My point

is: how are we supposed to work together if I can't trust you? I don't know for certain if you are being honest with me right now."

"I understand," he replied, "but I work with people all of the time who are not telling me the truth and are hiding things from me. I've even worked with people who wanted to kill me."

"I can understand that," she deadpanned.

"But you find a way to get around all of that and accomplish the mission."

"How? Especially if you don't follow the rules?"

"I don't trust rules. But I do trust my instincts and what they tell me about the people working with me. Rules can get you killed."

"So can breaking them."

"Agent Showers, have you ever had a one-night stand?" he asked.

She let out a sigh. "I'm trying to have an adult conversation."

"Perhaps it's not the best analogy, but hear me out. If you meet someone in a bar and you end up in the sack, you have certain expectations, maybe even certain demands, but you don't fall in love with that person and you don't share your most intimate secrets with them, even though you are doing something very intimate. You don't necessarily trust them either. You just do your job and move on. The same is true at work." He smiled, clearly happy with that explanation.

"You're making my head spin with your logic. Is that

what a one-night stand is to you?" she asked, raising a brow. "A job? And then you move on?"

Without waiting for him to answer, she said, "I guess that's one of the differences between us and why I work at the FBI and you work for Jedidiah Jones."

"Now my head is spinning," he said, mimicking her.

"When I was in college, a CIA recruiter came to see me. He told me that people who worked for the Agency were not obligated to follow U.S. laws when they traveled overseas. He bragged that a CIA employee could lie, cheat, steal, break into apartments, and even kill. The rules don't apply. That's what he said. That's the sort of folks he wanted working for him. People who think they are above the law. People like you."

"He was just being honest with you," Storm said. "As my mother used to say, 'You got to crack a few eggs to make an omelet.'" He finished his beer and waved to the waitress.

"I'm not a person whose moral code ends when I cross the U.S. border," she said. "Oh, another thing. I don't do one-night stands. So don't get your hopes—or anything else—up during our trip."

"Around you," he replied, "I'm always fully hopeful."

"I'm going to the ladies' room," she said. "I'll see you on the plane."

"Don't get confused and go into the wrong potty," he said, smirking.

"I only do that when I have to rescue you," she replied, leaving.

He noticed that she'd not left a tip.

"Lady friend troubles?" the waitress asked, returning to his table.

"She's a bit high-strung."

"Too skinny, too." The waitress bent over when she served him another beer, giving Storm an eyeful. "This one's on the house. My name's Eve. You know, the girl who ate that nasty apple. Why don't you stop in again when you get back from wherever you're flying off to." She walked away slowly, making sure that he got a good view.

The gate agent announced over the intercom that it was time to board the Heathrow flight. First class ticket holders hurried forward. Business class was next.

Storm checked his first class ticket. But he did not move. He had no interest in boarding early. If he did, all the passengers that came after him would see his face as they slowly made their way down the aisle, finding their seats and storing their luggage. Storm wanted to be the last on a flight. He wanted to sit as near the front of the plane as possible, and he wanted to be the first off every flight. This way, he could observe all of the other passengers and hopefully not call attention to himself.

When it looked as if the last passengers were on the walkway, Storm tossed a ten-dollar tip on the table and walked over to the gate. He'd not seen Showers and was curious where she'd gone.

"Welcome aboard," the agent said, taking his ticket. "Oh, you're first class. You could have boarded earlier."

"Nature called." He bent down to tie his shoe, stalling. Where was Showers?

Storm heard the sounds of someone running toward him.

"I've got a ticket." It was a woman, but not Showers. Storm noticed that she had a distinct Russian accent.

"Looks like you have three late-comers," Showers said as she stepped to the gate.

"Yes," the agent replied, "and all three of you are seated in first class. What a coincidence."

"Yes, indeed," Storm said.

CHAPTER EIGHT

Storm knew the instant that he saw her and heard the Russian accent. In her late twenties, she was wearing functional shoes, skin-tight designer jeans, and a dark gray sweater pulled over a low-collared, gray, wide-striped shirt whose tail peeked out. A professional women's dive watch was on her wrist. She wore no jewelry but did have a thin silver belt around her waist that Storm suspected could be an effective garrote in her well-manicured hands. He put her at five-foot-six and 119 pounds. She had long black hair pulled back from unblemished bronze skin. Her dark eyes were highlighted perfectly by thin brows.

Storm knew the SVR—the successor to the Soviet KGB—didn't believe women were emotionally stable enough to be trained as operatives. Instead, the Russian intelligence service used them as secretaries, couriers, and sometimes as prostitutes in covert operations. They also sent them abroad as *illegals*, giving them fake backgrounds and sending them into enemy countries to embed themselves in the local culture and gradually work their way into useful positions to spy. But they never used them as Vympel soldiers or on protective details.

If Storm was correct, this woman was not a native Russian but was from one of the Soviet's former republics whose intelligence services didn't share Moscow's machismo attitude. He suspected she worked for Ivan Petrov.

The overnight flight proved uneventful. Unfortunately, Storm found himself seated next to a rather plump middle-aged woman who drank four glasses of Riesling, fell asleep instantly, and began snoring with an open mouth.

As soon as the flight landed, Storm exited, keeping an eye on both the late arriving passenger and Showers. After clearing Customs and Immigration, he ducked into Heathrow's Virgin Atlantic clubhouse, where he used his laptop in one of the private rooms to send a photo to Langley of the female passenger. He'd snapped the picture with his cell phone when she'd gotten up to use the toilet after dinner on the transatlantic flight. The agency's facial recognition program identified her in less than a minute.

Antonija Nad was a former member of the Special Operations Battalion in the Croatian armed services. The BSD, as it was known, focused on airborne assault and behind-enemy-lines combat. It was one of the most respected special forces units in the world. It was also one of only two European forces that allowed women to fight in specialized units. She'd resigned from the Croatia military a year ago to work for PROTEC, a security firm based in London.

He had guessed correctly. She had to work for Petrov.

Storm checked the time. By now, Showers and Nad

would have exited Heathrow. He walked to the airport's rental counters to get a car and an hour later pulled up outside the London Marriott Hotel Park Lane across from Hyde Park. Storm never understood why Americans booked rooms in American hotels when they traveled overseas. It was like eating McDonald's in Paris. But someone in the government, who had arranged the tickets and hotels, had gotten them adjoining rooms there.

Because Showers was still being briefed at Scotland Yard, she hadn't checked in. Storm decided to find a room elsewhere. He drove through the neighborhood until he spotted a cozy bed-and-breakfast a few blocks from the hotel. The grandmotherly owner at the antique reception desk said one room was available, which he rented with cash. *Jones had warned him to not trust anyone. He was taking his advice.*

The flat was on the second floor of what used to be a high-end Hyde Park row house, with huge rooms. But that had been when the sun never set on the Union Jack. Since then, the building had been divided into small units barely bigger than a double bed. He'd stayed in worse. It was clean and had Internet access. Best of all, no one would know he was here.

Before he'd left Langley, Storm had collected crime scene photographs taken by the FBI. Taking a seat at an oak desk from the 1850s that faced his room's street window, he sorted through the photos, stopping when he reached a batch that had been taken on the roof of the Capitol Police headquarters, where the sniper had hidden.

The shooter had used a bag of sugar to support the barrel of the 9.8-pound Dragunov rifle. The bag was a readily available prop that no one would consider suspicious if he was seen carrying it. The Dragunov was a gun that could easily be disassembled and hidden in a briefcase.

The Dragunov's barrel had been equipped with a flash suppressor to help hide the shooter's location. But it didn't have a silencer. This meant the sniper had not been worried about the sound of the gunshot.

Like all professionals, the assassin had known that there would be two actual sounds when he pulled the trigger. The sound from the initial bang—the muzzle blast—would be masked by the noisy, rush hour street traffic around the headquarters building. The second sound would be the sonic crack that a bullet makes as it flies through the air. The bullet would create a sonic wave behind it as it sped forward. Anyone hearing the crack would look forward in the same direction as the bullet was going, not backward where it had come from. There was no need for him to use a silencer. Only the muzzle flash mattered, especially at dusk.

Storm looked at snapshots of the Dirksen Building taken from the sniper's viewpoint. The distance was roughly four hundred yards, or the length of four football fields, the equivalent of 1200 feet. Storm knew the Dragunov was most effective between 600 meters and 1300 meters, or 1,970 feet and 4,270 feet, which meant the fatal shot actually had been taken much closer than during combat. It would have been an easy shot for a skilled marksman.

He turned to a photo of the Dragunov and examined the

weapon. Ordinarily, the rifle's stock was wood with a hole cut out of its center to make the gun lighter. Someone had modified the rifle in the photo by attaching a shorter, solid wooden stock to it. *Why?*

He tucked the photos away, stretched out on the bed, and used the remote to turn on a television hanging from the ceiling. He flipped channels until he found the BBC's twenty-four-hour newscast. Agent Showers suddenly appeared on the screen with a uniformed bobby on one side and a man identified as a Scotland Yard detective on her other. The announcer said:

"The FBI has sent one of its agents to London to interview Russian oligarch Ivan Petrov as part of its investigation into the recent murder of United States Senator Thurston Windslow. The senator was slain in his Washington, D.C., office on Capitol Hill by a sniper who remains at large. The agent, April Showers, refused to comment, but sources tell the BBC that the FBI considers Petrov to be a 'person of interest' because of his close relationship with the slain senator."

As he and Showers had both feared, someone at Scotland Yard had tipped off the British press about their arrival. Showers was paying a price for playing by the rules.

CHAPTER NINE

The cell phone that Jones had given him rang shortly after 12 P.M. London time, waking him from a short power nap.

"We've been invited to have tea with Ivan Petrov," Showers said.

"He must have been impressed with your BBC appearance."

"Did you rent a car?" she asked, ignoring his comment. "It'll take us about three hours to get to the Duke of Madison's estate outside of Gloucester."

"Your buddies at Scotland Yard didn't offer to drive us?"

"Are you going to rub that in all day?"

"Probably," he replied. "I'll meet you outside the hotel in ten minutes."

"I can just knock on your door when I'm ready," she said. "We're in adjoining rooms, aren't we?"

"I'm out sightseeing. I'll pick you up at the front entrance."

For a moment, Storm wondered if he was being too paranoid. Maybe he was overreacting because of Tangiers. But he couldn't help himself. While he was in England, he could not afford to let down his guard. The older man sitting in Hyde Park on a bench reading the Times *was not really reading the* Times. *The woman behind him when he was on the sidewalk was not really walking her dog. "Trust no one," Jones had said. It was his mantra.*

He'd rented a Vauxhall Insignia because the German-made car, which was similar to a Buick Regal, was as common in England as a Honda in the U.S. It wouldn't draw attention. After Showers's BBC debut, of course, their arrival was hardly a secret.

Showers exited the hotel dressed in an attractive gray pantsuit, carrying a light jacket and her briefcase. Storm had entered the address of the Duke of Madison's estate into the Vauxhall's onboard GPS. He glanced at the rearview mirror as he began weaving through London's congested streets. Eventually, they reached the M-40, the main thoroughfare that would take them west to Gloucester. About four miles outside of London, Storm spotted a black Mercedes-Benz lurking two cars behind them.

"What did you learn at Scotland Yard?" he asked.

"They told me Petrov was having financial problems. The Russians have frozen most of his fortune in Moscow."

Storm focused on watching the Mercedes. Showers read through a briefing paper about Petrov. When the voice in the GPS warned that the car was only a mile from the exit that would take them to the Duke of Madison's estate, Storm suddenly pressed on the brakes and brought the Vauxhall to a crawl. Angry drivers honked and swerved around them. At first, the driver of the Mercedes slowed down, too, but then he realized that Storm was testing him. It would be obvious that the Mercedes was tailing the Vauxhall if it also came to a crawl.

As the Mercedes sped up, Showers looked up from her paperwork. "I noticed them, too, when we first left London. Nice work."

The windows of the Mercedes were tinted, but as the car passed them, Storm made a peace sign. He envisioned the occupants giving him the finger. Showers scribbled down the license tag and then used her cell phone to enter the car's license plate into an FBI computerized database in Washington, D.C. The vehicle was registered to the embassy of the Russian Federation in London.

"The Ruskies seem to follow you everywhere we go," Storm said. "They must enjoy watching you from behind."

Showers sighed.

They reached the gated entrance to the Duke of Madison's estate a minute later. Two security guards, with patches on their black berets that identified them as employees of PROTEC, checked their passports and then let them pass.

"Did you notice they were armed?" Storm asked, as the Vauxhall bounced over cobblestones toward the manor house.

"They're called 'manned guards' in England," Showers said, "and yes, I saw their weapons."

"Regardless of what they are called," he said, "security guards are not supposed to be armed in Britain. Maybe we should call your buddies at Scotland Yard and report them for breaking the rules."

Ignoring the dig, Showers said, "According to my briefing

papers, the manor house is about five miles up this road. The entire estate consists of ten thousand acres. The main house was built in 1532 with stones cut from a nearby quarry and was designed to show off the Duke of Madison's vast wealth."

"How'd the duke's heirs lose it?" Storm asked.

"Bad bets in hedge funds and London casinos," she replied. "Your kind of people."

The three-story mansion came into sight. A carved stag and the duke's coat of arms were sculpted in marble above each window.

A man and woman were waiting. Storm recognized Antonija Nad from their overnight flight.

"I'm Georgi Lebedev," the man said, extending his hand as they stepped from their rented car. "I recognize Special Agent April Showers from the BBC."

Showers blushed.

"Yes, she's becoming quite the celebrity here. I expect the queen to invite her over any day now," Storm said. He introduced himself as Steve Mason from the State Department.

"He's only here as an advisor," Showers added. "Seen but not heard."

Lebedev said, "This is Ms. Antonija Nad, our chief of security."

"Yes," said Storm. "We were on the same flight from Washington this morning."

"I didn't notice," Nad replied.

She was lying.

"I didn't notice you either," Showers said.

She was lying, too.

"I always notice beautiful women," Storm said.

He was not lying.

Nad gave Storm a slight smile.

He noticed she was carrying a CZ P-01 semiautomatic pistol in a holster on her belt. "I thought it was illegal for manned guards to carry weapons in England," he said.

"It is completely against the law," Lebedev said, "but under an old English law, a nobleman, such as a duke, has the authority to arm his knights for the protection of his lands and his serfs. Obviously, Mr. Petrov is not a duke, but when he purchased the estate, we were able to persuade the duke's heirs to sign a document that gives us permission to carry weapons while we are on the grounds here. Quite frankly, I'm not sure it would pass legal muster if someone complained, but no one has."

"Does this mean Ms. Nad is a knight?" Storm asked, looking at her dark eyes.

"It means I can shoot you if necessary," she replied.

Lebedev led them into the manor house. As they walked, Showers said, "I didn't realize Russian oligarchs made it a practice to have English tea."

"Please don't refer to him as an oligarch," Lebedev replied. "It's not a compliment in Russia. And please don't assume that because we are Russians, we only drink vodka."

"I meant no offense," Showers said.

"I'd rather have a good shot of Putinka, any day, than to drink English tea," Storm volunteered.

"Ah, you're familiar with Russian vodkas," Lebedev said. "I'm sure we can find some Putinka for you."

"I suspect Mr. Petrov's tastes are more along the line of Kauffman," Showers said, showing off.

"First you mention the most popular vodka in Moscow and then you mention the most expensive. I'll ask one of our servants to pour you a sample to see if you palates match your knowledge."

"None for me," said Showers. "When I'm working, I stick to something nonalcoholic. Tea will be fine."

"Then I will drink her shots," Storm said.

They walked through a massive dining room and exited the house, entering a garden courtyard.

"We'll be having what the English call low tea, which is an afternoon snack, as opposed to high tea," said Lebedev, "which is more of a meal."

"I don't see Mr. Petrov," Showers said.

"He'll be joining us shortly. Please be seated."

They sat in chairs on opposite sides of an oblong table covered with a white linen cloth. The head spot was left empty. Storm noticed that it also had a chair larger than the others, to support Petrov's girth. Three men wearing formal attire brought out silver trays with fresh strawberries dipped in chocolate, egg salad finger sandwiches, and warm scones with Devonshire cream. Nad and Storm didn't take any. But Showers and Lebedev sampled the offerings. A fourth servant poured tea for the women, but brought shot glasses to the table for the men.

Ivan Petrov entered the courtyard through a side door in the mansion. "Don't get up," he said. "I apologize for being late, but when you have businesses in different time zones, sometimes it's difficult to keep a normal schedule." He spotted the shot glasses.

"Ah," he said. "I'm so glad our American friends are not sticklers for English tradition. But I'm surprised that you didn't want an imported beer, Mr. Mason."

The reference to beer showed that he'd had Nad run a background check on him. Did they also suspect that his real name was not Steve Mason and he wasn't a State Department employee?

"Mr. Lebedev has proposed a challenge," Storm explained. "One shot glass contains Kauffman and the other Putinka."

"I'll play," said Petrov. "But first, are you a sporting man?"

"What are the stakes?"

"I'm extremely wealthy and you, sadly, collect a government salary," Petrov bragged. "How can we make this fair? Here's what I suggest. I will bet whatever British pounds I have on my person against whatever pounds you have in your wallet. This way neither of us will know the true value of the prize until we win. It will be part of the fun."

"Okay," Storm said.

The two men reached for the first shot of vodka simultaneously and swallowed the contents of the glasses in front of them.

Smacking his lips, Petrov said, "I believe the first glass was the Kauffman."

"I agree," said Storm.

Petrov ordered the servant to pour another round.

Again, Petrov went first, downing both shot glasses. "This time, it's the second glass," he said.

Storm followed. "And this time, I disagree."

Everyone looked at the servant. "Which glass did you pour the Kauffman into?" Petrov asked.

A glint of fear sparked inside the man's eyes.

"C'mon, man," said Petrov. "Be honest. You won't be fired. Or horsewhipped." He grinned. "Tell us which glass had the Kauffman."

"Your guest is the one who is correct, sir. I poured it into the first glass. The second was the Putinka."

Petrov laughed. "And so, my friend, you win." He reached into the jacket of his stylist coat and withdrew a leather wallet. "Unfortunately," he said, "I never carry money. No British pounds, no American dollars, no Russian rubles. Nothing. Look for yourself." He opened his billfold, exposing a dozen top-end credit cards but not a single bill. "This is because I have people who pay all of my bills whenever I leave the estate. It is one of the perks of being rich. You never touch cash. I apologize, but you win nothing."

"Only bragging rights," said Storm.

"And what would I have won?" Petrov asked.

Storm removed his own wallet. Unlike Petrov's, it contained a thick wad of bills.

"Ah, you are lucky," Petrov said, eyeing the cash.

"Not really," Storm replied. He extracted one of the bills. "Our wager was British pounds against British pounds and all of my currency is U.S. dollars. It appears as if each of us was trying to trick the other."

"Touché," Petrov said. He lifted a third glass of vodka and said, "*Za vstrechi!*"

"It means ..." Lebedev said, starting to translate.

Showers interrupted. "To our meet-up."

"Ah, do you know much Russian, my dear?" Petrov said.

"Just a few words. Enough to be dangerous."

"Indeed," Petrov said.

Storm noticed that Nad had not taken a drink. "You don't like vodka or tea?" he asked. "Perhaps a shot of rakija?"

"Now, that's a drink that I'm not familiar with," Lebedev said.

"It's popular in Croatia, especially in the military," Petrov said. "Our State Department guest has done his homework."

"Drinking slows the reactions," she said.

Petrov said, "My Nad is very, very dedicated." He glanced at his diamond-studded watch and said, "You have come here to question me about my relationship with Senator Thurston Windslow. At least that is what the BBC reported today."

He looked at Showers, whose cheeks began to blush.

Continuing, he said, "My lawyer, Mr. Lebedev, has reminded me that I am a British citizen and can claim certain protections as such. But I have nothing to hide, so I am willing to answer your questions."

"We do have one proviso," Lebedev announced. "Mr. Petrov's schedule is extremely hectic today, and as you know, English is not our native language. Therefore, we would like for you to tell us in general what information you require now, and then tonight, perhaps, you could submit your questions in writing? We can reconvene tomorrow."

As if rehearsed, Petrov chimed in, "I can tell you this. I was not in the United States when this terrible tragedy happened. I also considered Senator Windslow to be a close friend. I had absolutely no reason to wish him or his family harm."

"I'd like to learn more about your personal relationship," Showers said. "How often did you get together in Washington? Did you engage in any financial dealings?"

She was being purposely vague. She had no interest in tipping her hand.

"In Moscow," Petrov said, "we ask direct questions when we want direct replies. You want to know if I paid him a bribe."

His candor seemed shocking. But was it really? Petrov and his attorney had had plenty of time to plan their defense. Mentioning the bribe was clearly part of their strategy. But to what end?

"There have been rumors," Showers said, "of a six-million-dollar payment going from your London bank to the Cayman Islands and then to Senator Windslow."

"We can discuss this tomorrow," Petrov promised. "However, if that money was withdrawn from my bank, it was not authorized by me."

"You allow your employees to transfer six million dollars out of the country without telling you?" Storm asked.

Petrov glanced at Lebedev and said, "Only one or two of them. But the point is that I certainly never offered the senator a bribe. We were good friends. And there is no need for good friends to bribe each other. You do favors out of friendship, not for cash."

Petrov paused and then said, "If you like, I can save you considerable time by exposing the man who committed the crimes of kidnapping and murder in your capital. The man with bloody hands is Russian president Oleg Barkovsky. He is the villain you should be investigating, not me."

"Let's set a time to meet tomorrow," Lebedev said. "In the morning, Mr. Petrov will be delivering a speech at a student rally in Oxford."

"You should attend," Petrov announced. "I will be speaking about the murder of Svetlana Alekseev, the Russian journalist who was found dead in the elevator of her Moscow apartment building last month. She had criticized Barkovsky, and it is common knowledge that he ordered her killed. Just as he had your senator murdered."

"If you attend," Lebedev said, "you will see for yourselves how much loved Mr. Petrov is by the British people."

"Isn't it a dangerous for you to appear at a public rally," Storm asked, "considering there have been attempts here in England to kill you?"

"Especially," Showers added, "since your security detail is not allowed to carry weapons anywhere outside your estate."

Petrov replied, "I have full confidence in Ms. Nad's ability to keep me safe. She is an excellent marksman."

"Besides," Petrov said, "I'm not going to let that miserable bastard in the Kremlin keep me from speaking about atrocities being committed against my fellow oppressed Russians." He stood from the table and said, "Thank you for coming this afternoon. I will leave you to work out the arrangements for tomorrow."

"Before you leave us," Storm said. "I'd like a word in private with you."

Showers gave him a surprised and irritated look.

"I'm sorry, but this is impossible. I always include Mr. Lebedev in my private conversations."

"Then maybe the three of us can step into the main house," Storm offered. "It's a State Department matter, not related to the FBI's investigation."

"If you insist," Petrov said.

"Just a minute," Showers said. "I'm not entirely certain what my colleague has to say, but please know that he doesn't speak for the FBI or the Justice Department."

"Thank you," Petrov said. "This is rather unusual."

Lebedev fell in behind them as did Nad, leaving Showers alone at the table. She was furious.

"Do you really need a security officer with you?" Storm asked.

Petrov said, "You're right. I have nothing to fear from our guest. Please keep our FBI friend company in the courtyard."

As soon as the three men entered the house, Storm removed an envelope from his pocket and offered it to Petrov.

"A mutual friend asked me to give you a personal letter."

Petrov made no effort to accept it. Instead, he asked cautiously, "And does this friend have a name?"

"Jedidiah."

"You can give it to Mr. Lebedev," Petrov said.

"I'd rather give it to you."

"I will take it," said Lebedev, reaching up.

Storm flipped it aside, stopping him from snatching it.

"Jedidiah wanted you to take it personally," he said to Petrov.

The Russian hesitated and then took it from him.

Before Storm could say another word, Petrov turned and started to walk away.

"After you read it," Storm said. "We can discuss the gold."

Petrov stopped and looked over his shoulder.

"Perhaps. After I read it. Tomorrow then."

"Only this time in private—just you and me," Storm said. "Jedidiah believes you might have a leak in your organization."

A concerned look appeared on Petrov's face. "I see, and did he identify this leak for you?"

"Not by name," Storm said.

Petrov left him and Lebedev alone.

"I'll show you and Ms. Showers to your car," Lebedev said, opening the door to the courtyard.

Showers stood and Nad fell in behind as Lebedev guided them through the mansion to their parked rental outside.

"I will telephone you later tonight, Ms. Showers," Lebedev said. "Perhaps you can fax us your written inquires. Will you be attending the protest in the morning at Oxford?"

"I wouldn't miss it."

As soon as Storm and Showers were in the Vauxhall, Storm said, "Well, I thought that went just dandy."

Showers was so angry she couldn't speak until they had driven down the cobblestones and exited through the gated entrance. When they reached the main highway, she exploded.

"You rotten son of a bitch! I knew I couldn't trust you. How dare you pull that stunt. You embarrassed me. You went behind my back again. Every time that I think you're an actual human being, you prove me wrong."

"I was only following orders," he said.

"Oh, so now you're the one who suddenly is following rules. When it suits you. And what was all that macho crap with the vodka. I think this glass is the one, oh no, I think it was this one. My God, I felt like I was in some old spy movie."

He started to reply, but she held up both of her hands. "Just don't speak to me," she said. She reached for the radio. "The last thing I want to hear is your voice."

CHAPTER TEN

As soon as their guests were gone, Georgi Lebedev hurried to the manor house's extensive library, where Ivan Petrov was sitting behind an enormous, hand-carved desk reading the letter that Jones had sent him. The CIA director had written a personal note on a copy of the photograph that showed Jones, Windslow, and Petrov holding the gold bar: "We accept your proposal. Mr. Mason is my envoy and will handle all arrangements."

Lebedev said, "What did Jedidiah write? Is the CIA going to help us get the gold?"

"As we suspected, Mr. Mason is not a State Department liaison," Petrov said, avoiding the question. "Has Nad been able to identify him?"

"Not yet. She is taking his fingerprints from the shot glasses as we speak. She should have an answer shortly. But what of Mr. Jones and the CIA? Is it going to help us?"

Petrov said, "I will learn more tomorrow, but today, it is enough for me to tell you that Barkovsky's days are limited, and when the time comes, I will be the one who puts a bullet into the back of his head."

"*Vyshaya mer*," Lebedev said, which translated to "the highest measure of punishment." It was when a condemned man was taken into a room, made to kneel, then shot in the back of the head so that his face was blown away and made unrecognizable. It was part of the Stalinist tradition.

"You have not even told me where the gold is located," Lebedev said, "and we are like brothers, closer than brothers. Why would you share your secret with some stranger just because he arrives with a letter?"

"Do you take me for an ass?" Petrov asked.

"No, my friend."

"Then don't treat me like one," Petrov said. "I will talk to this Mr. Mason tomorrow, but I will tell him little, or nothing, until I learn what he has come to offer us."

"I say we screw the Americans. Nad is loyal to you. Let her get the gold. Do this on your own."

Petrov patted Lebedev on his shoulder. "And what happens when her loyal hired guards see mountains of gold before their eyes? Billions within reach. Can they overcome the temptation? Only men who believe in a greater cause can be trusted to recover the gold. You can't buy honor or loyalty. That's why I need the Americans. They will not betray their own country."

CHAPTER ELEVEN

Novo-Ogaryovo (President's Residence)
MOSCOW, Russia

President Barkovsky generally ate after nine o'clock Moscow time, in the company of his closest friends and young female playthings. But tonight he was dining alone and watching two men slugging and kicking each other in an Ultimate Fighting Championship event on cable television, in a private dining room adjacent to his bedroom. He'd just finished a *pirozhki* stuffed with boiled meat and sautéed onions when his chief of staff entered.

"We've just heard from our friend," Mikhail Sokolov said.

Barkovsky motioned Sokolov to sit, which he did, as the president refilled his wineglass and poured one for his guest.

"These American fighters are nothing," Barkovsky said, pointing to the television screen. "One of our Vympel soldiers could kill any of them with one quick blow. If I were not a president, I would fight in the ring myself and show these American bastards what real men are made of."

He took a large gulp of wine and asked, "What does our friend have to tell us?"

"Petrov had visitors in England today. An FBI agent and a man posing as a U.S. State Department employee."

"CIA?"

"Probably. But we have not been able to identify him."

"And what was the purpose of this visit?"

"The FBI suspects Petrov of assassinating Senator Windslow."

Barkovsky gave his aide a toothy grin. "This is excellent."

"The CIA man, however, asked to speak privately with Petrov."

The president put down his fork and wiped his fingers on a satin napkin. "And what did this stranger tell Petrov?"

"Our source did not know specifics. But it was about finding the gold."

Without warning, Barkovsky slammed both fists onto the dining room table and uttered an expletive. "Do the Americans understand what this means?"

"I'm certain the CIA will cover its tracks if it helps him. There will be no evidence that we can use."

"How is that possible? Aren't our officers as clever as Langley's drones? Tell London that we must identify this stranger. Now!"

Barkovsky let out a loud sigh. "Why do we still not know where the gold is hidden?"

"Petrov refuses to tell anyone, even Lebedev, his closest friend and advisor. And no one knows how he found where the treasure is hidden. Our friend says that Petrov is going to meet with the FBI agent and stranger tomorrow after he speaks in Oxford at a rally."

"What rally?"

"About the journalist killing."

Barkovsky waved his hand threw the air, dismissing it. "Let them demonstrate—in Oxford. Who cares about the goddamn British?"

For a moment, he didn't speak. He was considering his options. "No one knows how Petrov found the location of the gold. He has refused to tell anyone where it is hidden. But now it appears that the Americans might be about to help him find it. This changes everything. We cannot risk having it fall into Petrov's hands."

He was pensive for a few more moments and then added, "If we kill the Americans, they will simply send someone else. That leaves me only one other option. If Petrov will not talk, then he must be killed. Better that his secret dies with him than to have the Americans learn where the gold is hidden."

"There have been attempts on his life already and all have failed."

A smug look appeared on Barkovsky's face. "Do you think I am that inept? If I wanted him dead, he would be dead. Those attempts were meant to make him share his secret with someone else in case he was killed. But I underestimated his ego. Petrov is willing to go to his grave with his secret. So now it is time to let him!"

"If Petrov dies," Sokolov said, "you will never know where the bullion is hidden."

"That's not true," Barkovsky replied. "If he discovered it,

there must be a way for us to learn it, too. It will simply take more time."

"We could kidnap him. We could torture him."

"And the world would condemn me. They would demand his release."

"If you kill him, the world will also know, will it not?"

"Not if I give them a patsy."

"But who?"

Barkovsky said, "His guests—the FBI Agent who was on the BBC. And the mystery man from the CIA. Let them appear to kill him and the world will blame them and the United States."

"And the gold?"

"We will keep searching. What is important now is to stop the CIA from helping Petrov. Send word to London. We want Petrov killed and we want it to appear that the Americans did it."

Barkovsky raised his wineglass and tipped it against Solokov's. "To the success of the scheduled tasks!" he said. It was one of the first toasts that both men learned after they joined the Komsomol, the young Communist league. "A bullet in Petrov's head," Barkovsky said, raising his glass for a second toast. "And a pistol left in the hands of the Americans."

CHAPTER TWELVE

LONDON, England

"I'm filing a formal complaint against you as soon as we get to the Marriott," Showers said. "I no longer wish to work with you."

"I understand why you're upset," Storm said in an understanding voice. "I would be furious, too. But you'll be wasting your time if you complain to your supervisors. Trust me, it will be you who will be called home to Washington."

"Trust you?" Showers said. "That's a joke. And what makes you so smug that you think I'd be called home? They sent me here to solve the murder of a U.S. senator."

"You don't want to complain. This came from the top."

"The top of what?"

"The White House."

"Then tell me what you and Jones are doing, so we can work together. You owe me that much."

"It's above your pay grade."

Showers took a deep breath and said, "At this moment, I would love to shoot you."

He stopped in front of the Marriott.

"How about a Taser?" he said. "If it really makes you feel better."

"Just go crawl into whatever hole you're sleeping in in London," she said. "I wish I'd never met you."

Storm actually felt sorry when she slammed the car door and disappeared inside.

When he reached his room at the bed-and-breakfast, he removed the false fingerprints that he had applied earlier that morning. He had used his computer to download a copy of someone else's prints from the database at Langley and had copied them onto the flesh-like material that he'd been given from the CIA's science wizards. When Petrov's chief of security, Antonija Nad, checked the shot glass, she would discover the identity of someone else—someone she already knew.

Herself.

His cell phone rang.

"Someone's been in my room," Showers said, in an exasperated voice. "While we were with Petrov. I thought you should know in case someone followed you and searched your room too."

"Thanks for caring enough to call," he said.

"I told you, I play by the rules," she said. "Even if you don't."

"Where are you calling from?"

"The Marriott lobby. I assume they bugged my room. I didn't bring anything with me to check. Since you're a private eye and part-time spook, I thought you could come over and remove them. Either that or I've got to call in a team from the embassy."

"I'm coming over."

Storm grabbed his backpack and made the five-minute walk to the hotel. He waved her out of the lobby onto the street.

"Let's walk," he said. "It will be safer."

For fifteen minutes, they crossed through a series of streets, often doubling back and then going down a different route. When they were convinced they were safe, he asked, "How do you know someone was in your room?"

"I left papers on the desk in a loose-leaf binder. They were FBI press releases about the senator's murder. I put a penny on page six."

It was an old trick. When the intruder picked up the binder, the penny fell to the floor. Even if he spotted it, there was no way for him to know what page it had fallen from.

"Are you certain the maid didn't move the papers?" he asked.

"Haven't you insulted me enough today?" she said.

"I'm sorry."

"I've been thinking while we were walking," she said. "Should we clear it of bugs or use it to misdirect them? Whoever 'them' is."

He was impressed. She was thinking more like an intelligence officer than a cop.

He saw they were passing by a pub. "Let's go inside and get a drink. It's been a very long day. I'll pay."

"Do you really think buying me a drink is going to make me feel better about what you did today? About cutting me out and going behind my back?"

"A couple drinks might be the only things that do help,"

he said. "Besides, I'm hungry and thirsty. C'mon. What happened wasn't personal. If there'd been a better way to handle it, I would've."

"Just one drink," she said with a sigh. "And only because I could use it."

It was a neighborhood joint with dark wood paneling and a regular crowd who noticed strangers. He ordered fish and chips and Showers had a chicken poppy-seed wrap. He told the waiter to bring them drafts of London Pilsner.

She seemed to relax after she'd finished her first beer.

"First time someone's bugged your hotel room?" he asked.

"They taught us about it in the academy," she said. "But this is the first time."

He raised his second glass of beer and tapped it against hers. "Welcome to the cloak-and-dagger side."

"I can see why you enjoy this. It's more entertaining than writing down questions for Petrov and faxing them to him tonight."

"Why are you bothering to send him anything? He's not going to admit he was involved. He's playing you, trying to find out what you know."

"And what makes you think he's not playing you—in whatever you're doing?"

"Oh, I'm sure he is. Everyone is after something."

"I don't expect Petrov to confess," she said. "That's not how the game is played. My goal is to get him to say something that I can later prove in court was a lie. Then we can indict him for lying to a federal agent and for being part of a criminal conspiracy."

Storm shook his head in disbelief. "April," he said tenderly, calling her by her first name, which he'd never done before. "Do you really think the Justice Department is going to charge Petrov with a crime? He has influential friends. He's an oligarch. He lives in London."

"I know you think I'm naïve," she said. "But I told you before and I'll say it again because I genuinely believe it. No one is immune from justice. Yes, our system is flawed. Yes, it is much harder to bring down wealthy and well-connected criminals. But it can be done, as long as there are people who believe in our system and don't give up. As long as we fight for it. Truth eventually triumphs."

Storm smiled.

"Do you think this is funny?" she asked.

"Oh no, I wasn't laughing at you. I was thinking about how the words 'And the truth will set you free' are inscribed in the lobby of the CIA."

"Saying those words and believing them are two different things."

Storm said, "Why are you so sure that justice triumphs in the end? Who taught you that: a Sunday school teacher, a minister?"

He suddenly noticed tears welling in her eyes. "Actually, my father did. He was the most honorable and bravest man I've ever known."

"I'm sorry. I didn't mean to upset you. What was he like?"

"Why? So you can make him the butt of some half-witted joke?"

"No," he said. "Because I really would like to know."

"My father was a Virginia Highway Patrol officer," she said. "I adored him. I was a daddy's girl. One night, he pulled over two men who were hopped up on drugs and speeding in their car. He could tell something was wrong with them and then he heard someone whimpering. He made the driver open the trunk and there was a naked ten-year-old girl in it. The men had followed her from a convenience store, kidnapped her, and both repeatedly raped her. The passenger came out of the car with a handgun and shot my dad. Even though he was mortally wounded, he managed to kill them both. My father died saving that girl's life."

"Then your father was a brave man."

"He's why I decided to go into the FBI. People like those two men are monsters, predators. They destroy the weak, the innocent. People like my dad are all that stand between the public and the predators. They're the real heroes. They put their lives on the line every day helping others."

Storm raised his glass and said, "A toast to your dad." She could tell he was serious, so she joined him.

They ordered another round.

"What about your father?" she asked.

"Actually, this might surprise you," Storm said. "In fact, I know it will. Are you ready?"

She gave him a puzzled look.

"My father is a retired FBI agent."

"Oh my God!" she exclaimed.

The pub's owner appeared at their table with two shot glasses and a bottle of whiskey. "You two are Yanks, aren't ya?" he asked in a booming voice that echoed throughout the pub.

Storm nodded and the owner said, "We got a bit of a tradition here. You Yanks are always on the telly with your fingers pointed up at the sky screaming your lungs out about how you're number one—when you don't even know what real football is. So when we get a good-looking Yank couple like you in my fine establishment, I feel obligated to give you a taste of real English whiskey, not that horse piss they serve in the New Country." He laughed loudly and so did the pub regulars.

"Now," the pub owner said, "this here is a bottle of whiskey distilled in England to commemorate the royal wedding of Prince William and Catherine, and we'd be much obliged if you joined us in a toast to the royal couple and would take great umbrage if the two of you refuse."

He slammed down the two shot glasses and filled both to the brim. He filled one for himself, too, and hoisted it in the air.

"Will you drink to them with me?" he asked, good-naturedly.

"It's the least we can do," Storm said, "given that you lost a war to us."

The pub owner faked an angry look and announced: "To Prince William and the lovely Catherine, his bride!"

Storm downed it, but Showers hadn't lifted her glass.

"What's this?" the pub owner declared.

"C'mon," Storm said, encouraging her.

She reached for the shot glass and, much to his surprise, downed it easily.

Everyone applauded.

"It would be impolite for me, as host, to let you leave my

establishment without also raising a glass to your lovely lady here," the pub owner said, glancing at Showers. He refilled the shot glasses and quickly lifted them. "To the beautiful young, red-haired maiden sitting here who has to have a bit of Irish in her—judging from her green eyes and fair skin."

Showers smiled, and the three of them downed the shots as the other pub patrons continued to look on.

"And now," the pub owner said, "I'm going to leave you alone with a final word." He broke into a huge grin and said, "Them shots of whiskey is five pounds a piece, so I'm adding an additional thirty pounds to your bill. Welcome to London, you Yanks!"

The crowd erupted into laughter and clapping as the pub owner bowed and walked back to the bar, where he declared that it was time for karaoke. A thin man from the bar immediately leaped onto a small platform in the pub's corner, turned on a portable karaoke machine, and began mangling, "Lucy in the Sky with Diamonds."

By the time Storm and Showers left the pub three hours later, they had consumed more shots of whiskey sent over by friendly bar patrons in admiration of various British royalty and American presidents. At one point, Showers had seized control of the karaoke microphone and belted out a surprisingly good version of Lady Gaga's "Born This Way" that left the crowd clamoring for more.

As they made their way to the Marriott, they locked arms to support each other.

"I didn't know you were a Lady Gaga fan," he said admiringly.

"Some of her lyrics are poetic," she replied. "Have you ever even heard one of her songs?"

"What sort of music do you think I listen to?" he asked.

"That's easy," she said. "Country Western."

Storm replied, "It's not that I'm dishonest, I loathe reality." It was from one of Lady Gaga's videos.

A stunned Showers began clapping.

Storm raised a finger to his closed lips. "Let's keep this our secret."

When they reached the Marriott, she said, "So where is your hiding place?"

"Are you asking me if you can come up to my room for a nightcap?" he said hopefully.

"Maybe," she replied. "Or maybe I'm just interested in where a spy goes to hide out."

"I'm not a spy, remember? I'm a private detective."

"Is that true? Is anything that you've told me tonight true?"

Before he could reply, she put her finger against his lips and said, "Just take me to where you're staying."

When they reached his room, she collapsed onto the double bed. He shut the door and tossed the room's key onto the nightstand. She waved him over. He sat on the bed's edge.

"I do find you reasonably attractive," she said. She reached over and ran a finger over his hand.

He'd bedded many women. All had been easy conquests. He couldn't remember most of their faces. The only one who had mattered had been Clara Strike. She had been more than a one-night stand. And she had broken his heart. How did he feel about April Showers? Did he want another broken heart? Where could this lead? When he had finished his job and found the traitor, he would be going back to a life of anonymity.

She leaned up and kissed him on the lips. He kissed her back, hard and passionately. He followed that kiss with another and felt the heat that always surfaces when a man and woman anticipate making love for the first time. The sheer joy of discovering a new body. Exploring each inch of flesh. To touch and to be touched.

"If we are going to do this," she whispered seductively, "I need you to do me a favor. I saw a coffeepot downstairs. I want you to go get me a cup of coffee."

"You want a cup of coffee?"

"Actually," she said, "it's an excuse. A polite way to get you out of the room because I've got to pee and I'd rather do that in private. It's a woman thing."

He rose and started for the door.

She sprang up, and as he stepped out of the room, she slapped him hard on his butt and laughed.

The moment he was in the hallway, she shut the door, locking it behind him. He realized that he'd left the key on the nightstand.

He gently rapped on the door and said in a quiet voice, "I can just go down and wake up the owner. She'll let me back in my room."

"Do you really want to disturb her at this hour?" Showers replied from behind the door.

He'd thought she was drunker than she obviously was. She'd outfoxed him.

She said, "Think of the scandal! A woman in your room. A woman who has been drinking. Who knows what I might say? It might even make the BBC since I'm so famous. What did you tell them? The queen was going to invite me over?"

With his training, it would take less than a minute for him to force open the door. But he didn't want to force himself on her.

"You should sleep at the Marriott," she whispered. "You can use my room if you want. Just be careful, they might have installed secret cameras as well as hidden microphones. You're naked butt could end up on some Internet site. Good night!"

CHAPTER THIRTEEN

omeone knocked on her door. She heard Storm ask: "Are you awake? I brought breakfast."

She slipped on a terry-cloth robe and let him inside.

"I got this from downstairs," he said. "It's an English breakfast. I've got scrambled eggs, sausage, black pudding, baked beans, and a slice of tomato." He waved the tray under her face.

She suddenly felt nauseous. And that made him smile.

"Since I spent the night elsewhere," he continued, "I took the liberty of ducking into your room at the Marriott and grabbing you some fresh clothes. There in the hotel bag." He dropped a plastic bag on the bed.

"How come you're so bright and cheery?" she asked.

"I had to take a very cold shower after you locked me out."

"Just one cold shower? I figured you'd need a couple."

"The shower was enough to lower my expectations."

"Cute," she said.

"I'm going to fill up the rental with petrol," he said in a mock British accent. "We need to leave in an hour in order to get to the protest rally. Enjoy your breakfast."

Showers was nursing the worst hangover she'd had since college as they rode to Oxford. She kept her eyes closed under her sunglasses and fought the urge to vomit each time the car hit a bump or pothole.

The anti-Barkovsky rally was being held in the grassy fields of Oxford University Parks, on the northeast edge of the thirty-eight independent colleges that made up the school. Storm parked on a dirt road near the Old Observatory, and they walked toward a stage that had been constructed specifically for the protest. The platform rose only two feet above the grass and was only large enough for a podium and four chairs. There were about a thousand protesters mingling around it. A young girl told them that everyone was waiting for Petrov, who was running late.

As was his practice, Storm surveyed the crowd and immediately spotted three men who seemed to be out of place at the rally. They were Eastern European and in their thirties. Most of the others in the crowd were younger students or older professors.

"Did you bring your Glock?" he asked Storm.

"Yes," she said. "You don't have to yell."

"I wasn't."

Just the same, he lowered his voice when he said, "I'm going to point out three men. If my hunch is correct, you may have to shoot them. If you can't, give me your gun."

"I'm not giving you my gun," she said. "And you don't have to point them out. The fact that they are wearing London Fog overcoats and the sun is out and it is hot makes them stick out. How do you want to handle this?"

Two black Mercedes-Benz S-Class 600 sedans with tinted windows appeared on a road to the right of the park, about two hundred yards away. When they came to a stop, Petrov and Lebedev stepped from the first car. Security Chief Nad stepped from the second. The two cars' drivers fell in behind the group, and Petrov and his entourage began walking toward the stage.

"I'll intercept Petrov and Nad," he said. "You keep an eye on those men."

"Do you think Nad and the two security guards are armed?" Showers asked.

"I sure as hell hope so." He started making his way around the crowd.

Storm had gone about twenty feet when he saw two golf carts speeding from behind the platform. Driven by two students, the carts were decorated with anti-Barkovsky placards and were en route to give the guest and his attendants a ride to the stage. Storm realized it would be impossible for him to reach Petrov and his entourage in time.

One of the golf carts delivered Petrov to the stage. Lebedev and Nad stayed in the back of it. The two bodyguards positioned themselves at the front of the platform, on either side of it.

Nad had only brought two men with her! Both wore PROTEC security badges on their dark blazers and berets. If they were any good, they would notice the three interlopers.

The three Eastern Europeans separated. One positioned himself directly in front of the speaker's podium. The other two moved to the left and right of the stage, taking spots directly in line with the two PROTEC bodyguards. Showers was on Storm's left and was keeping an eye on the suspect closest to her.

Storm zeroed in on the suspect in front of the podium. He would be the one responsible for shooting Petrov. The others would be tasked with killing his two bodyguards and then backing up their friend. Storm searched for Nad and noticed that she was not studying the crowd as she should have been. Instead, she was watching Petrov, who was now behind the podium being introduced.

The crowd began clapping as Petrov began to speak.

Picking up his pace, Storm began shoving spectators out of his way. "Move! Move!" he yelled. He was trying to start such a commotion that Petrov and his security guards would notice. Both guards did and slowly reached under their jackets. Nad spotted him, too, but Petrov was too preoccupied with his speech to take note. "Hey, Petrov!" Storm yelled. The Russian stopped mid-sentence.

Everyone was looking at Storm, except for the three attackers in their trench coats.

Storm yelled: "Duck!"

The Eastern European directly in line with Petrov screamed, "Traitor!" and pulled a .45-caliber pistol from under this jacket. He began firing just as Storm tackled him from behind. Petrov collapsed on stage.

The shooter's two companions drew Heckler & Koch MP5 submachine guns from under their coats and killed both PROTEC bodyguards with sprays of bullets.

Antonija Nad ran across the stage to Petrov, who had blood coming from his chest. Panic erupted. Some protestors hit the ground; others bolted in different directions, while some stood petrified with fear.

Storm was now lying on the back of the downed gunman. He grabbed the shooter's right hand, pinning his pistol against the grass. But the gunman was stronger than Storm had estimated. With his free left hand, the shooter pushed his body upward, knocking Storm from his back, but not before Storm was able to break the gunman's hold on his pistol.

Both men sprang from the grass to face each other. The shooter reached under his coat for a Russian military-issued knife, which he jabbed at Storm. In an expert move, Storm dodged the blade, grabbed the attacker's hand, and twisted the blade backward, plunging it into the man's chest. In a move known on the street as "running the gears," Storm jerked the blade upward, then sideways, then sideways again and finally down into his victim's stomach before releasing his grip. The shooter's lifeless body fell limp onto the ground while Storm reached for the gunman's discarded .45 handgun.

While Storm was subduing the first shooter, Showers had drawn her Glock and fired at the the assailant nearest her. One of her rounds had struck him in his skull, killing him instantly. That had left only one assassin alive, and when he'd heard Showers's pistol fire, he'd shot a burst in her direction from his submachine gun.

One of the rounds hit its mark, smacking into her shoulder. Her right arm became useless, her Glock falling from her fingers as she grabbed her wound with her left hand and fell to the grass for cover.

Storm fired at the gunman with the retrieved .45. *Rap. Rap.* Two rounds fired at the attacker's head. *Pop. Pop.* Another two at his chest. As he fell, the gunman's finger pinched the trigger of his submachine gun, emptying what remained of its thirty-round clip into the air and ground around him.

Storm ran to Showers, who was fighting to catch her breath. He got her to her feet, put her Glock into its holster, and looked for help.

"Hang on!" he told her.

During the melee, Lebedev had commandeered a golf cart and driven to one of the Mercedes. He was now racing the sedan across the park toward them. A wounded Petrov was being helped off the platform by Nad.

Leaping from the driver's seat, Lebedev opened the car's rear passenger door and yelled. "Bring Petrov here!"

Nad screamed, "He's still alive! We must get him to a hospital!"

Together they shoved Petrov's huge body into the sedan's backseat.

With his right arm wrapped around her waist, Storm hurried Showers toward the Mercedes.

"I'll take her, too!" Lebedev yelled.

"We'll follow in my rental," Storm said. "It's closer."

Lebedev pressed the accelerator and the giant Mercedes spit a rooster tail of grass and dirt from under its back wheels, leaving Nad and Storm behind.

Storm ran to the parked Vauxhall and had already

buckled in and started the rental by the time Nad joined him in its passenger seat. The Mercedes was nearly out of sight as he drove south toward St. Cross Road.

"Turn left," Nad ordered.

Storm glanced at the illuminated GPS screen in car's dash. Downtown Oxford was to his right. He hesitated but then spotted the Mercedes on his left just cresting a hill less than a mile away. It was heading away from Oxford, too. Away from the nearest hospital.

Storm felt a pit of dread in his stomach. He pressed the gas pedal, causing the Vauxhall's engine to scream. The speedometer registered 136 kilometers per hour and was still moving forward.

The Mercedes was now a half mile ahead, but Storm was making up ground. Without warning, the black sedan suddenly slowed and turned off the main highway onto a dirt path. It disappeared into a patch of woods.

Storm pushed the pedal harder.

"Slow down," Nad commanded.

He looked to his left in the English-made car and saw that she had drawn her CZ P-01 semiautomatic pistol and was now pointing it at his chest.

"I told you to slow down," she said. "And turn where Lebedev turned."

Georgi Lebedev pulled a pistol from under his jacket and leveled it at Showers seconds after he parked the Mercedes under the row of trees.

"Give me your gun," he told her.

Already in intense pain and holding her wound with her left hand, Showers grimaced and Lebedev realized that her right arm was useless. He reached across the car seat and snatched her Glock from the holster on her right hip.

"It's time for the truth!" he hollered at Petrov, who was sprawled across the sedan's backseat, moaning and clutching his abdomen. Blood dotted his white dress shirt.

"Where is the gold hidden?" Lebedev yelled.

"Gold," Showers repeated. "What gold?"

"Shut up!" Lebedev yelled.

"Georgi Ivanovich," Petrov pleaded. "Take me to the hospital! I'm dying."

"Tell me where the gold is hidden, then we will go to the hospital."

"But we are brothers," Petrov gasped. "Why are you doing this?"

"No, Ivan Sergeyevich," Lebedev said. "I'm your lapdog. You feed me scraps. But no more. Never again. Where is the gold?"

Petrov cut loose with a string of expletives.

Without flinching, Lebedev fired the Glock into the back car seat, near Petrov's head. The shot made a deafening sound inside the sedan, but it was not loud enough to drown Petrov's screams.

"The next one will be in your foot," said Lebedev. "And then your balls."

"Slow down or I will shoot you," Nad said. "Slow down and turn right at that stone house ahead."

The abandoned farmhouse was next to the dirt road where the Mercedes had turned moments earlier.

Instead of slowing, Storm jammed the car's gas pedal against the floor.

"I was wrong. I thought you and Lebedev would not show your hand until later," he said calmly.

"How long have you known?"

"When I saw the shortened Dragunov's stock. It had been cut down for a woman. But I should have known earlier. The moment I found the Capitol Hill Police officer's disguise hidden in a trash can outside the women's room, not the men's."

"You have made your last mistake," she said. "Slow down. You can't make the turn at this speed. You're going too fast."

She was beautiful. He had wanted her to be something other than what she was. But she wasn't and now he would have to kill her.

The car's speedometer topped out at 180 kilometers.

"You betrayed Petrov for gold?" Showers asked, fighting to remain conscious. The pain in her shoulder was excruciating and she was losing blood.

Lebedev replied, "Not just for gold. But for love."

"You bastard!" Petrov sobbed from the rear seat.

"Shut up," Lebedev said. "I have been telling Barkovsky about your every move for more than a year. Nad and me. We made a pact. We are going to be rich and together."

"Are you responsible for the kidnapping in Washington?" Showers asked. "Did you have Senator Windslow killed? I need to know if you're planning on killing me."

"Yes," Lebedev said triumphantly. "With Barkovsky's help, Nad and I arranged everything. I wanted the Americans to blame Petrov. We did not want Windslow to help him find the gold. We did not want the CIA to trust him."

His words sounded to Showers as if they were coming from a great distance. She fought to concentrate.

"I will never tell you where the gold is located, you bastard," Petrov yelled from the backseat.

"Oh really, comrade," Lebedev replied. He fired the Glock, sending a round into Petrov's foot, causing him to scream in agony.

With the turn from the main highway approaching, Storm looked confidently at Nad and broke into a huge grin. "Good-bye. Bitch," he said.

She gave him a confused look and tightened the grip on her pistol. But it was too late.

Storm jerked the Vauxhall's wheel to the right, sending the car speeding across the oncoming traffic lane. Its tires hit a slight hump at the asphalt's edge and the Vauxhall took flight, rising several feet above the ground, aimed directly at the farmhouse's old stone walls.

"This is your final chance," Lebedev yelled at a terrorized Petrov. "Tell me where the gold is and I will spare your life. I will drive you to the hospital. For all the years that I kissed your pompous ass, I deserve to know. Now, tell me, or the next shot will be in your crotch."

A crying and defeated Petrov spat out a series of numbers.

Lebedev punched the longitude and latitude coordinates into an app on his cell phone.

"It's near the Valley of Five Caves in Uzbekistan?" he said, making the statement sound like a question.

"Yes," Petrov cried. "I swear it. Now, save me, my brother, I'm dying."

Lebedev pointed the Glock directly at Petrov's forehead. "I believe you, my brother," he said. "If there is one thing that I have learned because of our years together, it is when you are telling the truth and when you are lying. This is my reward for wiping your butt."

He fired the Glock, spattering his best friend's brains across the sedan's back window and seat.

Satisfied, he turned his attention to Showers, who was now so weak and groggy that she could barely comprehend what was happening. Her body was in shock. Without emergency help, she would die.

"I will tell the police that you forced us at gunpoint to come here after the rally and that you shot and murdered my friend with your Glock. I had no choice but to kill you with my own pistol." He rested her Glock on his lap and picked up his own gun.

"You're insane," Showers responded, her voice a whisper. "No one will believe you."

"I will tell them that you shot him in the foot to torture him, trying to make him confess. I will tell them you went crazy. It will be the word of Petrov's oldest and dearest friend against a dead FBI agent who came here to avenge the murder of a U.S. senator. The British press will love it."

"My partner," she uttered.

"Don't worry about him. He'll be dead, too. Nad will see to it."

Lebedev leveled the gun at her chest.

"Good-bye, Special Agent April Showers," he said.

It was at that very moment that Lebedev heard the sound of a loud explosion coming from outside the Mercedes and momentarily turned his face to look out the driver's side window.

The flying Vauxhall nose-dived into the stone wall of the old farmhouse with a tremendous roar. It hit with such force that the vehicle seemed to burst into pieces of shattered glass, busted chrome, twisted plastic, and crumpled metal. The trunk of the sedan flew upward upon impact, and for a moment it appeared that the Vauxhall might topple end over end, but the rear axle crashed back onto the ground with a loud boom. Flames, smoke, and steam poured from under the demolished front hood.

The car's crumple zone, driver's side air bag, and the driver's seat belt had saved Storm's life. But Nad had not been so fortunate. She had not bothered to put on her seat belt and Storm had flipped off the car's passenger side air bags. Nad had not noticed and it had cost her her life.

The impact had launched her from the car's passenger's

seat, rocketing her through the windshield, ripping her unblemished face to shreds. Her head had hit the farmhouse's wall like a melon hurled at a hundred miles per hour. Her skull had burst open. Her spinal cord had been telescoped. Her broken body was now lying in an unnatural twisted position on the ground next to the burning Vauxhall.

Storm pulled himself away from the wreckage and fell facedown onto the long grass. He could not hear from one ear. There was blood dripping from it and from his nose. His right knee was throbbing. But he was alive.

Gathering his senses, his first thought was of Showers, and the black Mercedes parked a hundred yards down the road, under a clump of English oaks.

Much like a drunk staggering from a bar, he tried to steady himself as he slowly plotted a course to Nad's body. He spotted her pistol about eight feet away, next to the stone wall. He reached it and with great effort bent down and examined the handgun. It looked undamaged.

I must save April, he thought. I must get to her.

With tremendous willpower, fighting the intense pain that was streaking through his limbs, Storm began making his way from the farmhouse toward the parked Mercedes.

He had gone about fifty yards when he heard a loud crack.

It was the sound of gunfire.

And it had come from inside the parked car in front of him.

To be continued in *A Bloody Storm*...

A
BLOODY
STORM

CHAPTER ONE

TEN MILES OUTSIDE OXFORD, England
Present day

Flames from the engine licked across the Vauxhall's undercarriage and raced like a firecracker fuse toward gasoline squirting from the sedan's ruptured gas tank.

Derrick Storm was fifty yards away when the tank exploded, causing an ear-punishing explosion that sent the car's steel carcass flopping into the air before it came crashing down.

Only moments earlier, Storm had deliberately driven the speeding Vauxhall off the highway into the stone wall of an abandoned farmhouse, sending his passenger, a Croation vixen named Antonija Nad, through the windshield. She had been pointing a pistol at Storm at the moment of impact. Now her lifeless body was limp in the grass beside the burning car.

Storm had cheated death thanks to a seat belt, a driver's air bag, the car's crumple zone, and Nad's foolishness in not buckling up and in assuming that no one would be crazy enough to nosedive into a wall at nearly a hundred miles per hour.

Storm wasn't sure if his partner, FBI Agent April Showers, had been as fortunate as he was.

She'd been a passenger in a Mercedes-Benz that Storm was chasing. Its driver, Georgi Lebedev, was supposed to be taking Showers and a Russian oligarch to a hospital emergency room. She had been shot in her right shoulder. Ivan Petrov had been gut-shot.

Rather than driving to an emergency room, Lebedev had turned in the opposite direction, eventually pulling off the highway onto a dirt road and stopping under a grove of English oaks.

"April!" Storm yelled, as he hurried toward the parked sedan some forty yards away. He was moving as fast as a thirty-year-old man, who'd just survived a crash, could. His knees threatened to buckle. His entire body ached. Blood trickled from his ears. His skin shined with sweat and smelled of fuel and motor oil.

"April!" he hollered again.

Blood.

He could now see it splattered inside the Mercedes's windows. Storm tightened his grip on the semiautomatic pistol that he'd retrieved from Nad's corpse.

Whose blood was he seeing? And why had someone inside the vehicle opened fire on a fellow occupant?

Ignoring the shrill ringing in his ears and his shocked senses, Storm struggled to make sense of it all. The stunning and now dead Nad had been chief of security in charge of protecting her wealthy boss. Even in Storm's confused state, he realized that Nad had betrayed Ivan Petrov. So had Lebedev, who was the wounded Petrov's oldest and dearest friend. Gold—lots of it— had turned both of them into modern day Judases.

Storm didn't care about the gold. Only rescuing Showers. Assuming she was still alive. Assuming it was not her blood that he was now seeing.

Even though he was in top physical shape, by the time Storm reached the sedan, he was gasping for breath. He grabbed the car's latch, raised his handgun, and jerked open the driver's door.

The top half of Lebedev's body fell out. Half of his skull was missing.

That explained the blood.

Storm leaned into the car for a better look.

Showers was in the passenger seat, with her head leaning against the passenger window. She was clutching her Glock in her left hand.

"April!" Storm called.

She didn't respond.

Grabbing Lebedev's belt, Storm pulled the dead man's body from the car and slipped onto the blood-covered driver's seat. He touched Showers's neck and found a pulse. But it was weak.

The touch of his fingers caused Showers to open her eyes. She gave him a faint smile.

"I knew you'd come for me," she whispered. "I knew Nad wasn't clever enough to kill you."

"Hold on! I'll get you to the hospital," Storm said. Glancing over the front seat, Storm looked onto the dead eyes of Petrov. There was a bullet hole in his forehead, as well as his earlier chest wound.

Storm started the car's engine.

"Wait," Showers sputtered. "The phone. Get it!"

"What phone?"

"Lebedev's."

Stepping from the car, Storm found the phone in Lebedev's jacket. Since he was out of the vehicle, he quickly opened the car's rear passenger door and grabbed Petrov's elephantine legs. Someone had shot a bullet into Petrov's foot. Storm pulled the three-hundred-pound carcass from the Mercedes, leaving smeared blood on the leather seat.

Two lifelong friends, now killer and victim, lying next to each other under the oaks.

Back in the driver's seat, Storm jammed on the car's accelerator, causing the sedan to rocket from under the trees.

"April! You can't fall asleep!" he snapped. "Stay awake!"

"Sure thing," she replied unconvincingly. Her voice was robotic.

Alternating his glances between the road leading to Oxford and her face, Storm saw Showers chose her eyes and he knew that he was in danger of losing her. He reached over, put his hand on her leg, and squeezed it.

Showers opened her eyes. "Hands off the merchandise," she said.

Good. She still had a sense of humor.

"You wear a bullet well," he replied.

But the truth was that she looked wretched. Her white skin was ghostly and her blouse was stained red.

Showers was in shock and that could kill her. He needed to make her stay focused, to keep her grounded in the moment.

"What happened here?" he asked. "Who shot whom?"

"Lebedev," she said in a whisper, "shot Petrov. Something about gold."

Storm knew about the gold. Sixty billion dollars' worth smuggled out of the Soviet Union before it collapsed. But he hadn't told Showers. The CIA didn't want the FBI to know about it.

"April," he said, "if Lebedev killed Petrov, who shot Lebedev? Who killed him?"

"Too tired to talk now," she moaned. "Later."

"No, now, April," he said sternly. "Did you shoot Lebedev or did Petrov kill him?"

"Me. He was going to kill me. Blame me for Petrov's death."

The gunshot in her shoulder had crippled her right arm. *How had she outmaneuvered Lebedev?*

"He took my Glock from me. Used it to shoot Petrov," she said. He noticed that she was speaking in bursts, trying to concentrate and also save her breath. "He put my Glock on his lap. Got his own pistol. Was going to shoot me. Tell everyone I shot Petrov. There was an explosion. A noise."

"That was me crashing into the farmhouse," Storm explained. But he wasn't certain if she understood.

"Loud noise. Lebedev looked away from me. Turned his head. I seized my Glock. Left hand," she said, smiling. "Didn't expect that. Shot up in his face."

Storm asked: "Why did you tell me to grab Lebedev's phone?"

"The gold. Longitude. Latitude. App. Memory card."

"You shot him left-handed after you discovered where

the gold is hidden!" he exclaimed. "Outstanding! You're really incredible."

Through half-closed eyes and with an unsteady head, she replied, "I have my moments."

CHAPTER TWO

The Mercedes's GPS directed him to the emergency room at the John Radcliffe Hospital on the east side of Oxford. Storm bolted inside.

"I have a gunshot victim in the car!" he announced. "She's bleeding. In shock. But conscious!"

An intake clerk grabbed a phone, and within seconds an emergency assessment unit came rushing from behind double metal doors. An attendant pushing a "trolley bed" ran behind a triage trauma nurse and a physician's assistant. The three of them followed Storm to the still-running Mercedes, where he helped the attendant lift Showers onto the cart while the nurse and the medic worked on her.

"She allergic to any medicines?" the nurse asked.

"Don't know," he replied.

"How'd this happen?" she asked.

"She was shot at a protest rally at Oxford this morning."

"We've already had three others come through here who were in the crowd. Why are you so late?"

"Got lost."

The nurse noticed the blood on the interior of the car windows and also on him. "We'll take it from here," she said. "You need to sign in."

As they hurried by the intake desk, Storm overheard the nurse say, "Call Security." Before the receptionist could lift her phone, Storm handed her Showers's FBI business card.

"Left my car running," he said. "Be right back."

"Wait," she called after him. "There are forms—"

But he was already speeding away from the hospital.

From behind the wheel, Storm called Jedidiah Jones, the director of the National Clandestine Service at CIA headquarters in Langley, Virginia. "Showers has been shot," he said. "Just dropped her at the John Radcliffe emergency room in Oxford, England. You need to call."

"I'll put the FBI in touch with the hospital. They have her medical information from her personnel file," Jones replied. "I'll let our London embassy know. They'll get people out there. What about you?"

"Only bruises."

Storm recapped the morning's events at the Oxford rally and later under the English oaks.

Jones listened without interrupting and then said, "Obviously, Georgi Lebedev was a traitor in Petrov's camp. He was keeping Russian President Oleg Barkovsky informed about what Petrov was doing."

Once former pals, Barkovsky and Petrov had turned against each other after the oligarch had criticized the Kremlin leader in public. A furious Barkovsky had forced Petrov to flee Russia and had later sent assassins to kill him in England.

Jones said, "It all makes sense now. President Barkovsky must have bribed Lebedev. Because Petrov trusted Lebedev like a brother, he wouldn't have suspected that he would turn on him."

Storm said, "There's more. Showers found out where the gold is hidden."

"She did? Only Petrov knew its location, and he'd refused to tell anyone. How'd she pull that off?"

"Judging from the bullet hole in Petrov's foot, I'm guessing Lebedev forced the issue. Lebedev must have threatened him in the parked car. He probably said he wouldn't drive him to a hospital for his chest wound unless he spilled his guts—pun intended—about the gold. When Petrov refused, Lebedev showed him how serious he was. Showers was in the front seat during all of this and overheard their entire exchange. I'll send you the longitude and latitude coordinates for the gold from Lebedev's cell phone after I ditch this car."

"Delete them after you send them to me," Jones said, adding, "Do you need a cleaner?"

"Too late," Storm said. "I'm sure the car explosion has attracted a crowd by now."

"I'll call MI-6 and have the FBI pull strings with Scotland Yard. Both owe us. But it would be best if you disappeared. Hold on for a moment."

Jones was off-line for less than a minute. When he returned, he said, "About forty miles south of Oxford is a town called Newbury. There's a U.S. Air Force operation there under the command of the 420 Munitions Squadron.

I'm arranging a military flight to get you out of England into Germany and then home. Best to avoid commercial flights and passport controls. How soon can you get to Newbury?"

"An hour or less unless I get stopped."

"Don't. At least not before you send me those coordinates."

Jones had his priorities. Gold. Then Storm.

"Call me later," Storm said, "about April."

"April? She your girlfriend now?"

"Agent Showers," he said, correcting himself. "And she's not my girlfriend. She's my partner."

"Right," Jones said skeptically.

"Just make sure someone gets to that hospital."

Hanging up, Storm used the Mercedes's GPS to direct him to the closest shopping mall: Templars Square, less than four miles away. He parked in the garage across the street, leaving his blood-covered jacket in the car. Storm wasn't worried about trace evidence. He'd been dead, at least officially, for four years. The CIA had helped him "die" and vanish from the grid. He'd been happily living in Montana when Jones summoned him back for what was supposed to be a simple kidnapping investigation. If Scotland Yard or Interpol found traceable evidence in the bloody Mercedes, their investigators would compare the findings to records of living suspects. No one searched a cemetery for a killer.

In the parking garage's second-floor stairwell, Storm paused to examine Lebedev's cell phone. He found the directional app and forwarded the coordinates on it to Jones. As a backup, Storm also sent them to his own private cell phone. Satisfied, he deleted the app but kept Lebedev's phone for delivery to the tech experts at Langley. *Who could tell what else it might contain?*

Exiting the garage, Storm entered the shopping mall and went immediately into a public toilet to wash blood from his hands. He had it on his slacks, too, but they were black, so the stains were not so noticeable. He left the toilet and bought a pair of slacks and a shirt in a nearby clothing shop, then returned to the men's room to change.

Outside the mall, he flagged a taxi at the corner of Crowell and Hackmore Streets.

"Where to?" the hack driver asked.

"Air base at Newbury."

"That's a long ride, mate," he said, giving Storm a curious look.

"Got into a fight with my girl inside the mall," Storm improvised. "She won't drive me back to the base. She's Irish, and if I'm late, it'll be my head."

"Birds—or in the States I guess you call 'em broads," the driver said. "The nationality don't matter. They're all a bit loony. We're off to Newbury."

They'd gone about a mile when the cabbie started talking.

Storm leaned back his head and closed his eyes. He didn't want conversation.

"You heard about the shootings at Oxford this morning, didn't you?" the driver asked. "All over the radio. Three men started shooting at some Russian speaking at a rally. People got hurt."

"I've got a twelve-hour shift waiting for me and a girl kicking my balls," Storm replied. "I don't need to hear about someone else's problems."

The cabbie chuckled. "Then you take a little nap and leave the driving to me."

About forty minutes later, the cab arrived at the air base gate. Storm paid the sixty-dollar fare and then handed the driver another twenty. "My Irish girlfriend happens to be married," he explained. "I'd like to have a face that is easy to forget."

The driver pocketed the bills. "You Yanks all look alike to me, mate."

Storm was about to board a flight an hour later when his cell phone rang.

"She's out of surgery," Jones said. "The prognosis is good. A car will be waiting when you land."

CHAPTER THREE

"What's today?"

Those were the first words coming from Agent Showers's mouth when she awoke from the anesthetic.

"You was brought in yesterday morning, miss," a nurse sitting next at her bedside answered. "I'm supposed to fetch our matron now. You're quite the celebrity. You should see all the reporters hovering around, trying to get a story. They got cops at your door to keep them away. They told me not to talk to you, but I want you to know that I'm happy you're okay, and I don't want you to worry a bit, because I won't tell anyone about your bloke."

"My bloke?"

"Sure, your Steve," she replied. "Isn't he your bloke? I mean, I just assumed the way you was going on and on about him and mentioning his name. But don't you worry, ma'am. Lots of people are as mad as a box of frogs when they're gassed."

"What did I say?" Showers asked.

"The truth is that it sounded a bit randy to me, you

know. That's why I'll not be repeating it."

"And you're sure that I mentioned the name: Steve?"

"Oh, you did more than mention him. You had me blushing, but I'm really not one to gab."

The nurse hurried from the room, leaving Showers to clear the cobwebs from her head. Obviously, she was in a hospital, which she presumed was in Oxford. Bandages covered her right shoulder, there was an IV in her left arm, and she was attached to a monitor that was tracking her heartbeat, temperature, and blood pressure. She felt a remote device at her side and pushed a button that raised the back of the bed with a loud mechanical whine. A pain immediately shot through her shoulder. Her head was throbbing and she needed to use the toilet.

The nurse returned with an older, gray-haired woman who was being followed by two men in business suits. One had an American flag in his lapel.

"I'm Rachel Smythe, head matron at the hospital, and these men are from the American embassy," the matron said. "They insist on speaking to you. Do you feel up to it?"

"Who are you?" Showers asked the man with the flag lapel.

"FBI Special Agent Douglas Cumerford," he replied, while reaching into his jacket to produce his credentials. "This is Thomas Goodman. He's with the State Department."

Goodman didn't offer credentials, and Showers immediately suspected he worked for the CIA.

"Thank you, Ms. Smythe," Showers told the matron. "I'm okay to speak to these two gentlemen."

"I'll be sending the doctor around dear," Smythe said, "after these two officials are done. If you need anything, just push the remote buzzer." She and the nurse exited.

"Glad you're awake," Cumerford said. "We need to brief you before the Oxford police and Scotland Yard take your official statement. Obviously, Ivan Petrov's murder is making international headlines, and the shooting at the university rally is all over the BBC."

"You've spoken to Washington about this?" Showers asked.

"I've been on the phone with the director numerous times since you were brought into the hospital," Cumerford said. "He sends his best wishes for a speedy recovery."

Gordon removed an envelope from his navy blazer. "This is what we would like you to say in your official statement." He handed it to her.

"The director approved this?" she asked.

Cumerford said, "He did. In fact, he said that you are not to deviate from the text. Say exactly what is written and offer nothing more. I'm going to be with you during all questioning, as your attorney."

Gordon said, "We can't stress how important it is for you to say only what has been written for you."

Showers said, "And if I slip?"

"Don't," Cumerford replied. "The British media have been busy interviewing witnesses from the rally. They've told reporters three men started shooting at Petrov and his bodyguards. Two of the attackers had submachine guns. They killed Petrov's two bodyguards, while the third gunman tried to assassinate Petrov, who'd just started his speech at the protest rally."

Showers said, "That's exactly what happened."

Cumerford continued, "The witnesses told reporters that you drew your handgun and fatally shot the assailant nearest you. Meanwhile, an unidentified man tackled the attacker who was firing at Petrov and killed him. He then used that man's pistol to shoot the third assailant, but not before that gunman fired his machine gun and wounded you."

"That's accurate, too," Showers said, "except it wasn't an unidentified man. It was Steve Mason. We're working together. He's got credentials issued by the State Department."

Gordon replied, "Ms. Showers, there's a bit of a problem when it comes to Mr. Mason."

Cumerford jumped in. "It would be in the best interest of the Bureau and our country if the unidentified man who helped you yesterday remained exactly that. An unidentified man. The director would prefer that you not mention the name Steve Mason to anyone, including the Oxford police and the Scotland Yard detective who will be questioning you."

"Read the statement," Gordon said. "Stick to it."

Cumerford added, "The media knows this unidentified man helped you into the Mercedes that was being driven by Georgi Lebedev and that Petrov was put into the backseat. Witnesses also described on the BBC how this mystery man and Petrov's chief of security followed the Mercedes in a Vauxhall. That car was later found outside of town, where it had crashed. The bodies of Petrov, Lebedev, and Antonija Nad were found nearby. The Mercedes was later recovered in a parking garage at a local shopping mall. Hospital officials also have told the press that an unidentified man brought you into the hospital. The tabloids are calling him a Good Samaritan."

"Steve Mason, Good Samaritan," she said. "He'll love that tag."

Gordon said, "Let's keep him faceless."

Showers scanned the statement that Gordon had handed her. "You want me to tell the police that I blacked out while I was riding in the Mercedes and that I have no recollection of anything that happened from the moment that I left the rally until today when I woke up after surgery."

"That's right," Cumerford said.

Showers said, "You're telling me not to tell investigators what I observed inside the Mercedes. You don't want me to describe how both Petrov and Lebedev ended up dead."

In a stern voice, Gordon said, "You can't comment because you were unconscious. Say that, and life will be easier for everyone."

Showers asked, "Then how are you explaining the deaths of Petrov and Lebedev?"

"We're not," Gordon said.

"We don't have to solve this case, Agent Showers," Cumerford added. "These deaths are not an FBI problem. Just give the local authorities your statement. Our priority is to get you out of England as soon as you do that."

"Before the police can blow holes in my story. Scotland Yard isn't stupid," she said. "When they identify the Vauxhall, they'll know Steve Mason rented it."

"Did he?" Gordon asked her. "Were you there with him?"

Showers realized that she hadn't been at the airport when the car was rented.

"But there must be photographs of him somewhere," she

said. "This is Jolly Old England, home of cameras on every street corner. The emergency room here—surely, they have a picture of him bringing me in."

Gordon smirked. "I believe the camera here and the ones outside the shopping mall all malfunctioned yesterday. It happens."

Showers understood. Jedidiah Jones had worked his magic.

During the entire time that Storm and Showers had been in England, they had only been seen twice together. Once when they visited the Duke of Madison residence to interview Petrov and Lebedev, both of whom were now dead, and another when they got drunk at a local London pub. If their fellow pub revelers recognized Showers from the BBC and called the police, all they would be able to tell them was that she was drinking with a handsome Yank with brown hair and brown eyes who was in his thirties. That could describe anyone. Besides, by the time they called, she would be back in the USA.

Gordon said, "Let the British press and local cops come up with a plausible story."

Cumerford said, "There's speculation that Russian president Barkovsky is behind Petrov's murder. He's denied it, of course. But he's the media's main target. Not the FBI or any other U.S. agency. That's why the less said by you, the better. Save your explanations for when you are debriefed back in Washington."

"And when will that be?"

"There's a local detective and a Scotland Yard investigator

waiting downstairs to question you," Cumerford said. "We will let them in. You will give them your statement. As soon as they hear it and the doctor gives his okay, we will take you in an ambulance to a special flight home. I have been assigned to accompany you."

"I'll need a moment to use the bathroom," she said. "Then I'll lie to the investigators."

Cumerford and Gordon exchanged nervous glances.

They expected her to take part in a cover-up. She knew when she began at the FBI that these things happened in government, and that she might be called on to lie someday. She hoped she'd never need to. Showers had run her own background investigation on the mysterious "Steve Mason" when they first met and he claimed to be a private detective. There were no records about him anywhere—no legitimate driver's license, no private detective credentials. She had always known Steve Mason was not his actual name. It was a CIA legend. And Steve Mason had been careful not to give her any clues that might have helped her identify him. Until after they arrived in London. Until the night when they had gone on a long walk and ended up in a pub where they'd downed shots of whiskey and beers. She had told him about her father, a Virginia State Trooper who had been killed in the line of duty after stopping and fatally shooting two drugged-up predators who had kidnapped and raped a ten-year-old girl. Her father had saved that girl's life. Her father was Showers's hero, and when she asked Storm about his own father, he dropped his guard.

"My father was an FBI agent," he'd said.

If that was true, it was start. She would begin investigating as soon as got back to Washington. It wasn't much, but it was an opening. Jedidiah Jones had forced Steve Mason into her life. Judging from her loose tongue while under sedation, he had invaded her subconscious, too.

It was time for her to find out who this mystery man really was.

CHAPTER FOUR

Clara Strike was smiling. They were eating breakfast at an outdoor café in New York City on a beautiful summer morning. Storm was a down-on-his-luck private eye trying to stay one step ahead of bill collectors. The night before he'd nearly been killed. He'd been peeking through a window in a seedy trailer park, secretly recording a cheating husband in a compromising position. It had taken Storm four months to track down Jefferson Grout, but Storm was tenacious, although he didn't take much satisfaction in it. He'd longed for a better class of clientele—and better paying ones than cuckolded spouses. Two redneck neighbors in the trailer park had spotted him and emerged with guns blasting. An angry Grout had fired two rounds, too. But Storm had escaped. Clara Strike had entered his life the next morning, appearing in his office with a sexy smile and a seductive invitation. Over breakfast, she'd explained that Grout was actually a CIA operative gone rogue. The agency had been searching for him for a year. The fact that Storm had found Grout when the agency couldn't impressed her. Grout had been trained, as she put it, to "dance between raindrops." She'd asked for Storm's help and slipped him an unmarked envelope filled with hundreds. He'd been naïve that morning. He'd taken her money and jokingly asked her for a poison pill, a spy camera, a pen that was a gun, and an invisible jet. She'd laughed. It was her smile that still haunted him. He could still smell her perfume. He was looking into her face right now. A morning breeze tousled her hair. She was blushing. He rose from the café table and walked to her. He bent down and kissed her hard. When he looked up, he looked into her eyes—only it wasn't Clara Strike looking back. It was Agent April Showers.

The military transport's tires struck the runway, jarring Storm awake. He'd been dreaming. *Clara Strike. April Showers.*

He rubbed his tired eyes and felt the stubble on his chin.

It was Clara Strike who had introduced him to Jedidiah Jones, and it was Jones who had made him more than a private eye. Jones had recruited him as a contract operative. A tracker of men. It was Jones who'd sent him to Tangiers, where he'd ended up wounded, lying on a cold tile floor in his own blood. Tangiers had been a trap. Someone inside the agency had betrayed the operation.

A black Lincoln Town Car waiting on the tarmac whisked him to CIA headquarters.

"You look like shit." Jones said when Storm plopped into a familiar seat across from the spymaster's desk.

"Nice to see you, too," Storm said.

Jones closed a bright red file with the title "PROJECT *MIDAS*" emblazoned on it. "Things got a bit ugly in London, but you accomplished your assignment. You found the gold."

"Actually, it was April Showers who got you those coordinates," Storm reminded him. "And it almost cost her her life."

"It's all part of the game," Jones said. "She's a big girl."

"Easy to say when your butt is safe behind a desk."

Jones snickered. "You think I got this pretty face working as a desk jockey?"

It was true. Jones's nose had been broken so many times that even the best plastic surgeon couldn't have fixed it.

"Let's get to it," Jones said. "Before you left for London, I told you there were others like you who were living off the grid. The agency helped a few of them 'die.' Others simply disappeared into our version of a witness protection program."

Jones tapped his finger against the "PROJECT *MIDAS*" file. "I've found it useful periodically to call on our 'D or D' operatives to perform missions that must be completely untraceable to this agency and our government."

"D or D?"

"Disappeared or Dead."

"Who comes up with this stuff?" Storm asked.

Ignoring him, Jones said, "Trying to recover sixty billion in gold bullion and other precious commodities that once belonged to the Communist Party is definitely not something we want traced back to the agency or to the White House."

"I understand," Storm said. "We discussed it before I left for London. Technically, the gold belongs to the Commies who are still running around Russia, and anyone who goes hunting for it would be operating as pirates according to international law."

"That would be a position the international court might take," Jones said, "but I think a good lawyer could argue that the KGB leadership stole the gold when they had soldiers sneak it out of Moscow in the dead of night just before the entire country imploded. When the Soviet Union ceased to exist as a legal entity in 1991, so did the Soviet Communist Party, and since the KGB stole the gold, it really belongs to no one at this point."

"I don't think the Kremlin believes in finders keepers, losers weepers. Especially when you're discussing sixty billion."

"Especially when the country is being run by President Barkovsky," Jones added. "And he has access to nukes and is itching for a fight. That's why the U.S. government and this agency are going to walk away from all of this. We are not going to go after the gold, even though Agent Showers has discovered where it is hidden."

Storm looked at Jones's eyes and said, "You're talking officially, aren't you?"

"That's right. Officially, we're not interested. But I'm sending you and three other D or D operatives after it."

"And if I say no?"

"You can do that," he said. "You can go back to Montana. You can go back to being a faceless nobody who spends his days fly-fishing and remembering past adventures while he's letting his talents and his life go to waste."

"You make that sound appealing," Storm said.

"C'mon, Storm, isn't it time for you to face reality? To face the fact that you aren't someone who can live off the grid. You need the action, the excitement, the adrenaline rush. Besides, in your heart, you're someone who cares—not only about helping people but about your country. You can put on that tough guy mask for the likes of Agent April Showers, but you don't fool me. Clara Strike saw through it, too. That's why I had her recruit you to work for us. It's why I need you now."

Storm thought about what Jones had said. It was true.

"Can I assume the coordinates that I sent you from Lebedev's cell phone checked out?" Storm asked.

Jones spread an enlarged satellite photograph across his desk. "We won't know if the gold is there until we have eyes on the ground," he said. "But the pieces seem to fit." He pointed to a tiny circle that he'd drawn on the photograph. "The longitude and latitude coordinates from Lebedev's cell phone pinpoint a location here, about fifteen miles from the Valley of Five Caves in Uzbekistan. It's part of the Molguzar mountain range south of the Jizzakh region."

"Not a frequent flyer hot spot," Storm said.

"Uzbekistan caves are famous in Eurasian countries. The Great Silk Route that linked Europe and China used to pass through Uzbekistan, and there's a legend that Alexander the Great hid huge amounts of gold and treasure in a cave in the mountains."

"Their version of El Dorado?" Storm said.

"Right. Maybe the KGB decided that if treasure hunters since 323 B.C. hadn't been able to find any gold, it was a safe spot for the Soviet Socialist Republic's treasure."

Jones pointed to a jagged line on the recognizance map.

"This is an old, long-abandoned logging road. We think the soldiers used trucks to bring the gold up into the mountains."

"And you expect me and a handful of other D or D operatives to carry out sixty billion worth of gold?"

"Don't be stupid. We have contacts in Kazakhstan with a fleet of Russian-made Halo helicopters, the most powerful in the world, but how we get the gold out is not your concern," Jones said. "All I need you and your team to do is locate the cave, see if the gold is hidden inside it, and then get out."

"Mind if we pocket a few kilobars as mementos?" Storm said. "Remember, finders keepers."

"Ivan Petrov told me the gold was hidden inside cargo containers that were transported out of Moscow. The containers are marked 'Toxic Waste' to keep anyone from looking inside. When you find the cave, you look in the containers and then come back home—with empty pockets. Simple as that."

Jones removed a men's wristwatch from his desk drawer and tossed it to Storm. "A present."

"Let me guess," Storm said. "It's a gold detector."

"No."

"A laser beam that can cut through locks on the containers when we find the gold."

"No."

"A secret gun that—"

"It's a wristwatch," said Jones.

Storm raised an eyebrow.

"Okay," said Jones. "It's also a worldwide tracker. I can find you no matter where you are."

"I'm not sure I want you keeping track of me twenty-four hours a day," Storm said.

"If you pull the stem to set the watch, it sets off an emergency rescue signal that means you are in trouble and need help. Immediately."

"No poison pill?" Storm said. He slipped it on his wrist and asked, "What if I actually need to set the time?"

"You never will. It automatically corrects itself no matter where you are."

"A watch that works and a tracker. What will they think of next?"

"For you, a poison pill."

"Who else from your D or D file have you chosen for this operation? And are you giving them watches, too?"

"You'll meet them later today, and no, you've got the only watch," Jones said. He opened the "PROJECT *MIDAS*" file and removed three photographs, which he handed to Storm.

"The first team member," Jones said, "will be using the name Dilya. She is a native of Uzbekistan. After it broke free from the old Soviet Union, Islamic jihadists moved in. Dilya worked undercover for us. In return, we helped her vanish. She'll serve as your guide and interpreter."

Her photograph showed a stern-looking woman in her thirties with a jagged scar cut across her left cheek.

"She got that scar," Jones explained, "while being interrogated by government officials. What's tragic is that she was actually helping her own government at the time but couldn't tell anyone. She was working on the same side as the people who cut her."

"And she didn't break her cover?"

"No. Dilya is a very tough woman."

Storm glanced at the second photo. It showed a short, round-faced man wearing thick glasses.

"He'll be introduced to you as Oscar. He's a Russian geologist."

"Former Commie?" Storm asked.

"Probably still is one, but he liked U.S. dollars. He supplied us with scientific information before the Soviet Union collapsed. He's familiar with the gold bullion and can confirm if the kilobars are the ones that were stolen from Moscow."

The third photograph was of an American. "You know this operative and he'll know you," Jones said. "On this mission, he'll be called Casper."

Storm did recognize him. They'd worked together before Tangiers. Casper's specialty was killing people.

"If I work with Casper, he'll know I'm alive," Storm said.

"And you'll know he is, too. I wouldn't have put you two together if it weren't absolutely necessary."

Strong and intimidating, Casper was the type you'd want with you in a bar fight but would never introduce to your parents—or your girlfriend.

"You've picked Dilya as a guide," Storm said. "Oscar is a scientist who can confirm the gold is real. Casper can kill anyone who gets in the way. Why do you need me? I'm a private eye. Tracking down people is what I do."

"I need you to watch the other three," Jones replied. "You I trust. With that much gold at stake, I'm not sure about the others."

CHAPTER FIVE

"We've been driving more than an hour," Cumerford said. "Let's stop and grab some coffee."

"Just make certain it's someplace where I won't be recognized," Showers replied.

They had slipped out of the John Radcliffe Hospital in Oxford shortly after eight that morning. The original plan was for Showers to be discharged as soon as she gave a statement to the local police and Scotland Yard. The FBI wanted to get her out of England immediately. But the doctors treating her objected, saying it wasn't safe to discharge her on the day after she'd undergone emergency surgery for her shoulder wound. Showers had reluctantly agreed to spend one more night at the hospital but had been eager to leave this morning.

She'd gotten dressed in blue denim jeans and T-shirt, donned a baseball cap, and put on dark glasses. Cumerford had arranged for word to be leaked to the television crews and reporters lurking outside the hospital's emergency entrance that Showers was about to be released. Hospital officials had hustled a female patient into an ambulance, which had sped toward London. To make the decoy more credible, Thomas Gordon, the CIA operative working undercover as a State Department employee, had followed the ambulance in the U.S. embassy–owned car that he and Cumerford had driven to Oxford. While the media was chasing him and the ambulance, Showers and Cumerford had slipped through a hospital side door into a rental car. They managed to leave Oxford without anyone seeing them.

Or so they both thought.

Showers was not going to London. The Bureau had instructed Cumerford to drive her to the Royal Air Force base in Lakenheath, where the U.S.'s Forty-eighth Medical Squadron was based. It had flights with medical personnel on board in case she suffered a relapse. The base was seventy miles north of London, which was another plus. By the time reporters realized that they'd been fooled and started the drive to Lakenheath, Showers would be gone.

The bullet had broken Showers's right collarbone. But it had been shock that had almost done her in. Had she not gotten to the hospital in what doctors called "the golden hour," she would have died. Her right arm was now in a sling and she was taking pain pills, but she had not suffered any permanent damage, although there would be a nasty scar to remind her of how close she'd come to death.

"I don't need to fly back on a medical transport," she complained.

"Washington insisted," Cumerford said. "You don't have a choice."

"Just like I didn't have a choice about my statement," she replied.

"Did you know the Good Samaritan called the hospital to check on you?" Cumerford asked.

"What?"

"Steve Mason, or whatever the hell his real name is. He'd been specifically ordered not to risk calling. But apparently he's not someone who colors inside the lines."

"No, he doesn't think much of rules," she said. "Why didn't anyone tell me?"

"You were sleeping. Apparently, when they didn't put his call through to you, he said a few things to the hospital staff that upset their English sensibilities."

Showers fought the urge to smile.

As they neared the intersection of the A14 and M11 roadways, Cumerford noticed a road sign that had two yellow, bending palm trees emblazoned on it, with a bright red background.

"There's what the Brits call a service area ahead," he explained. "We can pull in there and get something. Most of these service areas have a food court. That would be a smarter place for us to stop than getting off the main motorway and going into a pub, where you might be recognized."

"I come to England and end up eating at McDonald's."

"The BBC has been showing photos of you almost every hour for the past two days," he said. "They're calling it the Oxford Massacre. The Brits aren't used to gunfights, especially at peaceful college demonstrations."

To Showers, Cumerford seemed like an okay guy. He'd

been a special agent about five years longer than she had and had done a stint in Washington, D.C., before being sent to London. It was a cushy assignment reserved for FBI agents who were rising stars.

"I'd kill for a good cup of coffee" he said. "The Brits may know how to make tea, but they're lousy at brewing a simple cup of coffee. It's one thing I miss."

"My stomach is a bit upset. I'll just use the bathroom."

They pulled off the A14, and Cumerford parked near the front of the main service building. It was a modern, one-floor structure with large glass windows. Inside were five fast-food eateries, including a McDonald's and a Kentucky Fried Chicken, located in a half-circle food court mobbed with customers.

"I'm going to use the head, too, before I get my coffee," Cumerford said. "I'll meet you in the food court when you are done. Don't make me come looking for you."

He shot her a smile.

The restrooms were to the immediate left of the entrance, about twenty feet from the food court. When Showers walked into the women's side, there were two girls washing their hands at a row of sinks. She slipped by them into an empty stall and struggled to unbutton her pants with her left hand. She struggled with the button and zipper and silently chuckled. She'd had an easier time fatally shooting a man with her left hand than she had dropping her jeans. As she sat down, she heard the girls at the sink depart. In the quiet, she let out a loud sigh. She was exhausted, but mostly frustrated, because she knew her shoulder injury was going to take her out of the action. She'd accomplished what she'd been sent to England for. She'd solved the double murders in Washington, D.C., that she'd been sent to England to investigate. She would explain to her superiors that Lebedev and Nad had orchestrated the kidnapping of Matthew Dull and the assassination of his stepfather, Senator Thurston Windslow. She didn't know why Storm and the CIA hadn't told her about the gold. She wasn't supposed to know about it. But she'd been drawn into that aspect of the case when Lebedev started torturing Petrov in the back of the Mercedes. She suspected that "Steve Mason" already was scheming with Jedidiah Jones about ways to recover the gold. But she wouldn't be part of that now. She'd be stuck at a desk tending her wound. She wondered if she would ever see Steve Mason again or if he would simply disappear just as suddenly as he had appeared in her life. Regardless, she was determined to investigate him as soon as she got back in Washington. If his father was a retired FBI agent, there had to be some thread she could follow.

Buttoning her pants proved as difficult left-handed as loosening them. When she finally managed to complete the task, she opened the stall door, pulling it toward her.

From nowhere, a huge figure appeared in front of her. Showers stepped back and reached for her right hip with her left hand. It was where she normally kept her Glock holstered. When her fingers felt nothing but fabric, she realized that Cumerford had not returned her Glock when she was discharged that morning. She had only one useful arm and no weapons.

For a large man, he moved quickly. Showers saw the

flash of his hand, felt a jab into her neck, and then a strange warmth just before she passed out. He caught her limp body as she started to collapse.

"You got her?" a nervous woman watching from the doorway to the women's room asked. She was dressed as a nurse, with a stethoscope dangling from her neck. She had been stopping women from entering the restroom, explaining that a medical emergency was being addressed inside.

"Yes," the hulking figure replied.

Speaking into a tiny microphone tucked under the sleeve of her blouse, the nurse said, "We're ready here. Where's the other American?"

"He just walked out of the men's room and now is standing in line at McDonald's," a male voice replied in her tiny earpiece. "He's got two customers ahead of him."

From the interior of the food court, it was impossible for Agent Cumerford to see the entrance to the women's restroom or a side exit near it that opened into the parking lot.

But Cumerford was not alarmed. Women generally took longer in restrooms than men.

"Let's go now!" the woman ordered.

The man she'd been speaking to immediately left his post in the food court and walked briskly toward her.

"Medical emergency," the nurse said, taking the lead. "Stand aside please."

The gaggle of women patiently waiting at the restroom doorway cleared an opening for the foursome. Within seconds, Showers had been hustled outside and tucked into the rear seat of a sedan with tinted windows.

By the time Cumerford paid for his coffee and collected his change, he was beginning to become suspicious. He scanned the food court, but there was no sight of Showers. He hurried over to the women's restroom but didn't want to yell inside for Showers, and he couldn't walk inside without creating a scene. Cumerford noticed a rest area security guard coming through the front entrance, reporting to work, so he hurried up to him.

"I'm traveling with a female friend who was discharged this morning from a hospital," he said. "She's been in the women's restroom for a long time and I'm worried she might have fainted or is having trouble."

The male guard used his portable radio to call a matron, who approached them about a minute later.

"This man's lost his woman friend in the loo," the guard explained. "Says she's just been discharged from the hospital and is wearing a sling."

"Broken arm?" the woman asked.

"Broken collarbone, an accident," he replied, catching himself before he said "gunshot."

"I'll check," the matron said cheerfully, only to return moments later.

"Sorry, mate," she said. "But there's no women in the loo wearing a sling. No Yanks at all. Maybe she's gone into the food court."

Grabbing his cell phone, Cumerford stepped away from them and called his supervising agent at the embassy in London.

"Showers has disappeared!"

"What? How? Weren't you with her?"

"Not in the bathroom. We stopped at a service area."

Cumerford felt a tug on his arm. It was the matron.

"A couple said they saw your lady friend being carried out of the loo a few minutes ago. There was a nurse with her. She was unconscious."

"A nurse?"

"A nurse and two gentlemen. One was carrying her. He was a big fellow."

Speaking into his cell phone, Cumerford said, "Oh my God! Someone's abducted her! We've lost Agent Showers!"

CHAPTER SIX

President's Office,
Senate Office Building inside the Kremlin.
MOSCOW, Russia

Hanging on the wall directly behind President Barkovsky's desk inside his Kremlin office was the Russian Federation's coat of arms. The red seal had a double-headed, golden eagle in its center. In one sinister talon, the bird was clutching a scepter. An imperial crown was in the other talon. There was an overlay of Saint George on a horse about to slay a dragon in the center of the crest.

Barkovsky hated both his antique presidential desk and the seal, but especially the seal. It had been adopted in 1993 by his predecessors, after the collapse of the Soviet Empire. The reformers had stripped away the more familiar hammer and sickle and its motto: "Workers of the World, Unite."

"What does Saint George slaying a dragon have to do with modern Russia?" Barkovsky frequently complained to visitors. The legend had been brought back from the crusades in Libya. Why had the country's leaders put a crusader on a national emblem when there were so many better choices? Barkvosky felt he might as well be on that seal, but certainly before St. George. He had done more for Russia.

Barkovsky had just returned to his office after having a light lunch, when there was a rap on his door and his chief of staff, Mikhail Sokolov, entered, saying: "I have news."

"First answer me this," Barkovsky replied. "I wanted Ivan Petrov interrogated and killed. I wanted the Americans blamed for his murder. What do our people in London do? They sent three assassins to shoot him at a public rally! How is that blaming the FBI? And then they failed to kill him! And now Petrov and Lebedev are dead, and only the two Americans survived."

"Petrov was not supposed to be killed at the rally," Sokolov explained. "The plan was for our men to ambush Petrov and the Americans after the rally when they were returning in a convoy to Petrov's English estate. Petrov's security chief was helping us. She was supposed to make it look like the two Americans killed Petrov and two of his security guards before they were fatally wounded. Only the security chief and Lebedev were supposed to survive the attack. They would be the only witnesses and would interrogate Petrov about the gold before killing him."

"If that was the plan, then why did our men begin shooting at the rally?"

"Because they were recognized by the Americans in the crowd before Petrov began his speech. This Good Samaritan— this unidentified CIA man—was about to confront one of them. Our man panicked and began shooting."

"It's a total disaster. Now the entire world is blaming me, and why not? The men who London hired for this job were all ex-KGB, and all were total idiots. This has become an international incident. And we still have no idea where my gold is located."

"Ah, but we do. That is the good news that I have come to report."

"You know where my gold is? Where is it? How do you know?"

"We do not know the exact spot yet, but we will. Our people in England have abducted the woman FBI agent," Sokolov said.

"How does that help me find my gold? What use is she to me now that Petrov is dead?"

"She knows where your gold is hidden."

"That's impossible," Barkovsky replied. "The BBC is reporting that she was unconscious in the car after the shootings at the rally. She has no idea what happened between Petrov and Lebedev or how they ended up dead."

"The BBC is lying. Petrov told her where the gold is located before he died."

"How can you possibly know this?"

"Because we have confirmation. We have a friend helping us—someone who our intelligence service hasn't heard from for many years."

"We have a spy in the FBI?"

"No, in Langley. One of our best recruits has resurfaced after four years. We'd thought we'd lost him because he stopped all communication with us and disappeared. But now he is back and is helping us again. He sent word early this morning that the CIA is forming a team to go after the gold. The CIA is forming this team because the female FBI agent—April Showers—told them where the gold is located. She must have been conscious in the car when Lebedev interrogated Petrov. That is why we have kidnapped her."

Barkovsky let loose a stream of expletives. "We warned the Americans to stay away from my gold, but Mr. Jedidiah Jones thinks he can defy me and get away with it."

"Mr. President, even if the FBI agent doesn't tell us where the gold is located, we will still be able to find it because our friend—our mole—is on the team that Jones has selected to locate your gold. Without realizing it, Jones will be leading us to your gold."

Barkovsky broke into a menacing grin. "We have both the female FBI agent and a CIA mole." He hesitated and then asked, "But is this spy of ours reliable? How do you know this isn't a provocation by Jones? One of his many CIA tricks—especially if this spy has been silent for years and only now has resurfaced?"

"It's true, our friend vanished four years ago," Sokolov said. "But before that, the information he gave us was one hundred percent reliable. In one of the last communications, he warned us about an operation in Tangiers. We were able to use his information to foil the CIA's plans. Americans were killed and Jones's operation was a complete failure."

"We can use our mole to corroborate the information we

get out of the FBI agent, and vice versa," Barkovsky said. "This is brilliant!"

"Yes, but first we must get April Showers out of England. We can't afford any more mistakes. Where should we send her to be interrogated?"

"Take her to wherever this CIA team goes. Do it there."

"For what purpose, may I ask?" Sokolov said.

"I want Jedidiah Jones to know when they recover her body that she was executed because of his decision to go after my gold."

"We embarrassed him in Tangiers," Sokolov said. "We will do it again."

"I do not want the FBI agent or members of the CIA team killed until we have my gold. No mistakes this time. Once I get my gold, then I want them all dead. I want to send this arrogant Jedidiah Jones a message."

"Everyone but our friend, the mole, of course," Sokolov said.

"No, kill him, too," Barkovsky said. "There is only one reason a spy betrays his own country. There is no romance, no mystery. It is always for the money. And a man who can be bought is not a man who can be trusted. After we have the gold, he is expendable."

"But he might be useful later," Sokolov protested.

"Jones is too smart for that. If only one person survives and escapes, he will know that person is a traitor. Why else would he be alive?"

"Then we will kill all of them and the FBI agent, too. This time she will not escape."

"I do not want any witnesses. No survivors. I want to piss on Mr. Jedidiah Jones, and I want him to know that I am doing it."

CHAPTER SEVEN

A military flight delivered Storm to a U.S. base in Germany, where he boarded a privately owned aircraft chartered by the CIA. It took him to an airfield in Kazakhstan. Although the Kazakhstan government denied that it allowed U.S. flights to operate within its borders, a backroom deal had been cut to allow the CIA to use specific airstrips for its covert operations in return for U.S. foreign aid, and this was one of those operations.

Storm found a late model Range Rover waiting at the Kazakhstan airfield, with a woman standing next to it. From the photograph that Jones had shown him, he knew it was Dilya.

"Welcome to Kazakhstan," she said, extending her hand. Storm estimated she was five feet, five inches tall and about 120 pounds. She had short black hair and a firm, no-nonsense grip. Even though she was a native of Uzbekistan, she spoke with a proper British accent.

"Grab your gear and get in," she said. "I'll drive you to our staging area, to where the others are waiting."

"Did you study in England?" he asked as they were driving from the airfield.

"The Soviets didn't allow us to travel when I was a child. But all of our schools relied on English textbooks. That is why we speak with an accent. The audiotapes we heard were from London. I speak three other languages, and there is not a trace of a British accent in my voice then. Only when I speak English do I sound British."

She glanced at him and said, "You will stick out when we go into remote mountain areas. You don't look like men here. People will think you are a Russian, and everyone here hates Russians because they tortured us for decades."

"I'll wave an American flag."

"Tell them you are from American television. We love American TV here. If you want to get women excited, tell them you are from *Dancing with the Stars* and are thinking about making a dance competition in Uzbekistan. You will be a hero!"

"Thanks for the pointers," he said. He noticed the scar that cut across her cheek. It was illuminated by the dash lights as they drove through the night's blackness. She noticed that he was looking at it.

"What do you think of my decoration?" she asked. "A little memento. Here they always cut a woman on her face. That way, every day when she looks in the mirror, it reminds her of what they can do, of their power. And everyone who sees her knows that it is dangerous to associate with her." The car hit a bump that caused them both to bounce in their seat as Dilya turned off the main highway onto what looked to

Storm like a cow path that would guide them up a mountain.

She said, "You've never been tortured?"

"Only by former girlfriends"

The Range Rover arrived at a one-room farmhouse with rough stone walls and a wooden roof. It was completely isolated from any neighbors. Dilya parked and explained, "The American inside is called Casper and the Russian is called Oscar. I will introduce you." He followed her through the wooden front door.

A bespectacled man glanced up from a table where he was studying a map. Storm recognized him as Oscar. On the other side of the room, sitting on the edge of a bed, smoking a cigarette, was Casper.

Oscar stood, Casper didn't. Oscar spoke. Casper glared.

"You must be Steve," the ex-Soviet geologist said.

"Nice to meet you, Oscar," Storm replied. He glanced at Casper and said, "We meet again."

"Hello, *Stevie*," said Casper, accenting his name in manner that was clearly meant to belittle.

The last time they had met, Casper had had black hair. Now it was completely white and pulled back into a ponytail. He'd added a new tattoo to his collection. This one was on his right arm and showed a skull with a snake coming out of one eye and a knife jabbed into the other.

"Thought you got killed in Tangiers," Casper said, ignoring Jedidiah Jones's rules about revealing anything about past missions.

"Disappointed?"

Casper sneered. "All I know is that Tangiers went bad

and I heard you were the reason."

"It did go bad," Storm replied, "and I was thinking that you might have had something to do with that."

Casper rose from the bed, and Storm saw a U.S. Marine Corps Ka-Bar knife on his belt. The two men locked eyes as Storm readied himself for a fight.

"I lost good people in Tangiers," Casper said. "Good men who shouldn't have died."

"I ended up on the floor with my gut riddled with bullets, while you were miles away sitting in a bar nursing a beer," Storm replied, "so don't lecture me about casualties."

"This really isn't the time or place for you two to argue," Oscar said in a quiet voice.

Dilya stepped between Casper and Storm and in a belittling tone said, "We wouldn't have been chosen for this assignment if Jedidiah Jones didn't trust us. You need to be professional. You can resolve your personal disputes after we find the gold."

"Scarface is right," Casper grunted. "We'll settle our personal score later, *Stevie boy*."

Storm couldn't imagine why Jones had paired him with Casper. He only knew that he'd have to watch his back when it came to him. As for the other two: Dilya seemed trustworthy. He wasn't certain about Oscar. Did Jones have some reason— besides the fact that they were all officially "dead or disappeared"—for putting them on the same team?

"Everyone gather around," Dilya said, assuming command.

They each took a position on one side of the square table. "We are here at the base of these mountains," she said, placing her finger on the map. "We will drive as far as possible tomorrow morning up into the mountains, and then we will hike across the border into Uzbekistan. Our orders were to go this way." She swept her hand across the map to where she had marked a bright red X. "That is where the gold is hidden. However, we are being diverted."

"What are you talking about?" Oscar said.

"Yeah," Casper said suspiciously. "Why the last-minute change in plans?"

"As you know, there is no way for us to contact Langley from the base of this mountain, but while I was at the airport, I received an urgent call from Jones. He gave me additional orders."

"I don't like the smell of this," Casper grumbled.

"I was with Jones yesterday, and he didn't say anything to me about a change in plans," Storm added.

"You have been flying with orders to stay off the air since you left Germany," she reminded him. "It seems that a friend of yours has been kidnapped in England."

"Agent Showers?" Storm exclaimed. "Kidnapped! How's that possible? She's in a hospital recovering from a gunshot wound."

"She *was* in a hospital in Oxford, but she was kidnapped while she was being driven to an English air base to fly back to the States."

"Whose got her? Where is she now?"

"According to Jones, she is being flown to Jizzakh, a city not far from our original destination in the Molguzar Mountains," Dilya said. "He has ordered us to go to Jizzakh and rescue her."

"What?" Oscar said indignantly. "I'm a geologist. I'm not risking my neck because some careless FBI agent got herself kidnapped."

In a move that surprised even himself, Storm grabbed the front of Oscar's shirt, jerking him off his feet and slamming his head down on the map.

"You're talking about a partner of mine," he said. "And she is not careless and we will go rescue her, is that clear?"

"Please release Oscar," Dilya said in a matter-of-fact voice.

Storm turned him loose, and the Russian stood, clearly angry. "Touch me again, and I will kill you," he sputtered.

"With what?" Casper said. "A rock?" Reaching down, he pulled his knife from its scabbard and flipped it in the air, causing it to turn over so that he could catch it by its blade. "I can loan you this, if you think you can take him."

Oscar looked at the extended knife and then at Storm.

"Huh, just like I thought," Casper said, expertly returning the blade to his belt. "I didn't think you had the nuts." He looked at Dilya and said, "This Commie geek has a point though. We were recruited to help find the missing gold. If this FBI broad needs to be saved, why doesn't Jones send in the marines?"

"We're the closest," she said.

"And we're untraceable," said Storm.

"You mean expendable," Casper complained.

"This woman knows the location of the gold," Dilya said. "If she talks before we can rescue her, we could be walking into a trap."

"We either need to rescue her or silence her then," Casper replied.

"We're going to rescue her," Storm snapped. "No one is going to harm her."

Casper rested his palm on his knife and said, "I'm not like our little Commie friend here, Stevie boy. You grab my shirt and push my head down on the table and I'm going to come up swinging. I'll give you a souvenir just like our Uzbek princess here has."

"Why don't you two just drop your pants and get this over with?" Dilya said. "This is not a democracy. Jones has given us an order and all of us, for various reasons, have to listen to him."

Casper removed his hand from his knife and said, "Where are they holding this broad?"

Dilya jabbed her finger down on the map. "This is the city of Jizzakh. Jones has arranged for transportation and a satellite tracking device to be waiting for us on the other side of the mountain after we cross the border tomorrow morning. He has told me to use GPS to get our team to where the woman is being held captive. When we reach the location, I am supposed to turn over leadership to Casper."

"Casper?" Storm asked.

"Yes," she said firmly. "Jones was very clear about this. We are not to try to call or communicate with the Agency while we are in Jizzakh, because our signals will be picked up by the Uzbek authorities. Jones said it is up to Casper to formulate a plan to rescue Agent Showers."

"Jones clearly doesn't want you to screw this rescue up

like you did in Tangiers," Casper said.

Although he was boiling inside, Storm kept himself under control.

Dilya said, "We rescue Showers first and then go after the gold."

"Assuming she's still alive," Oscar said.

Casper grinned, revealing a missing front tooth. "Better be nice to me, Stevie boy. You're girlfriend's fate is in my hands now."

"That's right, this time you'd better plan a perfect rescue."

Storm was worried. Not for himself, but for Showers. He didn't want to think about what might be happening to her at this very moment.

CHAPTER EIGHT

Where was she?

April Showers stayed perfectly still. She didn't want her captors to know she was conscious. She needed to assess her situation. *How long had it been since she'd been kidnapped in England? How long had she been sedated?* Through half-closed eyes, she carefully checked her surroundings. It was dim in the small room, but there didn't seem to be anyone watching her. *Good.* She opened her eyes fully and searched for a video camera. There was none that she could see.

The chamber that she was in felt cool and damp. A low-wattage bulb dangled from the center of a concrete ceiling. The walls were also made of concrete. There was a metal drain in one corner and a water hose coiled around a stainless steel hanger bolted to a wall. She saw meat hooks attached to the high ceiling and realized that she was being held in a room where animals were slaughtered. The smell confirmed her suspicions. It was a putrefied mixture of a hundred foul odors. Flies landed on her skin. When she tried to swat one, a pain shot through her right arm. In her drug-induced stupor, she'd forgotten that she was recovering from her wound. She felt her shoulder. Someone had applied fresh bandages. Her right arm was dangling at her side. She could move it, but not without great pain and with only limited mobility. She was wearing the same jeans and T-shirt that she'd been dressed in when she left the hospital. Only her baseball cap was missing. Her sling was still around her neck. With her left hand, she guided her right wrist through it. That felt better.

Showers used her left hand to sit up. She had been lying on a thin mattress that had bloodstains on it and smelled of urine. A leather collar had been fastened around her right ankle. The binding was connected to a two-foot short chain anchored into the floor. If she had a knife or something sharp, she could cut the collar. But she could not break the chain. There was only one entrance into the room and it had a solid door. There were no windows. Escaping was going to be difficult.

She pulled her legs up to her chest. *When were they coming?* She had no concept of time, and that frustrated her. *Was it night? Was it day? Were they sleeping?*

Showers had never been a patient person, and after several minutes of aimlessly swatting at flies and wondering what might happen next, she decided to take charge of her situation.

She screamed, unleashing her pent-up rage.

"Here I am! C'mon inside."

She waited, listening. But there was no reaction. Only silence. She decided to try again.

"Hello!" she called. "Let's get this party started."

Still no reply.

There was no way for her to know that Hasan Sadikov was only a few yards away, resting on a metal folding chair outside the room. His back was facing the door and he was reading.

Books were Hasan's escape. He ignored Showers's calls and instead focused on the novel. He wanted to read another thirty pages before he would stop to interrogate her. The wait would be a good thing. He'd done this many times before and had always found that his victims were uncomfortable with uncertainty. The imagination could be worse than the reality, especially with Westerners. They'd watched too many horror films.

Hasan was teaching Showers a lesson, too. He wanted her to understand that she had no control over her current situation. She was at his mercy.

It had become quiet inside the slaughter room by the time he finished reading and placed his book into a well-worn satchel that he had brought with him. It was time to go to work. He stood, unlocked the door, folded his metal chair together, picked up the satchel, and carried it and the chair into the room.

Showers still had her face pressed against her knees when he entered. She quickly lowered her legs.

"I think we should speak in English," he said politely. He moved close to her, opened his chair, and took a seat. To Showers, Hasan looked completely unremarkable. He was a middle-aged man of medium height with a belly that hung over his belt. He reminded her of a man you might see riding the bus to work or walking with his children in a store. He could have been anyone.

"I've visited the United States," he said, smiling. "New

York, Washington, D.C., and, of course, Orlando. Have you been to Disneyland?"

"Disney World," she said, correcting him. "Disneyland is in Anaheim, California. Disney World is in Orlando."

He ran his right hand through his black hair. He turned his neck from one side to the other, as if he were a boxer getting limber before a fight.

Showers said, "I'd like to use the toilet." She was testing him.

He paused, considering her request, then said, "I am a reasonable man." He called out, and a younger man entered the room. "Bring us a pail."

"I'd rather use a bathroom," Showers said.

"Of course you would, because then you could try to escape from this room. But a pail will have to do."

The aide placed it next to Hasan's chair, and he slid it with his foot toward her.

"You can do it here. I'll wait," he said. "I might even turn my head."

Considering how much trouble Showers had had when she'd undone her pants in the bathroom at the English service area, she decided to wait. She kicked the pail back over to him. "I'm not using that."

He shrugged.

They were playing a power game, and she apparently was going to lose.

"When I was in the United States," Hasan continued, "I kept hearing a phrase. It was 'I have good news and I have bad news.'" He grinned, clearly pleased with himself, and continued, "The good news is that I am not a cruel man. I am not a terrorist. I have no interest in holding you hostage for years for ransom or sacrificing you for the glory of Allah. If it matters at all, I was raised Eastern Orthodox."

"Obviously, you slept through Sunday School."

"A sharp wit," he said. "I like that. It makes my work challenging."

He placed the satchel in his ample lap and removed an old Panasonic microcassette recorder from it. After checking to make certain it contained a tape, he switched it on and placed it on the floor.

"My employers will want to know exactly what you said to me and how you said it. I have been hired to make certain you tell the truth."

Hasan shook out a cigarette from a hard pack and offered her one.

"I don't smoke," she said.

"Neither do I. It's a nasty habit," he replied, lighting his cigarette, and slowly exhaling.

His denial didn't make sense, and she wondered if her exhaustion was clouding her thoughts. Suddenly Hasan leaned forward and stuck the burning tip of his cigarette into her neck. She screamed and jerked back as the smell of burned flesh reached her nostrils.

He eased back into his chair and sucked on the cigarette until its tip glowed again.

"Now for the bad news," he said sternly. "I will hurt you much more than that."

Showers was breathing rapidly.

"I don't think you have ever been interrogated," he said, "but I know you have thought about it. Everyone does. 'Can I keep quiet? Or will I break?' It is a fool's question. Do you know why?"

She shook her head.

"Because everyone talks. They talk or they die. The only real uncertainly is how long it will take for you to tell me what I want to know. For me, it doesn't matter. A minute, an hour, a day. But for you, well, it matters a great deal." He looked at the red tip of the cigarette and leaned forward. She instinctively pulled back. He flashed a toothy grin of yellowed teeth.

He said, "Tell me, do you like to read?"

She nodded.

"Good," he said. "I love literature. I try to read a book every day. I have done this since I was six years old. I do it because I want to learn. I am always trying to improve my mind and reading can help you deal with problems. Have you ever read Solzhenitsyn's *One Day in the Life of Ivan Denisovich*? No? It is an important book, a very important book about life inside a Soviet prison camp where people were abused. And if you had read it, then perhaps you would have learned something from it that would be helpful to you now."

She stayed silent.

"Do you know what Solzhenitsyn said about Americans after he was exiled from the Soviet Union and had lived in your country for many years? He said Americans lacked the moral fiber to defeat Communism. He said you didn't have the stomach for it."

She drew a deep breath and responded, "Maybe you

missed it, but the Cold War ended and we're still standing—unlike Communism."

"Defiant. I like that. The challenge."

By now, the cigarette was spent, and he dropped it on the floor and stepped on it. He reached into the satchel and removed a spool of heavy white cord.

She watched him intently.

He said, "There was a reason why I mentioned books. It's because I believe a person should strive to improve themselves in their chosen profession. Consider my field, for example. I could use the same interview techniques whenever I interrogate someone, but then how could I improve? This is why I am always searching for something more efficient. This cord, for instance. Do you know how many positions a human body can be tied into that can cause extreme pain?"

She did not answer.

"The Japanese have incorporated the use of knots and ropes and pain into their sexual customs. They call it Kinbaku or Sokubaku—sexual bondage using ropes. Did you know that?"

Again, she kept silent. He was showing off.

He grinned again and said, "What's the matter? As you Americans say, 'Cat got your tongue?' Or did I say that wrong, too?"

He placed the spool on the floor and took a new item from his bag. It was two strands of electrical wire. "Electric shocks, especially applied to a person's private parts can be extremely painful, but everyone who watches television knows this. There is no imagination involved. It's mundane torture."

He put down the wire and said, "You see, a true professional, such as myself, attempts to tailor the various tools at his disposal to the unique personality of the individual being questioned. It's my job to find just the right motivator to insure that you will tell me what I need to know. You should be grateful that I am not some brute, but a true professional, because I'm actually doing you a favor. It is incredible how much pain some people can tolerate, but I can save you from that by recognizing your deepest fear and tapping into it. It is quicker, more humane, really. Why, I will be doing you a favor. You should thank me, really."

"I'll thank you if you undo this chain and let me go," she said.

He looked into Showers's eyes and smiled. He said, "I have used all sorts of devices on women such as you. They scream, but then, so do men." Hasan removed a clear plastic bag filled with soda crackers from the satchel. "This looks refreshing, doesn't it?" he asked. "Hardly an instrument of torture. Are you hungry?" He opened the bag, took a bite of a cracker. "But in the right hands—someone knowledgeable, well, let me tell you a secret." He shook the bag and its contents. "If I put this bag over your head and crumple up little dry crackers in it, eventually you have to breathe them into your lungs and those crumbs will scratch your insides. You will start spitting blood." He finished the remainder of the cracker and placed the bag onto the floor. "Now, are you still hungry?"

This time, he withdrew a pair of stainless steel shears from his case. "Mutilation—cutting off toes, fingers, or a man's sexual organ—can be effective. Disfigurement terrifies people—especially women—and it is pitifully easy. The chopping off of a hand or foot. The gouging out of an eyeball. The scarring of a cheek. Have you ever smelled your own flesh burning...? Well, yes, you just did." He smiled again and added, "All it takes is a cup of gasoline and a match."

He placed the clippers in the row that he had created neatly on the floor. Next from the satchel came a small wooden club. "Beating people is perhaps the most pedestrian form of persuasion, and the most common."

She realized he was showing her these articles not only to intimidate her but to observe her reaction.

"Actually, I am mistaken," he said in a sinister voice, "just like when I said Disneyland and meant Disney World. You see, beatings may be a common form of torture, but you could argue that there is another practice that is used just as frequently in jails and prisons. Sexual violation. Rape."

"I've heard enough," Showers said. "You're a big, brave man with your little bag of horrors, especially when you are facing a woman with a useless arm who's chained to the floor. If you get into trouble, all you have to do is call your goons from outside. But you don't fool me. I see right through you. You're nothing more than a sadistic little pervert, a bug, a piece of human garbage who gets his kicks out of picking on helpless people who can't defend themselves. Does it make you feel important? Does it make you feel potent?"

Showers watched as Hasan blushed. At the FBI academy, she'd been told that it was important for agents dealing with hostile witnesses to take command of the interview and then to both intimidate and befriend a witness. Now she was on the other side. She was the witness, and she suspected that Hasan had not read the same textbook, nor did he plan to play by the FBI's rules.

"Torturing you," he said, "is going to be very enjoyable for me."

"That's just what I would suspect a bug like you to say," she replied.

CHAPTER NINE

"It's not going any further," Storm declared.

Dilya pushed the Range Rover's gas pedal and the car's engine roared, but even with its four-wheel drive and climbing ability, the SUV had reached its limits. Switching off the engine, Dilya left the keys in the ignition and stated the obvious: "From here we go on foot."

The four of them moved to the vehicle's rear gate, where they collected their gear. All were wearing hiking boots and had sidearms. In addition to his backpack, Casper was carrying a twelve-gauge pump shotgun on a sling, Dilya had a sniper rifle, and Storm was armed with an AK-47. Oscar, meanwhile, was carrying a bag of various geological gear.

"How far to the border crossing?" Storm asked.

"Only three miles," she replied. "We don't have to climb to the top of these mountains. There is a pass that cuts through them, but it will take us at least two hours to reach because of the terrain. It's important for everyone to watch their footing."

Storm asked: "How long until we get to Jizzakh?"

"We'll be there by nightfall."

"That'll give them plenty of time to interrogate your girlfriend," Casper said, taunting him. "Maybe they'll give her a pretty little scar on her face, too—after they've passed her around like a bicycle."

"You talk too much," Dilya said. "Save your breath for climbing the mountain."

"Are there border guards?" Oscar asked.

"Only occasional patrols. There are so many miles of border in these mountains that it would be impossible to watch every pass."

Dilya led. Oscar immediately began following her, but both Casper and Storm hesitated.

"After you, sweetheart," Casper sneered.

Storm shook his head, indicating no. He did not want Casper behind him, and Casper knew it. He chuckled and fell in behind Oscar, leaving the rear to Storm.

There was no formal trail and the incline soon grew steep, but not so much that they needed to be roped together. The tops of the mountains were covered with deep snow, which they avoided where possible. About a half hour into their trek, they came to a mound of loose rocks that they needed to climb. It required them to use their hands to help pull them forward as they scaled a series of jagged rocks on all fours. Dilya scrambled up the surface with ease, but Oscar lost his footing and a half dozen fist-sized rocks broke loose and shot down the incline behind him, nearly hitting Casper and Storm.

"Sorry," he called to them.

Casper cursed, and Storm immediately regretted his

decision to be at the bottom of their line. He knew what was about to happen, and a moment later, he found himself dodging another rock that came bouncing down toward his face. It was followed by another, larger stone that barely missed him.

"Oops," Casper said. "My bad."

When they reached the top of the loose rocks, they began walking on a goat path that soon led them to a cut between the mountains. The air was thin, and all of them were struggling to catch their breath. Dilya suddenly raised her hand and they stopped. She dropped to her knees. The rest did, too. About three hundred yards ahead of them were two men in Uzbek border patrol uniforms. Both carried automatic weapons. They were smoking cigarettes and talking.

Casper duckwalked to where Dilya was hiding.

"Give me the M-24," he said, referring to the American military-issue sniper rifle that she was carrying. "I'll kill them."

"There are two of them," she said.

"Yeah, so? I'll drop the second before he figures out what happened to his buddy."

"No," she said firmly. "You could miss. One might escape. We will wait."

"I never miss," Casper said. "And they could be here for hours."

"And for what reason?" she replied. "This is a routine stop for them. This path is well known. We will wait."

Casper let out a sigh in disgust and moved back nearer Storm. He sat, leaned his back against a rock, and closed his eyes, but he couldn't help but taunt Storm. "Tick, tick, tick," he whispered. "Every minute we're stuck here is another minute for them to play with your lady friend. Maybe they'll just pull off a fingernail, or maybe they'll take a complete finger or even her hand. How do you like the nickname 'Stumpy'?"

Storm moved up to where Dilya was watching the guards through field glasses, which she immediately handed to him.

"Every moment we're stuck here counts," Storm reminded her.

"These two men are part of a twelve-man squad. They ride in a truck to known crossing areas and then fan out searching for drug runners and other illegal aliens. If Casper shoots them, their companions will know. We cannot save your friend if we are discovered."

Through the field glasses, Storm saw one of the guards flick a spent cigarette. The guard then turned, and the two of them began walking away from the pass.

"We'll wait fifteen minutes for them to rejoin their comrades and leave. Then we will cross into Uzbekistan. I only hope that the guards did not discover our new vehicle hidden on the other side of the border. It is a long walk down the mountain to the nearest town."

Storm thought about Showers. Alone, being interrogated in Jizzakh. He was not a deeply religious man, but he said a silent prayer that there would be a car waiting and that Showers would still be alive when they reached her.

Minutes later, the unlikely foursome walked gingerly through the pass and started down a narrow footpath. Coming down the mountain proved more taxing than climbing it. Gravity tugged at them, pulling them close to the path's edge, trying to make them hurry their footing and break into what surely would be a fatal run.

They watched for the border guards but didn't see them.

After about an hour, Dilya said, "There!" She pointed to a clump of trees. Storm caught the reflection of the sun off the windshield of a four-wheel drive Chevy. When they reached it, they shed their gear and paused to catch their breath.

Oscar disappeared into the trees to pee. Casper inspected a diagram that had been left inside the SUV along with a handheld satellite GPS. This left Storm and Dilya together. They walked to a large rock jutting from the terrain, and Dilya took a drink of water then handed her canteen to Storm.

"It's beautiful," Dilya said, scanning the picturesque plains that spread for miles before them from their mountain perch.

He knew better than to ask, but couldn't help himself. "Why did you get involved with Jones?"

"When the Soviet Union collapsed, more than two million Russians ran back to Russia because they knew what would happen if they stayed here. But we had grown dependent on their handouts and there was chaos. People were starving. My country is mostly Sunni Muslim, and the Jihad Group, which is linked to Al Qaeda, soon began launching terrorist attacks because our government became friendly with Americans. My parents, husband, and daughter were murdered in a bomb blast in a café. I wanted to die, but first I wanted to kill as many terrorists as possible. Jones' people found me. They helped me infiltrate the Jihad Group."

She made it sound simple—like signing up for Terrorism 101. But Storm knew better. He was familiar with the Jihad

Group, and it was one of the most secretive and deadly of all the extremists. One of the group's top commanders, a radical known simply as the Viper, was why Storm had been sent to Tangiers. Jones had needed Storm to help track down the Viper, and the CIA had learned that the terrorist was meeting in Tangiers with another Al Qaeda operative. For years, the northern Moroccon city had been known as a safe haven for spies and terrorists. Jones told Storm that as soon as he was able to identify where the Viper was hiding, an agency team would be sent to capture or kill him. Casper had been part of that "kill team." It had been housed separately from Storm's group in Tangiers, waiting for a greenlight. But a day after Storm landed in Morocco, he and the others with him had been ambushed. Everyone but him was killed. It had been a trap and the Viper escaped.

"Do you know the Jihad Group?" she asked him.

"Yes, the Viper is a truly evil man."

"They all are."

Oscar emerged from the bushes and Casper finished with his map. "You girls going to chat all afternoon or are we ready to go kill someone?" Casper asked.

Dilya said, "Why must you be so unpleasant?"

"Actually, Scarface, I've been on my best behavior just to impress you." Looking directly at Storm, he added, "Tick, tick, tick."

CHAPTER TEN

"Let's begin with the most obvious question: Where is the gold?" Hasan asked Showers.

"What gold?" she replied.

Hasan chuckled. "So this is how we will play our little game." He scanned the various torture devices that he'd carefully placed in front of him and then yelled something in Uzbek. Two men hurried into the room. One carried a metal folding chair, which he set up directly across from Hasan. He hoisted Showers from the mat and forced her into the chair. The guard jerked her injured right arm behind her, sending a jarring pain up her shoulder, but she refused to scream. He handcuffed her wrists in back of the chair.

The other guard brought a large truck battery with jumper cables into the room and dropped it near her feet.

"Didn't you say shocking people was mundane?" she chided.

"Consider this foreplay," Hasan hissed. "I will get more creative as our evening together progresses."

At least now she knew it was nightfall. Hasan rose from

his seat, walked behind her, reached down, and suddenly grabbed her right shoulder, digging his thumb into her wound.

Showers screamed. He pressed again, clearly trying to separate the collarbone that the hospital surgeons had labored to repair. The pain was so intense, and she was so exhausted that Showers mercifully blacked out.

"Langley has a bird's-eye view of the dump where they are entertaining the FBI broad," Casper announced as Dilya drove the SUV toward Jizzakh. "Intel says there are currently only four men inside the building."

"Four?" Oscar replied.

"What sort of building is it?" Dilya asked.

"A slaughterhouse," Casper said, chuckling. "I didn't think Muslims ate meat."

"Muslims practice *Halal*," Dilya said. "We don't eat pork or any meat that has blood in it. Nor do we drink alcohol."

"Pity for you, Scarface. No booze to help you sleep during those lonely nights," Casper said. "Maybe we can get together after this little escapade and I can introduce you to a friend of mine named Jack Daniel's"

"Does this mean women only find you attractive when they are drunk?" she asked.

"What's your rescue plan?" Storm said.

"KISS," Casper replied, smacking his lips at Dilya. "It stands for Keep It Simple Stupid. When we get there, our little scientist friend here will stay outside and shoot anyone who tries to come in to help the other tangos."

He grabbed the barrel of his shotgun and said, "I'm going to take my little friend here and blow open the door."

"You don't have C-3?" Dilya asked, referring to plastic explosives.

"Don't need it," he replied. "A few rounds of double-aught buckshot fired into the hinges and my boot heel will do the trick. And I'll still have a few left over for the tango inside."

"That's your plan?" Dilya said. "Shoot the door and then run inside?"

"Well, it's a bit more sophisticated than that. I'm also going to have lover boy here toss in some flash bangs." He was referring to Storm. "When those bangs explode, there will be a very, very loud noise, a blinding flash, and a shock wave that will knock whoever's inside on their asses like they were standing next to a giant speaker at a heavy metal concert."

Casper paused. He liked being the center of attention and being in charge. "Now," he said, "I figure Scarface here has more time firing an AK-47 than our lover boy. As soon as I blast that door, and while the flash bangs are turning everyone into blind mutes, she fires off a series of bursts that will serve as ground fire, killing anything in our way. Amid this confusion and chaos, yours truly will charge through with my reloaded shotgun, followed by her and the AK-47 and lover boy here bringing up the rear with his Glock. Obviously, lover boy here will need to use his little popgun because the only other rifle we've got is the M-24, and that isn't going to be worth a damn in close-range fighting. I'll assume you can fire a handgun, right?"

Casper glanced at Storm with disdain and didn't wait for

him to respond. Instead, Casper said, "Not that it matters, because Dilya and me should be able to take down all four of the tangos with you and Oscar just tagging along for the ride. We'll rescue the FBI princess and then go get the gold. KISS."

Storm asked, "What's to keep them from killing Agent Showers the moment you blow open their front door?"

"Absolutely nothing," said Casper. "But there's no way we can sneak into that building undetected."

"He's right," said Dilya. "Our best hope is that—during all of the confusion—they will either ignore her or attempt to use her as a hostage. We should have the element of surprise."

"Unless," said Casper, "we've got another Tangiers situation here. Isn't that right, lover boy?"

Dilya said, "It's a good plan."

"I wasn't asking for a critique, Scarface."

Showers gagged for breath and opened her eyes just in time to see one of the two guards in the torture chamber lowering the metal pail that she'd been offered earlier to pee in. He'd splashed water onto her face, waking her and also creating a better conduit for electricity, since her feet were now in water. They'd removed her shoes and socks. The pain in her shoulder was excruciating. She felt certain that Hasan had rebroken her collarbone.

Hasan was fiddling with the large truck battery that was next to her. Reaching over, he connected one of the wires from the battery terminal to the metal chair that she was sitting in. He held the other in his hand. Now that she was awake, he was ready to begin. He held the clasp in front of her face. "Where is your smart tongue now? Do you wish to stick it out at me?"

She clenched her jaw.

"Let me think," he said, clearly enjoying himself. "Where should I clip this?"

Although her wrists were handcuffed and her right foot was attached by a leather collar and chain to the floor, Showers's left foot was free. She aimed it for his groin and kicked. Her curled bare toes hit their mark, causing Hasan to instantly double over, gasping in pain. "You bitch!" he sputtered

"Careful," she said. "You might shock yourself."

Hasan lunged forward from his crouched position, extending his left hand. Just as he was about to grab her injured right arm, a loud boom echoed from outside the room, followed quickly by five other identical booms and then two deafening explosions that made Hasan believe the entire building was collapsing.

Dilya peered through the smoke caused by the flash bangs and spotted a dazed man standing ten feet inside the building with an automatic rifle at his feet where he'd dropped it. Both of his hands were on his ears. She fired a burst from her AK-47 and his body fell backward.

Casper charged down the hallway, stepping over the dead sentry, and burst through a half-opened door into the room where Showers was being interrogated. In an expert move, he dropped to one knee while simultaneously shouldering and firing his shotgun. The blast literally blew the guard closest to him from his feet, ripping a gaping red hole in his chest. The second guard was still drawing his sidearm when Casper's second round of buckshot sent him crashing dead to the floor.

In a panic, Hasan reached for his satchel.

Showers screamed: "Look out!"

But when Casper swung his shotgun toward its new target, Hasan yelled, "Don't shoot!" and immediately raised his hands.

Dilya and Storm rushed inside and tended to Showers, retrieving the handcuff keys from Hasan, freeing her hands, and removing the collar from her foot.

"Did he hurt you?" Storm demanded.

"Yes, but I can move. He broke my collar bone again."

Storm swung and planted his right fist squarely in the torturer's jaw, cracking it and causing Hasan to spit out a tooth and cough blood as he staggered sideways.

"How gallant," Casper deadpanned.

Dilya said, "There's no time for this! Let's go!"

Casper aimed his shotgun at Hasan.

"You just can't shoot him in cold blood," Showers said.

"Wanna bet, sweetheart?" Casper replied.

"He was torturing you," Storm said.

"Just handcuff him," she pleaded.

Storm reached for the handcuffs that he'd tossed on the concrete floor, but before he could retrieve them, Casper unloaded a round of buckshot into Hasan's head, literally causing his face to disappear.

Showers gasped.

"We won't be needing those handcuffs now," Casper said, grinning.

Storm flashed Casper an angry look.

"Now, now, now," Casper said as if he were lecturing a small child, "let's not get your panties in a wad. Remember Jones put me in charge of this rescue."

"Time to move," Dilya yelled. They ran from the room, down the short hallway, and outside into the parking lot where a nervous Oscar was pacing with his gun drawn. Dilya took the wheel while Casper jumped into the front seat. Both handed their weapons—the AK-47 and the shotgun—to Oscar, Showers, and Storm, who were in the back seat.

"There's a medical kit in the rear compartment," Dilya announced.

Oscar put the rifles in the back and grabbed the kit. "I have first aid training."

"Finally, something you're good for," Casper.

"Give her morphine," Dilya ordered. "For her shoulder."

As their vehicle began to exit the lot, a blast of bullets peppered the car's front hood, blowing out the SUV's front tires and causing steam to burst from under the hood.

"Who's shooting at us now?" Oscar yelled.

"On the roof!" Storm replied. "Another tango!"

Casper shoved open the front passenger door and leaped out shoulder first, twisting in the air so that he was now facing the building behind them with his handgun raised. He'd emptied the semi-automatic clip by the time he hit the packed ground.

Casper's shots, however, sailed by the lone figure on the

roof, completely missing him. The shooter aimed his AK-47 at the helpless American prone on the ground. Just as he was about to unleash a fatal burst, Storm emerged from the SUV with his Glock drawn. Firing upward, his first round struck the tango's chest with such force that it lifted him off his feet, causing him to instinctively squeeze the AK-47's trigger.

Bullets smacked into the ground around Casper, but the shooter's aim had been misdirected and the worst that the CIA-trained killer suffered was the sting from bits of flying dirt popped loose from the hardened terrain.

The rooftop assailant fell dead.

Casper rose slowly, with a torn shirt and a bleeding scrape on his massive shoulder but no busted bones. Their vehicle hadn't fared as well.

"We're done with this ride," Dilya declared as she stepped from behind the wheel. "Nice shot," she added.

"He saved your life," Showers hollered at Casper as she exited the rear seat, followed by Oscar.

Reloading his handgun and brushing off his arms, Casper looked at Storm but offered him no thanks.

"Grab the gear," Dilya said. "We've got to keep moving."

"Let's take their vehicle," Oscar said, pointing to a new Range Rover parked by the slaughterhouse.

"No!" Storm objected. "It's too easy to track." Eyeballing the street, he spotted a half dozen Russian-made, Lada 4 x 4 SUVs parked about a block away. They were part of a delivery fleet for a national chain of Uzbek bakeries.

Storm ran to one, forced open its door, and hotwired the ignition. "She's ugly," he yelled, "but the engine sounds solid."

They carried their weapons and equipment to the well-worn Lada.

"I should've known better than to trust INTEL. Every time I do, it nearly gets me killed," Casper complained. "If I'd had my shotgun, that son of a bitch on the roof never would have gotten the drop on me."

"It's not the size of a gun that matters," Flowers said flatly, "but the man using it." She smiled appreciatively at Storm.

"You're just damn lucky someone was willing to save your ass," Dilya added.

Storm took the wheel. About a mile from the slaughterhouse, a white police car with bright green and blue stripes came speeding toward them on the opposite side of the two-lane road. Once again, Casper drew his Glock but the car zipped passed without slowing.

"They didn't give this old truck a second glance," Storm said. "Must have figured we were making a morning delivery."

"Good choice of getaway vehicles," Dilya said.

Addressing Showers, Casper said, "Now you know why I didn't leave any witnesses behind, sweetheart. The cops won't have any idea what happened and probably will blame it on terrorists. If there was a witness, they'd know it was Americans."

Showers didn't reply. The morphine was taking hold and her eyes were growing heavy. She began to nod off. Somewhere in the distance, she felt a man's hand move her head onto his shoulder. Storm had moved into the backseat, turning over the driving to Dilya.

She leaned against him and slept.

CHAPTER ELEVEN

They drove South from Jizzakh toward the Molguzar mountain range, with everyone except Showers taking turns behind the wheel, so the others could sleep. Daybreak found them still traveling, following directions on the handheld GPS navigation device that had been programmed with the coordinates that would take them to the gold. Their course eventually brought them to a gravel road that snaked up the mountain. Eventually, they were forced to leave it and make their own trail. The ride was slow and jarring as the four-wheel delivery truck climbed over the rough terrain, often being forced to detour because of boulders that had fallen and downed trees that blocked their route.

As they came nearer and nearer to their destination, they began to feel a sense of anticipation. It was hard to imagine so much gold bullion in such a desolated spot, hidden for more than twenty years.

Dilya stopped the vehicle at what looked like a landslide about a tenth of a mile from where the cavern of gold was reportedly stashed. They would have to walk across the rocks. They exited the old truck.

It was now Oscar's turn to be in charge, and he grabbed his backpack of geological gadgets and demanded the GPS from Casper, who had been navigating as Dilya drove. Casper relinquished it begrudgingly and fell in step behind him, with his shotgun slung on his shoulder. Dilya went third, while Storm held back with Showers.

"You feel okay to walk?" he asked.

"Just point me to the start line."

They began crossing the rocky terrain together. "I haven't thanked you for rescuing me," Showers said.

"Nothing I won't be bringing up in front of you every day of your life," he said.

"So what do I have to do to pay my debt?" she asked.

Storm thought for a moment about how she'd tricked him in London after they'd been drinking in a pub. He'd believed they were going to spend the night his hotel room bed, but she'd innocently asked him to fetch her a cup of coffee, and when he stepped into the hallway, she locked the door.

"The next time we check into a hotel together, I get to keep all the room keys," he said.

"What makes you think that will happen again—us checking into a hotel room?"

"I'm an optimist."

"An optimist would have come up with something better than having control of the room keys."

"Okay, how do you feel about whipped cream and pickles?"

"Pickles?" she repeated.

"Kiwis."

She shook her head in disgust. He was impressed at how well she was taking this.

"Ouch!" she cried, suddenly lifting her heel.

He hurried to her, taking her left arm to steady her.

"What did you step on?"

She kissed his cheek. "Not a thing," she said, breaking free.

Showers started walking and said, as if nothing between them had just happened, "What's the story about the gold? I know we are looking for bullion, but that's about it."

"If the coordinates from Lebedev's cell phone are correct, we're about to find sixty billion in gold that once belonged to the old Communist Party in the equally old Soviet Union. It was hidden here by soldiers after the KGB snuck it out of Moscow before a failed 1991 coup."

Showers said, "How are five people—one with a bad arm—supposed to haul sixty billion in gold out of here in a Chevrolet?"

"We're not. We're just supposed to confirm it is here. Jedidiah Jones has a plan to haul it out with helicopters from Kazakhstan. We look, but don't touch, and definitely don't sample."

"Jones is going to do this under the nose of Uzbek authorities?" she asked skeptically.

"Jedidiah wasn't real forthcoming about that, but he did mention several times that we had to keep our hands in our pockets."

"That should be a familiar location for your hands," she replied.

Storm had been so focused on rescuing Showers that he

had not dwelt much on what might happen when they actually found the gold. Each kilobar was worth at least fifty-seven thousand dollars, and his job on this trek— according to Jones—was to make certain no one got greedy.

He drew his Glock and handed it to her.

"I already know you can shoot left-handed," he said.

"You think I might need to add some notches on it," she asked.

"Jones warned me that I might. I don't trust Oscar, and I'm not even sure how Dilya is going to react to that much gold."

"And Casper?"

"I told you once that I got wounded in Tangiers. I've always suspected that someone sold us out. Someone betrayed us. Casper was on the kill team that Jones sent in. He went off the grid right after that mission went bad. If I had to guess, Casper sold us out."

"But he's blaming you for Tangiers."

"The best defense is a good offense."

"Do you have a plan if someone gets sticky fingers?" she asked, quickly adding, "I'm talking about the gold bars, not your pockets."

"It depends on who it is. Oscar isn't much of a threat, but Casper and Dilya know how to use weapons and have killed before. They're the ones we have to watch."

"And what about you?" she asked. "Should I be worried about you and the gold?"

"I'm not a big fan of gold," he said. "Or diamonds."

"Diamonds are a girl's best friend."

"Lucky we're searching for gold then. I'd hate to have to

shoot you, especially since we just rescued you."

"I knew you'd find a way to bring that up again."

"After that kiss, I'm rethinking the whole whipped cream and pickles fantasy. Maybe adding some ice cream and pie, too. Or a female midget."

"You are sick."

They walked in silence for a few minutes because the altitude was stealing their breath. Storm said, "Jones said he had a reason for sending everyone on this mission. Everyone but you had a purpose. He told me that he didn't trust the others."

"You already said that," she replied.

"What if he wasn't talking about the gold?" Storm replied. "Why would he put me in charge of stopping someone from stealing a few bars of bullion? He can always track them down."

"Your job is what—finding out who isn't trustworthy?"

"Maybe even more specific than that. Casper thinks I screwed up Tangiers. I think he double-crossed the agency. Dilya told me yesterday that she infiltrated the Jihad Group, and I was sent to Tangiers to track down its leader. Is it a coincidence that Casper, Dilya, and I all have ties to Tangiers?"

"What about Oscar?"

"He's not mentioned Tangiers, but Jones always suspected that it was Russian Vympel soldiers who attacked my team there. Oscar had Russian KGB connections."

"What soldiers?"

"The KGB's elite forces, like our SEALs. Jones was convinced that the Russians were responsible for Tangiers."

"Why would Jones put four people together knowing

that one of them is a traitor?"

"If my hunch is correct, this may be about more than the gold," Storm said.

The others were fifty yards ahead of them. By the time they caught up, Oscar, Casper, and Dilya were standing in front of a steep ledge that jutted straight up for at least a hundred feet. Oscar doubled-checked the GPS coordinates and then looked at the sheer rock wall. "If this GPS location is accurate, the gold is a few hundred feet behind this rock wall. There must be a cave in there."

Casper grabbed the GPS, snatching it from Oscar's hand. "Let me look."

"This little Russian bastard is telling the truth," he said. "There's got to be a cavern behind this wall of rock."

"This area is composed of large granite slabs," Oscar said, "but there are deep cracks in the rocks that often can lead to inner chambers, some quite large. I'm not sure how the soldiers got truck cargo containers filled with tons of gold up here, but if there is a cavern, the only way to enter it will be through a crack somewhere in the granite."

"We just crossed over rocks that looked like rubble," Dilya said. "Is it possible the KGB dynamited the entrance? Sealing in the gold."

Oscar said, "That would be logical."

"What exactly do you mean by 'a crack somewhere in the granite'?" Showers asked.

"A hole, an entrance, perhaps small, perhaps big," Oscar replied. "If the soldiers destroyed the main entrance, there should be smaller cracks. Maybe not big enough for a truck to drive through, but big enough for us to walk through."

"Should be a crack? That's real scientific. Thanks for giving us your expert opinion," Casper said. Rather than returning the GPS to Oscar, he clipped it onto his belt.

"How do we find the entrance?" Showers asked.

"Look for water or a stream that suddenly disappears into the ground. Look for steam rising from a hole. Caves are warmer than the air outside them. Look for red dirt—iron-rich soil that has been removed from a cave."

Dilya checked the time. "We've got about an hour left before sundown, so let's spread out. Oscar and I will go to the left. The rest of you can go to the right. If we find something, we'll get each other. But we don't go into any holes alone."

"That's the only way that—" Casper started to say, but Showers cut him off, not wishing to hear another crude comment.

"If you want to go ahead without us, go," she told him.

Casper didn't wait around for a discussion. Instead, he began walking to their right.

"If we're lucky, he'll wander into a cave and never come out," Storm said.

Oscar opened his backpack and removed four flashlights. "You'll need these if you see an opening. But again, wait for everyone. It will be safer. Caving is dangerous."

Showers and Storm began walking in the same direction as Casper. Dilya and Oscar went in the other direction.

For thirty minutes Storm and Showers moved slowly through the terrain, partly because it was rough climbing and she had only one arm. They didn't see any obvious openings and it was beginning to get dark. They were just about to turn back when suddenly Casper's head poked out from behind rocks about ten feet in front of them.

"I found an opening!" he yelled.

They hurried over to him. The crack would have been impossible to see if Casper hadn't climbed between several large boulders. It was an opening about seven feet tall and two feet wide.

"I don't have a flashlight, so I only got about fifteen feet inside, but the opening gets bigger as you go deeper," he said. "Give me one of your flashlights and I'll explore it while you go get the others."

"We're supposed to wait," Showers said.

"What are you afraid of? You think I'm going to cart out sixty billion in gold in my pockets between the time you go get the others and come back here? I'm simply going to save us time in case this opening proves a dead end."

Storm handed Casper his flashlight and he vanished through the crack. "I'll go get the others so you can rest," Storm volunteered. "You still have my Glock, right?"

Showers lifted her sling. His handgun was hidden behind it, tucked in the waistband of her jeans so she could draw it with her left hand.

Storm was able to backtrack quickly without Showers. He found Dilya and Oscar returning to the sheer wall.

"Casper's gone into an opening," he said, catching his breath.

The three of them began running and soon reached Showers, who was sitting outside the cave's mouth. The sun was nearly completely down.

"Has he come back?" Storm asked.

"Nope. Gone like a rabbit."

"Or a snake," said Oscar, taking command. "I'll go into the hole first, Dilya next, then Agent Showers, and finally you. He pointed at Storm. "There could be water, making it slippery, and be careful of drop-offs. You need to watch your heads so you don't knock yourself out, but also keep the light on the ground so you don't step off a ledge."

"How about vampire bats?" Storm asked facetiously. "Just to keep things interesting."

"If you've never been in complete darkness," Oscar continued, "then you are in for a surprise. In a cave there is no light, no sunshine, not even starlight."

"Like a coffin," Dilya said.

Oscar reached into his bag and gave Storm a new flashlight since he had given his to Casper. The Russian then vanished into the opening with Dilya at his heels.

"Vampire bats, coffins, total darkness, steep ledges, and Casper the ghost lurking around," Showers whispered to Storm as they entered the cave. "I might have had better odds being tortured."

Their flashlights cut through the darkness, illuminating a narrow passageway. Storm guessed they had gone about fifteen feet inside the mountain when the crack started to expand and break in different directions. Oscar continued down the main one with everyone on his footsteps. Storm checked his watch as they made their way forward. He wanted to time how long they'd walked. When they'd traveled another twenty minutes, Oscar came to a stop and declared, "We've reached a chamber!"

They crowded up next to him and all shined their flashlights into the blackness. The chamber was at least thirty feet wide, hundreds of feet long, and forty feet high. It certainly was a big enough opening to hide sixty billion dollars of gold packed into cargo containers.

"Nearly all caves are made of calcite, the crystal of calcium carbonate," Oscar explained. He shined his flashlight down and the light reflected back. About ten feet below them was a large pool of water. The roof of the cave was covered with stalactites; water drizzling along the walls had created cave draperies.

"The white that you are seeing is pure calcite," Oscar said. "Other minerals, mostly iron, are responsible for the orange and red stains."

"It's beautiful," Showers said.

"Yes," added Dilya, "but there are no gold bars, no tanker containers."

"If Casper had not taken the GPS, I would be able to tell if this cavern is behind the wall of granite," Oscar complained.

"You mean this GPS?" Casper's husky voice called from behind them. He held the GPS up in front of his flashlight for them to see. None of them had heard him approaching them. They shined their lights on him. His face was dirty, and in their flashlight beams, he looked even more menacing.

"You're standing right where this GPS says there should be truckloads of gold," Casper said. "And there ain't no Commie gold bars anywhere around here. There's nothing but water and rocks."

"Could the gold be under the water?" Dilya asked, shining her light down at the pool beneath them. "Maybe when they destroyed the entrance, they created a dam."

All of them pointed their lights at the water, but saw nothing except their own reflections staring back.

CHAPTER TWELVE

"Ivan Petrov must have been lying when he gave the coordinates for the gold to Lebedev," Storm said.

"But I heard Lebedev say that he knew Petrov was telling him the truth about its location," Showers said. "The two men had grown up together. They were like brothers."

"Brothers don't shoot each other in the foot and then between the eyes," Storm replied. "Brothers don't kill each other for gold—usually."

"I've checked all of the other tunnels except for one, ladies," Casper declared. "They're all dead ends and there is no gold hidden in any of them."

"How about the one you didn't check?" Oscar asked.

"It goes in the opposite direction of us. It goes away from the coordinates. That means this cavern we're looking at has got to be where the gold was put—unless Petrov lied."

"You're the geologist," Storm said, turning his flashlight so that it illuminated Oscar's face. "Don't you have some sort of equipment that can tell us if the gold is here?"

"It's got to be under the water," Dilya said. "We have no

idea how deep this cavern is. Let's go back to the surface. We need rope. We might even need diving equipment. But one of us has to go down there in the water for a better look."

"I agree," said Oscar. "Let's go back to the surface and call it a night."

As they walked toward the cave exit, Casper took the lead, with Oscar following him to make certain he kept on course. But Dilya hung back to get one final glimpse of the pool of water.

"The gold is down there. I feel it," she said as Showers and Storm stepped by her in the tunnel.

As Casper neared the cave's opening, he could see faint moonlight coming from outside. He stepped from the cave with Oscar and Showers close behind him. All three of them were blinded by a brilliant light.

"Drop your weapons!" a male voice ordered them.

Still inside the cave passageway, Storm froze. The bright light was coming from a spotlight. Someone outside had ambushed them.

Storm instinctively reached for his Glock, and then remembered he had given his handgun to Showers. He took a step backward away from the cave's entrance and felt the barrel a pistol pressing against his back.

Dilya said, "Time to leave the cave."

Instead, he slowly turned to face her.

"Who's out there?" he asked.

"Friends," she replied, "of mine, not yours. Now, move or you'll die here."

Dilya had betrayed them.

Rather than turning around, Storm stayed facing her with his hands raised and took several steps backward into the light. He moved deliberately, and just before he stepped from the cave, he stopped.

"Why are you doing this?" he asked her.

"Why does it matter?" she snapped.

At that second, Storm turned sideways, causing the bright spotlight to flash into her eyes. Storm had been intentionally keeping his body between the blinding light and Dilya's face, shielding her with his shadow.

In that same instant, Storm grabbed Dilya's wrist with his right hand and the gun with his left hand turning its barrel away from him. It was a rudimentary disarming technique taught by U.S. Special Forces, and it, and Dilya's momentary blindness, resulted in Storm taking the upper hand.

Freeing the pistol from her grasp, he pushed her in front of him at the cave's entrance.

"Now, let's go say hello to your friends," he said.

Dilya walked from the cave into the spotlight, with Storm holding the pistol against her head with his free hand.

"What do we have here?" a man's voice asked.

"A hostage," Storm replied.

"And I have three."

Storm looked to his left and saw the red dots from laser-guided gun sights dancing on the chests of Showers, Oscar, and Casper, who were standing in a line at the cave's opening.

"You can have the gold," said Storm. "In return, we go free and we take Dilya with us until we reach the border."

Dilya yelled something in Uzbek.

"Do you know what she just said?" the man asked.

Because of the spotlight in his face, Storm still couldn't see the man, and he had no idea how many others were out there with him, although he'd counted four red dots aimed at his team members. Two of the lasers had been pointed at Casper.

"She just told me to shoot her," the voice said. "This is how loyal she is to our cause. And do you understand why she is willing to sacrifice herself? Because she knows she will be martyred. I don't expect you to understand that kind of faith."

"I have faith in what will happen when I pull this trigger," Storm replied.

Agent Showers jumped into their conversation. "Who are you?"

"The Jihad Group," the man said. "And the American who is pointing his pistol at my sister's head once tried to track me down."

"The Viper," Storm said aloud.

Dilya again yelled something in Uzbek.

The Viper replied with a single command in Uzbek, and the crack of a rifle broke through the night air. Oscar collapsed on the rocks, shot through the chest. It had happened so quickly that Showers and Casper, who were standing on either side of him, didn't have time to react until the Russian's dead body hit the ground.

"The next to die will be FBI Agent Showers," the Viper said.

"Go ahead," Showers said. "You're going to kill us anyway."

"Actually, you are more valuable to me alive right now," the Viper said.

"I'd rather die," Casper announced, "then have my head cut off on YouTube by a bunch of camel-screwing Haji extremists."

Storm looked at Showers and saw that all four red dots were now on her torso. The Viper wasn't bluffing. She would be the next to die unless he released Dilya.

He made eye contact with Casper, and for once, the two men seemed to be on the same wavelength.

"Now!" Storm yelled. With his left hand, he grabbed Dilya's throat and pulled her sideways toward the ground, as he began firing his pistol at the spotlight illuminating the cave entrance. Everything instantly went black.

At that same moment, Casper threw himself in front of Showers, shielding her with his own body while knocking her down, as the Viper's men began firing. Bullets ricocheted off the rocks, making pinging sounds.

In the sheer darkness, Storm felt Dilya's body become limp and felt warm fluid flowing onto his left hand that was still clutching her throat. She'd been fatally shot in the neck.

For a second it was completely quiet, and then the booming sound of Casper's shotgun erupted. The first boom was followed immediately by another and another. The well-trained killer was using the red laser sights on their enemies' guns to identify where they were hiding in the darkness. Casper's final blast was answered with the primordial scream of a man whose body had just been ripped into by buckshot.

It became silent again, and Storm noticed there were no

longer any laser sights aimed at the cave.

The Viper yelled out in Uzbek. And when one of his men replied, Casper fired his shotgun at the man's voice. His shot drew a round of rapid return fire from the Viper's pistol. Storm immediately answered that with his own handgun, aiming at the muzzle flashes.

And then there was silence.

Out of habit, Storm had counted his shots, and he knew he had only one round left in the gun that he'd taken from Dilya. He had no idea if Casper, Showers, or the Viper and his men were still alive.

No one wanted to speak, because that would reveal location. The evening's already faint moonlight was now obscured by clouds. Storm slowly crawled in the direction of Showers and Casper, picking his way around the chest-high boulders that edged the cave's entrance. When he reached the spot where he had last seen his teammates, his hand touched a body and he froze.

Was it her?

He felt a man's hair and glasses. *Oscar.*

"April?" he whispered.

"Over here," she replied.

Using his hand as a probe, he felt a boulder rising up in front of him and made his way around its edge. Tucked between large rocks were Showers and Casper. They'd taken shelter on the ground.

"You hit?" Storm asked softly.

"No, but Casper is. Bad."

"How bad?"

"One in the leg. One in my abs," Casper replied. "But I can still shoot."

"How many are still left?" Showers asked.

"Can't tell."

As if on cue, they heard a man screaming and then the rapid fire of a gun. It was followed by another man crying out.

"What's happening?" Showers asked.

Storm carefully inched up from where the three of them were hiding and peered over the huge boulder in front of him, in the direction of where the sounds had come from. He saw nothing distinguishable, only boulders. He inched his way out of their hiding place and crawled several feet forward, then stopped behind another large stone. Using it to shield his body, he peered over its jagged surface. Nothing. And then there was a movement, but it was so slight that he questioned whether his mind might be playing tricks on him. He hadn't seen the outline of a man, rather it appeared as if one of the boulders ten feet in front of him had actually moved, as if the ground around him were coming alive. He picked a single rock and locked his eyes on it. Two minutes later, he was just about to write it off as paranoia and exhaustion, when the rock seemed to rise up and move forward, ever so gradually.

Storm raised his pistol and aimed it at the stone. If it moved again, he was going to fire.

As he stared at the rock, he felt the blade of a knife pressed against his throat and the warmth of breath in his ear. The words were in Russian, but Storm didn't need to understand the language to know the meaning. He released his grip on the pistol.

The man holding the knife at his throat forced him to his feet and called out in a loud voice. Another Russian responded and Storm heard the sounds of people moving. Showers and Casper were being dragged from the rocks behind him.

The beams from the headlights of an SUV shined on them. The vehicle was one of two that the Viper's men had driven along an alternate route to the cave entrance. The spotlight that Storm had ruined had been attached with a long cord to one of their vehicle's batteries.

The headlights made it possible for Storm to see the "rock" that had been moving in front of him. Five bushy monsters now surrounded Storm, Showers, and Casper. They were not rocks. They were Vympel soldiers wearing Ghillie suits, elaborate camouflaged outfits favored by special forces. Their heavy outfits were designed to make them impossible to see when they were on the ground.

"I thought these bastards were a KGB myth," Casper said. "I never saw them coming."

The four men standing guard wore earpieces and had been wearing night vision goggles. Their leader came forward from the parked SUVs, where he had turned on the headbeams.

"Why didn't they just kill us?" Showers asked.

"I'm guessing that's their plan," said Storm, "but first they want to make certain that the gold is here. We're still the Russians' best chance at finding it."

Their leader issued a command in Russian, and three of the soldiers disappeared through the cave entrance, leaving the leader and two men behind to watch their captives. As they waited, the leader stepped over to Oscar's body and began digging through the backpack that the geologist had been carrying before he was killed. The soldier removed a small device, putting it in his pocket.

"A tracking device," Casper said. "That Russian prick was helping them."

Because of the dark makeup on their faces, it was impossible to see any facial expressions. Only their eyes showed through. They said nothing, and that made them appear even more fierce.

The three soldiers had positioned themselves across from Showers, Storm, and Casper. While two of them watched with their guns pointed at the trio, the third stepped forward to frisk them. He started with Storm and did it quickly, expertly removing his extra clips of ammo. Satisfied, he moved to Showers, beginning with her ankles, moving his hands up her legs, but he hesitated when he reached her waist because her right arm was in a sling. As he began to check her, Showers screamed in pain.

"I'm wearing a sling!" she yelled. "How can I shoot anyone?"

He stepped back, surprised at her outburst.

The leader said something in Russian, and the soldier moved on to Casper. They'd already stripped him of his beloved shotgun, but he was still wearing his Ka-Bar knife on his waist.

Storm looked at Showers, and she moved her right arm slightly, pulling the sling away from her abdomen. Without moving her chin, she looked down, signaling him.

In that instance, Storm understood.

"You Commie bastards are supposed to be invincible," Casper said loudly, "but you look like a bunch of candy-asses to me."

"Oh my God!" Showers screamed hysterically. "I don't want to die!" As the soldiers watched, she threw her good left arm around Storm's neck and cried, "Kiss me one last time, darling!"

The Vympel leader yelled, "Nyet!" But Showers clung desperately to Storm.

With her now blocking the soldiers' view, Storm reached between the sling and her waist, where he felt the familiar metal grip of his Glock. Somehow she had managed to slip the gun back into its hiding place before she'd been captured.

"Now," he whispered.

Showers spun to his left as Storm pulled the handgun and began firing. His first target was the leader. Afraid that the Russian might be wearing a protective vest, Storm fired directly at his face. His first shot found its mark. Leaping to his right, Storm fired at the surprised soldier guarding him, who reacted by raising his submachine gun. Storm's shots whizzed by the Russian's head as the soldier pulled the trigger, popping off two rounds as he'd been trained to do, rather than firing a full, ineffective burst in a panic. One round nicked Storm in his thigh. Its sister sailed past his chest, striking a rock. Before the soldier could squeeze off another pair, Storm fired his Glock, killing him.

While Storm was busy firing at two of the soldiers, Casper attacked the Russian sent to frisk him. Although

Casper was wounded, he released a crippling left hook into the soldier's jaw while simultaneously slipping the Ka-Bar knife free with his right hand. Assuming the Russian was wearing an armored vest under his mountain man attire, Casper curved the blade so that it would puncture his attacker's side.

He thrust his knife with such force that its hilt pushed into the wound. Casper pulled it upward and then sideways and down, ending the man's life.

"Nice shooting, deadeye," Casper called to Storm.

They had successfully killed the leader and two soldiers outside the cave, but there were still three inside it searching for the gold. Storm checked his leg. It was a flesh wound, but the gunshots that Casper had taken earlier, during their exchange with the Jihad Group, were much more serious.

Bending down, Casper retrieved his shotgun from the Russian who'd taken it from him earlier. "I'm bleeding out," Casper said. "You two get going. I'll keep the other three pinned in the cave as long as I can."

"No," Showers said. "We're not leaving you behind."

"It's my choice," Casper replied. He looked at Storm. "I thought you'd betrayed us in Tangiers. I blamed you for what happened."

"I thought you were the traitor," Storm replied.

Casper chuckled. "And it was neither of us. Dilya was working for the Viper all along, and Oscar was a mole for the Russians. They're the ones who sabotaged Tangiers."

He let out a painful groan and reached for his side.

"You don't have to be a hero," Showers said. "We can

get you down the mountain."

"To where?" he replied. "I'll be dead by the time we hit the main road. Besides, I want to die a hero and I owe you."

"You don't owe me anything," Storm said.

"You saved my life when you shot that bastard on the roof of the slaughterhouse."

"Then we're squared," Storm said.

"Not yet, deadeye. Not until after you leave and those rats come peeking out of their hole. I never loved anything as much as this shotgun so there's something fitting about me holding it when I die and go to hell. Now get out of here before I change my mind."

CHAPTER THIRTEEN

Storm drove the SUV down the mountain at daredevil speed, dodging rocks, trees, and drop-offs that seemed to jump before the vehicle's beams.

They had gone less than a half mile over the rocky terrain when headlights appeared behind them.

"Casper?" Showers asked, but she already knew the answer. "Hurry," she said.

"I'm not Sunday driving," he replied. "But if I go any faster, I'll rip out this car's bottom."

The SUV's undercarriage banged against a rock, nearly knocking both of them from their seats. Mercifully, they reached a gravel road a mile later. The SUV chasing them was close enough now that Showers could see the outline of the driver and a passenger.

"Casper must have killed one of them," she said.

Her sentence was punctuated by a bullet sailing through the rear window of the SUV. Shards of glass flew by her face. The Russian in the SUV's passenger seat was leaning out his window firing his machine gun at them.

Storm handed his Glock to her and she started to fire, just as Storm swerved to avoid plunging off the narrow road. Her first shot hit their own SUV's back side window and the second the interior of its roof.

"Shoot them, not us," Storm said. "We're the good guys."

"They're less a threat than your driving," she replied.

The gunman chasing them fired another burst of rounds, peppering the rear of the SUV.

Showers spun around in the front passenger seat, so that her back was now pressed against the dash, and lifted her left hand so she could fire through the busted rear window. She emptied the rest of the magazine, causing the attacking vehicle to pull back.

"I must've hit one of them," she declared. "Give me a new clip."

"I don't have any. They took them? Remember? Getting frisked?"

"Time to get creative," she said, climbing between the bucket seats into the SUV's rear compartment.

"Anything there?" Storm asked as she rummaged through the back. "An AK-47, rocket launcher, cannon, bombs? Peanut butter sandwich?"

"Actually, there's only this," she said. She lifted a bag of crème cookies.

Storm glanced in the rearview mirror and saw Showers throwing them one at a time with her left hand at the approaching SUV. Several exploded onto the windshield.

"You've got to drive faster," Showers yelled.

"I hate backseat drivers," he replied.

She slipped into the front passenger's seat and said, "Drive faster."

"Look at this road," he complained.

They were racing down a one-lane gravel path that had steep drop-offs on its one side. One wrong turn and they would plunge off a cliff.

"Well, he's going faster," she said.

"I'm still in front, aren't I?" Storm said, checking his mirror.

"At least he's not shooting now," she said. "I must have wounded him."

"With a cookie?"

"No, the Glock."

"Maybe they're out of bullets."

Just then the Russian fired another round at them.

"Obviously, they brought along extra ammo," she said.

Storm swerved, and the wheels of the SUV sent gravel flying from the roadway's edge. Showers pressed her left hand against the Range Rover's ceiling to brace herself as he turned quickly around another curve.

Despite Storm's driving, the vehicle behind them was gaining ground. Within a few seconds, they were so close that Showers could see the Russian's eyes as he aimed his machine gun at them. At this distance, he wouldn't miss.

"This is not how I planned to die," Showers said.

"A white picket fence," Storm said, swerving, "a rocking chair, grandkids running around while you sipped lemonade. Was that your plan?"

"No, but it certainly wasn't dying on a Uzbek mountain

next to someone whose real name I don't even know."

"Planning your own death is overrated," Storm said. "Trust me. I've done it."

Showers braced herself for what she thought would be her last breath as Storm swerved again and waited for the inevitable.

Just as the Russian was about to fire, the SUV that he was riding in turned into a giant fireball. The explosion lifted the vehicle from the roadway and completely engulfed it in flames. It crashed down and bounced off the cliff, tumbling down the mountainside in flames.

"What was in those cookies?" Storm asked. He jammed on his brakes, causing the vehicle to spin to a stop.

"What the hell just happened?" Showers asked.

"Quiet!" Storm said. He turned off the engine.

Through the SUV's shattered windows, they heard a whirling noise hovering above them in the darkness.

"Jedidiah Jones!" Storm said. "He sent a predator." He glanced at Showers and started to explain, "You know, an unmanned radio controlled military drone—"

"I know what a predator is," she snapped. "What I don't know is how Jones knew we were being chased down the side of a Uzbekistan mountain by Russians."

Storm lifted up his wrist so she could see his watch.

"I guess no one in the FBI has one of these," he said proudly. "It's a tracking device. When Dilya pulled a gun on me in the cave, I turned it on and it sent Langley a signal telling Jones that we were in trouble. This watch tells Jones exactly where I am at any time and in any place in the world."

"Glad someone is keeping track of you," she replied.

By the time they reached the bottom of the mountain, the morning sun was rising, and on the horizon they saw a Bell 206 helicopter flying low across the plains toward them. Storm turned off the road as the four-seat chopper landed. Within minutes, they were flying toward Kazakhstan, leaving the bullet-ridden SUV and the bodies of Casper, Oscar, Dilya, the Viper, his men, and six dead Russians behind them.

As they rode in silence in the chopper, Showers suddenly reached over with her left hand.

"Here. A present."

Storm looked at her opened palm.

It was one of the cookies from the SUV. It had fallen into her sling when she was heaving the others through the window.

CHAPTER FOURTEEN

They separated as soon as the CIA-contracted charter flight delivered them to the U.S. garrison in Wiesbaden, Germany. Showers was admitted to the hospital so doctors could repair her damaged collarbone, while Storm was given time to bathe and eat, but then was put on a flight back to Andrews Air Force Base. A car was waiting to take him to Langley.

Jones was leaning back in his squeaky desk chair when Storm entered his office and sat in the all-too-familiar chair across from the CIA spymaster.

"We didn't find any gold," Storm said. "No sixty billion in kilobars owned by the Communist Party. Petrov must have given Lebedev the wrong coordinates."

Jones leaned forward and said, "Is that what you think?"

Storm paused and then said, "You intentionally entered the wrong coordinates into our GPS in Uzbekistan. You sent us on a wild goose chase."

"For more than twenty years, that gold has been hidden in the Molguzar Mountains and no one has been able to find it," said Jones. "Why disturb it now? Especially since I know where it is and we can keep an eye on it with one of our birds."

Removing sixty billion in gold from a Uzbek cave would be a major operation that would not go unnoticed. There would be angry denouncements from Russia and Uzbekistan. The White House would have a major political problem on its hands—especially since Russian president Barkovsky remained in power.

"If you didn't expect us to find the gold," Storm said. "Why did you send us to Uzbekistan?"

"I thought you would have figured that out by now," Jones said.

Storm had, but for once he wanted to hear it from Jones. This time, he was the one playing dumb in their cat-and-mouse game.

"Tangiers," said Jones. "After it, I knew we had a leak. There were only four possibilities. Oscar, Casper, Dilya, and—you."

"You suspected me?"

"It's my job to suspect everyone. What did we really know about you as a person? Clara Strike recruited you because you were a skilled private eye. After Tangiers, I thought maybe the other side had gotten to you, corrupted you. You decided you wanted out. I was suspicious, but your death also gave me an idea. I decided to retire Oscar, Dilya, and Casper, too."

"Tangiers," Storm said.

Jones nodded. "When I learned where the gold was hidden, I decided fate had given me an opportunity, a chance to catch a traitor. I knew the mole would contact the Russians. Sixty billion was too big of a prize. And that is exactly what Oscar did."

"What about Dilya?"

"That's an irony, isn't it?" said Jones. "You throw out a net and who knows what you catch? Oscar told the Russians about Tangiers. Dilya tipped off the Viper."

"Twice betrayed," said Storm. "What kind of spying operation are you running when two of your recruits are secretly working for the other side?"

Jones shrugged. "Good traitors are hard to find."

"Why did you suspect Casper?" Storm asked.

"Casper had a habit of getting drunk and bragging. I thought maybe he had inadvertently talked to the wrong people."

"Casper got killed and we nearly did."

"But you didn't, did you?" Jones said. "Before you begin feeling sorry for yourself, remember you came back to work for me because you knew someone had betrayed you in Tangiers. You wanted revenge. And I couldn't afford another Tangiers. It was a price I was willing to pay."

"Casper might feel otherwise."

"In a strange way," Jones said, "fate brought us full circle from Tangiers. We learned that Dilya and Oscar were traitors. We missed the Viper in Tangiers, but his body was found dead on the mountain. The Vympel soldiers apparently cut his throat. You and Casper were cleared, and we now know where the Russian gold is hidden. It's a win-win-win in my book. The only question that remains is this: Are you done? Are you going to disappear back in Wyoming?"

"Montana," Storm said.

"No matter. Are you going to go back off the grid or are you going to do what you do best?"

Storm rose from his chair. "Right now, I'm going to take some time off."

"Take as long as you want," Jones said, opening his desk and removing an envelope. "This will help." He slid over the package and Storm picked it up, knowing that it contained hundred-dollar bills.

Storm removed the wristwatch that Jones had given him and put it on his desk. "I won't be needing this."

Jones said, "I'll keep it for next time. There's a rental car parked outside." He handed Storm a set of keys.

"Is it bugged?" Storm asked.

"You figure it out." He stood and extended his hand.

As the two men shook, Jones said, "Agent Showers will be flying in tomorrow. I understand she will be placed on a mandatory one-month medical leave of absence. She'll have time on her hands, just like you."

Storm found the rental parked outside. Jones had splurged. It was a cherry red Corvette ZR1, a $110,000-plus convertible with a 638 horsepower, supercharged V-8, the fastest production car ever made by General Motors. It was not the type of car that passed unnoticed—the suburban-friendly vehicles that Jones insisted that his operatives drive.

Storm fired up its engine and enjoyed the loud muffler growl as he exited the CIA en route to the George Washington Parkway. His private cell phone rang.

"Hello?"

It was Showers calling from Germany.

"I need a lift from the airport tomorrow?" she asked.

"I'll check my schedule," he said.

"I'm expecting more than a ride?"

"Like what?"

"Dinner."

"No cookies in Germany?"

"Just be on time." She hung up.

He turned into one of the scenic overlooks on the parkway and look down at the Potomac River. He searched his cell phone until he found what he wanted. When he had been in London in the parking garage, he'd sent Jedidiah Jones the coordinates for the gold. He'd also sent a backup copy to his own private phone.

Jedidiah Jones was not the only one who knew where the sixty billion in bullion was stashed.

His phone rang again.

"Listen," Showers said in a serious voice, "I really do want you to show up tomorrow at the airport. I'll pay for dinner if you want. Just don't go AWOL on me."

"The last time we met, you stuck me with the bill," he said.

"Trust me, it will be worth your while. See you tomorrow, and don't worry, you're not my boyfriend."

"And you're not my girlfriend," he said. "But I have a question. You got some time off coming, right?"

"They're forcing me to take a month off."

"I'm thinking about going on a trip."

"Where in the world are you going now?"

"Mountain climbing."

New York Times bestselling author

RICHARD CASTLE

STORM FRONT

From Tokyo to London, high-level bankers are being gruesomely murdered. The killer, Gregor Volkov, is Derrick Storm's old nemesis. Desperate to figure out who Volkov is working for, the CIA calls on the one man who can match his strength and cunning— Derrick Storm.

WILD STORM

Airliners are dropping from the sky, shot down by a terrifying futuristic weapon. The intelligence community is blindsided and scrambling for answers. But the terrorists have aimed their weapon at the one man who can't be brought down: Derrick Storm—who saves his own plane from certain doom, then is enlisted by shadowy CIA boss Jedediah Jones to track down the force responsible for the tragedy.

HEAT WAVE

A New York real estate tycoon plunges to his death on a Manhattan sidewalk. A trophy wife with a past survives a narrow escape from a brazen attack. Mobsters and moguls with no shortage of reasons to kill trot out their alibis. And then comes another shocking murder and a sharp turn in a tense journey into the dirty little secrets of the wealthy.

NAKED HEAT

When New York's most vicious gossip columnist is found dead, Heat uncovers a gallery of high profile suspects. Heat's investigation is complicated by her surprise reunion with superstar magazine journalist Jameson Rook. Sexual tension fills the air as Heat and Rook embark on a search for a killer among celebrities and mobsters, singers and hookers, pro athletes and shamed politicians.

HEAT RISES

The bizarre murder of a parish priest at a New York bondage club opens Nikki Heat's most thrilling and dangerous case so far, pitting her against New York's most vicious drug lord, an arrogant CIA contractor, and a shadowy death squad out to gun her down. And that is just the tip of an iceberg that leads to a dark conspiracy reaching all the way to the highest level of the NYPD.

FROZEN HEAT

Paired once again with top journalist Jameson Rook,
NYPD Homicie Detective Nikki Heat arrives at her latest
crime scene to find an unidentified body stuffed inside a
suitcase. Nikki is in for a big shock when this new homicide
connects to the unsolved murder of her own mother. Will
Nikki Heat finally be able to solve the dark mystery that
has been her demon for ten years?

DEADLY HEAT

Top NYPD Homicide Detective Nikki Heat and her
partner, journalist Jameson Rook, pursue the elusive former
CIA station chief who ordered the execution of her mother
over a decade ago. But their quest for the old spy unearths
an alarming terror plot that has already entered its
countdown phase. Complicating their mission, a serial killer
boldly names his next victim: Detective Heat.

RAGING HEAT

When an illegal immigrant seemingly falls from the sky,
NYPD Homicide Detective Nikki Heat's investigation into
his death quickly captures the imagination of her boyfriend,
the Pulitzer Prize-winning journalist, Jameson Rook. But
when Rook's inquiry concludes that Detective Heat has
arrested the wrong man for the murder, everything
changes...